Praise f
END OF THE WO

"Celt is a smart, convincing novelist, and her ambitious tweaks of the concept are fascinating and fun to grapple with. . . . Navigate[s] the loss of a friendship, the kind of pain that can feel like the end of the world."

—*Los Angeles Times Book Review*

"Adrienne Celt's new novel depicts a fraying world (climate crisis, political violence, social upheaval) that's frighteningly recognizable. It's a timely novel, as well as one that has great fun exploring what time itself is. Yet *End of the World House* asks a question that's timeless: How do we make a meaningful life?"

—Rumaan Alam, author of National Book Award finalist *Leave the World Behind*

"In this new novel from the ever-ingenious Adrienne Celt, a couple of close friends are visiting the Louvre when they find that the world as they've known it has ended. Marvelously imaginative and terrifyingly plausible, a time-bending funhouse riddled with rabbit holes, *End of the World House* is slippery and uncanny and infinitely enthralling."

—R. O. Kwon, author of *The Incendiaries*

"Mystery, time-travel, and love at the end of the world. What more could you want?"

—*Town & Country*

"Exhilarating. . . . This book about love, friendship, and the cruel nature of time is catnip for fans of *Groundhog Day* and Rumaan Alam's *Leave the World Behind*."

—*The Millions*

"The apocalypse has never been this fun . . . What do you get when you take *Groundhog Day*, add a dash of the apocalypse, a little French obsession, and mix in female friendship and romantic entanglement? This firecracker of a book that gets weirder and more bizarrely funny the more pages you turn."

—*Good Housekeeping*

"*End of the World House* is thoughtful, funny, provocative, and creative. . . . While there's a temptation to compare the book's time-bending elements to pop-culture products like *Groundhog Day* or the streaming series *Russian Doll*, there is also in Celt's never-ending museum an echo of the infinite library of Jorge Luis Borges and, in her ruined world where we can only do the best we can, of Samuel Beckett. The author has triumphed by rendering a personal tale against a backdrop of global significance."

—Washington Independent Review of Books

"A phantasmagoric thrill ride, Adrienne Celt's *End of the World House is* a story of apocalypse and art, but also of friendship and love and fighting for a sense of one's self in the face of modern-day alienation and precarity. I love this book for the way it reconsiders how time and space function within novels, how it made me think about memory and art-making, and also, for its acuity and its heart."

—Lynn Steger Strong, author of *Want*

"*End of the World House* showcases Celt's agile and humorous prose, as well as a knack for cutting descriptions. Celt renders our surreal daydreams—or perhaps our complacent nightmares—crystal clear. This novel is so much fun."

—*Chicago Review of Books*

"Brilliant."

—*PopSugar*

"Truehearted and affecting."

—*Kirkus Reviews*

"Adrienne Celt has crafted something brilliant with *End of the World House*. This book is an intoxicating mix of beauty, art, and mystery. Celt writes about the tangled threads of close friendship with tremendous skill and a wild amount of heart. It's a novel that's undeniably funny, unafraid to look at the messy ways we unwittingly complicate our lives as well as the lives of the people closest to us. A compelling look at intimacy and its myriad vulnerabilities, *End of the World House* is a stunner."

—Kristen Arnett, *New York Times* bestselling author of *Mostly Dead Things* and *With Teeth*

"[R]eading Adrienne Celt is like being granted access to a secret kingdom, another layer of reality you didn't know existed. Even mundane objects shimmer strangely under the intensity of her gaze. Haunted, romantic, unexpectedly playful, and unputdownable, *End of the World House* will change the way you think about the immortality of art, free will, the future and the past. Adrienne Celt is brilliant and I want to read everything she ever writes."

—Rufi Thorpe, author of *The Knockout Queen* and *The Girls from Corona del Mar*

"Adrienne Celt's writing is such a pleasure to read—fluid, funny, and smart—that the dazzling architecture of *End of the World House* almost feels like an extravagance. The story of a friendship ravaged by a ruined world, with shades of both *Russian Doll* and Rumaan Alam's *Leave the World Behind*, this is both a page-turner and a shrewd examination of intimacy and survival."

—Kristen Iskandrian, author of *Motherest*

"Adrienne Celt's *End of the World House b*rilliantly captures our swelling fears of the world we live in today, but it's way more than that. It's also a severely smart and surreal examination of friendship and capitalism that is both terrifying and beautiful and strikes deeply at readers' emotions. I loved it."

—Brandon Hobson, National Book Award finalist and author of *The Removed*

"An enjoyably mind-bending trip through an all-too-realistic depiction of the breakdown of society, Bertie's unexpected journey explores the power of relationships to shape our reality."

—*Booklist*

Also by Adrienne Celt

Invitation to a Bonfire

The Daughters

End *of the* World House

A Novel

Adrienne Celt

Simon & Schuster Paperbacks
NEW YORK LONDON TORONTO
SYDNEY NEW DELHI

Simon & Schuster Paperbacks
An imprint of Simon & Schuster, Inc.
1230 Avenue of the Americas
New York, NY 10020

This book is a work of fiction. Any references to historical events, real people, or real places are used fictitiously. Other names, characters, places, and events are products of the author's imagination, and any resemblance to actual events or places or persons, living or dead, is entirely coincidental.

First Simon & Schuster paperback edition April 2023

SIMON & SCHUSTER PAPERBACKS and colophon are registered trademarks of Simon & Schuster, Inc.

For information about special discounts for bulk purchases, please contact Simon & Schuster Special Sales at 1-866-506-1949 or business@simonandschuster.com.

The Simon & Schuster Speakers Bureau can bring authors to your live event. For more information or to book an event, contact the Simon & Schuster Speakers Bureau at 1-866-248-3049 or visit our website at www.simonspeakers.com.

Interior design by Paul Dippolito

Manufactured in the United States of America

1 3 5 7 9 10 8 6 4 2

Library of Congress Cataloging-in-Publication Data has been applied for.

ISBN 978-1-9821-6948-0
ISBN: 978-1-9821-6949-7 (pbk)
ISBN 978-1-9821-6950-3 (ebook)

For KBS

Part One

–1–

By the time they reached the Louvre, Bertie and Kate were nearly running. It wasn't unusual for their walks to turn into unplanned races—both were in the habit of strolling a half step in front of people, and when they were together this could become a problem. First Bertie would move in front of Kate, then Kate would pick up her pace to match Bertie's, and so on and so forth until they looked at each other and broke into a sprint. It had been that way since they were fifteen—that is, some fifteen years ago—and on ordinary days they both embraced it, competing to reach an imaginary finish line, celebrating whoever won. But today, despite wanting to arrive at the museum on time, their mutual fear of looking un-French was helping them to approach moderation.

At the end of the Rue de Rivoli, they slowed down and used each other as mirrors to readjust their outfits. A tug of the shirt when Kate lifted her eyebrow, and a twist of the skirt when Bertie sucked her teeth. The morning was hazy, with a fog that wasn't quite willing to resolve into rain but was heavy enough to sit on the women's hair and dampen their jackets. Kate reached into her bag for an actual mirror, which she used to apply a fresh layer of lipstick; they'd come to the museum at the invitation of a man Kate had met the night before in a bar, and she claimed not to have decided yet whether she wanted to impress him.

"What are your priorities, art-wise?" Bertie asked. She had a handkerchief around her neck, meant to look chic but also useful as a breathing filter when they passed through areas still smoky from the last round of bombs. The tracking app they had pored over on the plane attributed responsibility to a terrorist faction from the suburbs, who'd arrived via commuter rail wearing innocuous clothes and backpacks with gunpowder sewn into the lining. Now, Bertie shifted the knot of her handkerchief back to the side, into its more fashionable position. "Do you want to hear something dumb? I kind of want to see the *Mona Lisa*."

"That's not dumb," said Kate. "Everyone wants to see the *Mona Lisa*."

"I mean, that's why it's dumb. Usually it's surrounded by a huge crowd, like, hundreds of tourists all crammed around this tiny painting which is probably only an okay painting, and which they only like because it's famous."

"So what, are you going to commune with it? Now that you're the only one there?"

This had been the man's offer, as they sipped their drinks and watched him glimmer lasciviously: private entrance into the museum, which today was technically closed. If she was honest with herself, Bertie had, in fact, gotten a shiver of pleasure from the idea. *I deserve it*, she'd thought. *If not me, who?* But she wasn't about to be quite that honest with Kate, who would only make fun of her.

"Never mind," she said. "We can skip it, I don't care."

"No," said Kate. "We should see it. You're right." She snapped her lipstick shut and stowed it away again. "Do you really think people don't like the *Mona Lisa*?"

Bertie shrugged. “I just don’t think most people have really thought about it.”

They’d come to Paris because the tickets were cheap. First there’d been a spate of hijackings, and then the bombings, and a period of general unrest. No one would call it a world war, but that was semantics. Now the borders were opening back up, under the auspices of a cease-fire, and though most Americans were still too nervous to travel, a few of the tourist boards were giving it the old college try. Kate and Bertie chose Paris because they felt that the French advertisements did the best job of flirting with the overall sense that the world was ending without ever actually stating outright that this might be your last chance for a vacation.

Also, Kate was moving in a month. So this was kind of a last hurrah. Bertie knew it would’ve been smarter to put her money and energy into finding a place in the city, finally moving out of the dismal Mountain View apartment she’d only rented to be near Kate, but that would’ve meant recognizing that Kate was really going to leave. So she’d suggested a trip instead. Anyway, the commute from San Francisco was hellish, more so now that the 101 was gone and the 280 was the only freeway option between the city and the South Bay. It was like God died, the day they shut the 101 for good. People actually cried in the streets.

In principle Bertie was a cartoonist, but for years now she’d made her money doing illustrations for a large tech company in Silicon Valley—one that liked to appear lighthearted and approachable to the public so they could sell more ads. Which worked surprisingly well. Even cynical people seemed reassured by the company’s palette of bright colors and its dinosaur avatar, which Bertie had now drawn in a thousand absurd situations, including on a rocket ship and driving a school bus, as well as learning "I think, therefore I am" from René Descartes with a book clutched in its tiny hands. The company paid Bertie more than she felt she was worth, so she drew it any way they wanted, as many times as they wanted, along with a rotating multicultural cast of nameless humans who accompanied the dinosaur on its adventures.

Bertie was supposed to be working on a graphic novel, too, on her own time, but these days she rarely had the energy. Not because of her job so much as the malaise that lay over everything. Politics, global war, world hunger, just—everything. Kate had wanted to be an essayist, but that was years ago: she gave it up in favor of directing publicity and fundraising for a nonprofit that lobbied to improve the quality of school lunches. It was theoretically a more selfless career than Bertie's, but Bertie didn't see it that way. After all, Kate liked being in charge; she liked the power. Whereas Bertie was indifferent to her job, which sometimes made her feel like she had less self than anyone. At least if she'd hated it, she could've quit, but no one wanted to hear you complain about leaving your okay job with good health insurance—not at a time when the U.S. suddenly had honest-to-God refugees streaming towards the coasts from the South and the Midwest, finding not much in the way of aid or sympathy. So she kept going every day, sometimes enjoying herself, sometimes spending whole afternoons reading the comment threads at the end of online advice columns, letting rage and disappointment wash all over her in order to reach the rare and blissful moments of catharsis.

That morning the crowd around the glass pyramid in the

Cour Napoléon was sparse, just a few tourists taking photographs of the grounds and some Parisians passing through on their way to work. Near the fountain, a mother and her small daughter threw pieces of croissant to the birds, and a few yards behind them a group of four people was peering at something at the top of a tower, shielding their eyes with their hands. A few days before, when Bertie and Kate had walked by the same courtyard while heading to the Tuileries Garden, the space had been packed, including a line of museum-goers that snaked back half a block, but since the Louvre was closed today, most people had made other plans. The man from the night before had told them he had connections and could get them in for a private viewing if they showed up by eight-forty-five in the morning and gave his name—Javier—at the entrance. It sounded like a delicious secret, almost too good to be true. They'd found Javier at a jazz club somewhere in the Fifth Arrondissement, an old place stuck in a cellar which boasted a surprisingly good band and a crowd of middle-aged Frenchmen who were eager to dance with youths from abroad and buy them red wine for five euros a glass.

The mist finally turned into a drizzle, and Kate took Bertie's hand.

"Oh, hi," said Bertie, and in answer Kate gave her hand a squeeze, the same gentle greeting they'd shared for years, but now at a castle, in Paris, in a light Parisian rain. They stood there for a second, admiring the cornices and balustrades, the judgmental statues and the omnipresent pigeons. Bertie thought it was impressive that so many pigeons remained in the city when the songbird species were all in decline, but then again pigeons were willing to eat garbage, so perhaps they were more fit to survive. Later she would remember that the air in the courtyard smelled tinny, and that the crowd had gotten denser while they stood around. But in the moment she only felt happy to be there, slightly damp and still somewhat young, side by side with her best friend.

"Okay, are you ready?" Kate asked.

"What do you—?" Bertie started to reply, but before she could finish, Kate took off running towards the entrance, still holding her hand and almost pulling her arm from the socket.

"Jesus!" Bertie laughed as they whipped through a cluster of suit-and-tie pedestrians, earning several dirty looks. One man snarled as Bertie's shoulder slammed into his. "Sorry!" she called back to him, but he didn't seem to accept the apology, and muttered something under his breath as he turned away. On the other end of the courtyard, a different, younger man paused to watch the spectacle of them before turning to the side and wiping a drop of rain away from his forehead. He had no coat, and his hands were stuck in his jeans pockets against the morning chill. A round face. Later, Bertie would remember him, too, but it would take her some time to think why.

Kate stopped outside the pyramid doors and checked the time on her phone; neither woman had bothered to activate international service, so they couldn't call anyone or do anything outside the warm glow of the hotel Wi-Fi. But neither one owned a watch or a camera, either, so they still carried their phones wherever they went.

Now that she was over whatever momentary ebullience had made her start sprinting, Kate pulled herself together fast. Her face bright without being sweaty, her hair preternaturally smooth. She tugged on the door, but it was locked.

"It's only eight-thirty," she said. "What do you think we should do?"

"He's your loverboy," Bertie replied. She hadn't found Javier particularly appealing, with his shiny face and his subpar teeth, but Kate always made friends with everyone. "Didn't you get his number?"

"Hell no. Anyway, we weren't supposed to meet him until later. And," she held up her phone, "no service, remember?"

Around them, people were starting to stare. A few—other tourists, most likely—seemed interested, perhaps hoping that Bertie and Kate's presence indicated the museum might be opening after all. But the others looked obscurely angry.

Bertie shifted uncomfortably from one foot to the other. She had the sudden premonition that they wouldn't get in; that it was all a joke. Why had they believed a total stranger when he said he could do them such an enormous favor? Javier was probably off laughing somewhere, telling his friends the story of the stupid American women he'd met at a bar.

"Let's get out of here," she said, pulling on Kate's sleeve. "We can do something else today. It doesn't matter."

But Kate shook her off, and muttered, "Ugh, let me be." She had never liked being managed. It used to be a problem for her at work, though she'd long since jettisoned the issue into her personal life. Bertie backed away, trying not to be hurt, and turned to meet the eye of the young guy she'd noticed watching them earlier. His eyebrows lifted in surprise.

"Oh, wait," Kate said. "Now I remember." Without further explanation, she knocked three times on the glass, then twice, then three times again. From the dim back of a hallway at the bottom of the grand pyramid stairs, someone came into view. She looked like a security guard or a docent, in a dark fitted suit with a walkie-talkie on the front. The woman made a big production of unlocking the doors and then opening them just a sliver, sticking her head outside into the mist. "Qui sont vous?" she asked, and when both Bertie and Kate hesitated before trying to reply, she clicked her tongue in exasperation and switched to English. "You are . . . who?"

Kate frowned. "We're with Javier?" she suggested, as if not quite certain herself. But the security guard's whole demeanor changed.

"Oh. You come, then." She stepped back, holding the door to allow them inside, and both women slipped past her. A father and his teenage son, appearing from nowhere, tried to follow them in, but the guard waved her hand at them and said, "Shoo!" before closing the glass door and locking it. Bertie felt a quick wave of claustrophobia as the lock clicked into place, but it was soon overwhelmed by the immensity of the museum in front of them, and the grandeur. *Sometimes good things happen*, she thought, looking over her shoulder at the father and son who were frowning on the other side of the door. By the time she turned, the guard was bustling away down the hall, disappearing around a corner, and leaving Kate and Bertie alone. They looked at each other. "Okay, then," Bertie said.

—

When Bertie had to explain Kate to people who didn't know her, she sometimes called her "my bitchy friend Kate," even though it made her feel guilty afterwards; Kate was really more particular than bitchy, but that seemed like splitting hairs. The funny thing was, at a bar or a party Kate would be nice to anyone, even creeps like Javier. She built up lines of devoted followers who pointed her out to one another in a fond, "Have you met . . . ?" kind of way, and she was popular at the office, too, as Bertie had seen on afternoons when she came to pick Kate up after work. She made jokes and remembered people's birthdays; when everyone wanted to go to happy hour, she was often the first to say yes, and therefore the one elected to mother-hen everyone to a single location. But when it came to actual closeness, real affection, she could turn off her internal lights in an instant.

Bertie had experienced this firsthand back in high school, when Kate moved to her school district in the ninth grade—Kate's third school in as many years, since her stepdad kept getting relocated for work—and they spent a whole year skirting around one another, sticking to their separate social universes. Kate had purple hair back then, and Bertie naturally assumed that Kate was too cool for her, a sentiment Kate evidently shared for a number of months. Bertie hung out in the art room, which Kate did not, and Kate went to underground all-ages punk shows, which Bertie emphatically did not. The one time she'd tried to talk to her in those early days, Bertie had gotten out maybe one sentence about theatre auditions before she noticed Kate's eyes traveling down her body, taking in her loose curls and the cheap cotton skirt she'd bought at a folk festival, which had until that moment made her feel both international and elegant. Later Kate would explain that she wasn't being dismissive of Bertie so much as hippies in general, because Seattle had so many that they threatened to absorb you, like water into the spongy ground. But at the time, Bertie saw the look on Kate's face, and simply shut her mouth and walked away.

"Wait, what?" Kate had called out after her, but Bertie hadn't bothered to reply.

The change came in tenth grade, when they were seated at adjacent desks for the PSATs. Everyone taking the test had to show up at school on a Saturday morning, and people were full of test-day jitters, which only got worse when the administrators split them up alphabetically and placed them into classrooms with a randomly assigned moderator. Under the circumstances, familiar sights became somewhat surreal: maps and posters curling down at the corners as if left over from a lost civilization. Bertie didn't put too much stock in the PSATs, since they didn't count for anything except National Honor Society. But she was still susceptible to a general desire for success and admiration from authority figures, and so showed up with five spare pencils and a small hand sharpener as well as a water bottle and a baggie of snacks. "Brain food," her father told her. "Can't think if you're hungry." And in fact this statement stressed Bertie out more than anything, wondering if it was literally true.

The first portion of the test, which was multiple-choice reading comprehension, passed without much incident, and the students were given a ten-minute break, during which they milled around in the halls and asked one another how they thought they'd done. Bertie didn't feel like talking to anyone, so she nibbled on some cheddar crackers and drew a rabbit on the back of her hand with a ballpoint pen she found in her backpack. When the moderator told them to sit down and get ready for the second section, she was already at her desk, and she smiled at Kate in an idle way as the other girl slid into her seat.

"I hate math," Bertie said, more or less to no one, though Kate happened to be there.

"Me, too," said Kate with unexpected enthusiasm. "Screw math." Then she looked at Bertie's hand. "Hey, nice bunny, though."

"Oh, thanks," said Bertie. "I sort of forgot that was there."

"You're good at drawing."

"Am I? I like it." Privately, Bertie had always considered herself quite good, but not many other people had bothered to tell her so. Her teachers did sometimes, of course, but they pretty much had to. What was an art teacher going to do—look at a student's sketch and say, *Have you considered statistics, maybe?*

Kate and Bertie both smiled again, nervously, and then turned with everyone else to their test booklets. They were all trying to tamp down the suspicion that the answers they came up with here today would somehow determine the rest of their lives. Later Bertie would sometimes wonder what the questions had even been about: she thought she'd probably solved for X a lot, and offered the area of various shaded triangles. But as an adult, she couldn't quite remember if that constituted geometry or algebra or maybe even trig. What she remembered was how, on the day of the test, Kate sat up halfway through the math section and said, "Oh, shit," because her nose had started bleeding abundantly.

Kate dove for her backpack, but there wasn't much there to stop the flow; they were barely allowed to bring anything with them, lest they somehow secret in an answer key. Around her, other students were sneaking glances at the spectacle before going back to their tests, some going so far as to hold their hands up like blinders to shield themselves from the distracting view. Bertie fiddled with a bit of math, waiting for the moderator to do something—she was a teacher, after all, and this couldn't have been a complete surprise in a room full of neurotic teenagers. But Kate had covered her nose with both hands and then bent down, still softly repeating, "Oh shit, oh shit, this always happens."

Finally, Bertie leaned over. "You need to pinch the bridge of your nose and tilt your head back." Kate immediately complied, but the blood kept coming. "Okay," said Bertie. "One sec. Hang on." She looked with some apprehension at her test booklet, and the watch she'd placed beside it to keep time, before marching to the front of the room and telling the woman sitting there that she needed tissues right away.

"You were instructed to bring your own if you had a head cold," the moderator said. "We don't really have any. Budget cuts."

"You don't understand," Bertie said. "She's bleeding. Like, a lot."

"What?" The woman paled. "Who's doing what?"

"I said, she's *bleeding*," Bertie hissed through her teeth. The woman didn't appear to grasp the severity of the situation. "Can I be excused to get her some toilet paper, maybe?"

"Oh, God." The moderator stood up. "I can't actually let you leave the room. Or maybe—for the bathroom—but you could still meet someone—I mean, I'll go."

Bertie would've been amused at this point, if she weren't so offended. "You think I'm doing this to cheat on the test?"

"Of course not," the moderator said, having at least the grace to blush. "It's just the rules. They're for your own good."

"Like, I hit her or something? To cause a distraction?"

"Of *course* not—"

"Excuse me," said Kate. She was still sitting at her desk, head reclined, nose pinched. The front of her shirt was, by now, quite drenched in blood, and the sight of her sparked the moderator—who Bertie learned later was a chemistry teacher, and then carefully avoided for the rest of her school years—into action at last. The woman jumped up and ran out of the room, pausing at the door only to say, "Please continue, everyone, no chatting," before disappearing into the hall. The test takers all stopped to watch the empty doorway where she'd been, listening to her frantic footsteps patter across the linoleum. Then most of the room went back to their booklets, while Kate and Bertie looked at each other in disbelief.

Kate did eventually get a roll of toilet paper, which she unwound around her fingers and stuffed into each nostril. Periodically she would stop working to unplug a sodden mass of pulp and toss it into a trash can that had been placed beside her, but otherwise she continued scratching out her equations and filling in her answer bubbles, same as everyone. She and Bertie were both offered extra time at the end of the test, but neither of them needed it—Kate was mainly eager to get to her locker and change out of her bloody shirt. As they walked out of the room for the break before the evidence-based writing section, they glanced at the moderator, sitting flustered at her desk, and then at each other, rolling their eyes. After that, they got to talking, and had been friends ever since. Kate still called Bertie "Bunny" sometimes, although these days she did it less and less. Bertie wished she knew why.

—

After reassuring themselves that the security guard was not coming back to tell them this was all a joke and escort them out onto the streets of Paris, Bertie and Kate walked down the white stone steps of the Louvre and past the empty ticket counters, each footstep echoing back at them as light filtered through the glass pyramid above. Raindrops collected on the windowpanes, silently condensing on the cool surface and then sliding away. An unseen machine hummed in the distance somewhere, but otherwise the museum was quiet.

"This is a bit eerie, isn't it?" Kate asked, as they approached the grand spiral staircase to the bottom floor.

"Well, I don't know," said Bertie. But it was. Beautifully so, as if a Victorian ghost might at any moment step out from behind a pillar and beckon them towards their destiny. And uncomfortably, too—the walls both too aware and too inert, without the usual thousand voices echoing off of them and taking up space.

"Actually," Bertie said, "I did think there would be more—"

"Of a welcoming committee?"

"Well, no."

"More curators on hand to ask your opinion on the history of art?" Kate raised her eyebrows. *Ah, yes,* Bertie thought, lovingly. *My best friend the bitch.* Even now Kate had a way of articulating Bertie's least favorite parts of herself, making her observations so lightly it wasn't clear if she actually meant them as criticism or jokes. Though Bertie found it easier to take them as jokes.

"Aren't you charming," she said, slipping her arm through Kate's elbow. "I just thought it would be clearer which way to go."

"Hmm," said Kate. "It is kind of weird to be here like this, isn't it?" She stopped to examine a marble nymph, matched white-on-white with its plinth; anywhere else, Bertie thought, you'd mistake it for corporate art. Something that could sit next to a cooler full of seltzer and ginger ale, elevating the room without calling too much attention to itself. Though maybe she'd just been spoiled by spending so much time around corporations. "I mean, I wonder if this is how rich people experience the world pretty much all the time."

"Trying not to touch anything?"

"Well, sort of," said Kate. "I meant all alone."

Bertie felt a light ping against her heart.

"You're not alone," she said. "Not yet."

"Oh, well." Kate shot her a glance from the side of her eye. "Of course. But you know. Privately."

They moved on, Bertie releasing Kate's arm and walking half a step ahead. She had perfected a museum-going strategy during her art school years, when she would sometimes drive to the SAM in downtown Seattle after a particularly rough painting critique and wander past the tapestries, thinking about how they looked like early cartoons, and how maybe someday the pages of her own work—sketched, inked, colored by hand—would hang like this, if she ever finished making it. She liked to walk around in a loop, stopping only by impulse or instinct, pretending to be in a friend's old junk room or the basement at her grandmother's house, finding everything by surprise.

But she was having trouble drumming up the usual

excitement. Even here, in a palace of art, all of it unfamiliar, resplendent. There were three whole floors to explore, and three wings—Denon to the south, Richelieu to the north, and Sully, central, to the east—and all Bertie could think about was how everything was ending much too fast. She got a panicky feeling, ticking items from the future off the checklist in her head. Their flight left Charles du Gaulle the next night at ten p.m. and, due to the magic of time zones and international date lines, would technically arrive back at SFO just two hours after it took off. In a month Kate would be gone, starting her new job in Los Angeles, and Bertie really would be alone. She pinched her arm, so hard it hurt. But when Kate said, "What?" she just shrugged.

"Okay." Kate stopped in her tracks. "Enough of this moping. Let's go see her."

"See who?" asked Bertie. Then she caught herself. "I'm not moping."

"Of course," Kate agreed. "You would never."

"Her who?"

"You don't mope. You sacrifice yourself to a higher purpose."

"Kate."

"You lie on the train tracks of moral authority and tear your shirt open and ask, 'Do I not bleed?' "

"Screw you."

"You feel the smallest kernel of misbehavior like the princess and the goddamn pea."

So you admit that moving constitutes misbehavior, Bertie thought, but what she said was: "For the love of God, see who?"

"You really can't guess?" Kate asked. "Here's a hint: Madame Mystery."

It took a second for this to click, but then Bertie got it, and she felt a stirring of anticipation. "Oh," she said. "*Oh.* The *Mona Lisa.*"

"Aka your best friend, so long as no one else is around to annoy you by liking it too much."

"To be honest, you annoy me pretty much all the time."

"Yeah." Kate smiled. "But just this once, I think you can see past it."

—

For the entire trip, Bertie had been congratulating herself on avoiding the thought of Kate's move, deciding instead to stay "mindful" and "in the moment," as she was often encouraged to do at work. It turned out to be surprisingly easy when "the moment" consisted not of team meetings and windowless rooms, but instead of perfect baguettes served with fresh butter, or a plate of salty olives at a streetside café in Montmartre, accompanied by a cup of mint tea. On the first night of their vacation, she and Kate had smuggled a bottle of wine to the banks of the Seine, where they threw pebbles into the water and laughed with a group of teenage boys who rode past them on skateboards, spitting raps in a mishmash of English and French.

From a few meters away, one of the boys had shouted, "I love you!" his accent heavy and his voice hilariously earnest. He was smoking an e-cigarette as he rode in figure eights, his motions fluid and fugue-like; you could see on his face that he would never die. From his mouth came little puffs of vapor that smelled like pineapple, at least from a distance. Bertie realized she could be his mother, if she'd gotten started having babies early enough, at fifteen or sixteen, maybe.

"Which one of us?" Kate shouted back. Which sent the boys into hysterics. They fell all over one another, kicking their boards out and letting them slide a few feet away before jumping back on and disappearing around a bend. "Now we'll never know," Kate said.

"Maybe it was both of us."

"The whole pair of us."

"The wonderful pair."

The lights on the river were all moon shaped, wobbling. A firecracker went off many blocks away, or maybe it was something else, but for a moment Bertie allowed herself to believe it would always be like this, the two of them and a good sweet wine, and in the distance, fireworks. There was a percussive *pop pop pop*, and then a period of silence, before a burnt smell drifted over and eclipsed the pineapple scent of the boys. Bertie held a mouthful of wine until she got tears in her eyes and her tongue began to sting. She watched the waves lap at the concrete banks and felt Kate's head drop onto her shoulder. You could will something to be perfect, she thought. And it almost would be. Not quite, but almost.

—

They figured out that the *Mona Lisa* was on the first floor, in the Denon Wing, at the end of a grand salon, but got lost a few times on the way. Things around them seemed a little slippery; at one point they passed a bank of elevators blinking up and down between floors for no apparent reason. Bertie instinctively grabbed her phone from her back pocket and took a picture, thinking, *Proof.* Though, proof of what? She wasn't sure. A car opened its doors in front of them, and Kate made a move to get on, but Bertie grabbed her elbow and steered her away. "Maybe later," she said, watching behind her as the elevator slid smoothly shut again.

"Okay, but are we almost there?"

"We definitely won't be if we go up to some random floor." She aimed her phone at Kate and said, "Smile! Vacation smile!" Which made Kate roll her eyes and sigh, putting up a hand like a bedraggled starlet being hounded outside rehab.

Bertie still wasn't sure the *Mona Lisa* was such a great painting, but she was excited to see it in person at last. To attach a physical marker to something that had floated alongside her for so much of her life: the *Mona Lisa* showed up in *Looney Tunes*; the *Mona Lisa* was a clue in Sunday crossword puzzles; the *Mona Lisa* was screen-printed on an old sweatshirt her mom used to exercise in, huffing and puffing on the stair-stepper machine in front of the television. During art school, the work had been used as an example par excellence of the sfumato style of painting da Vinci championed during the Renaissance, where the lines between different structures and types of light were intentionally smoky and indistinct. Bertie didn't draw that way at all, but it interested her: the idea that everything blurs together, that there is no real distinction between one object and the next. One person and the next.

"Oh, thank God, I'm dying of thirst," Kate said, spotting a

water fountain and leaning over it for a drink. Bertie stood next to Kate and let her weight fall onto the wall behind her. In high school, Kate's mom was always trying to get them to drink more water in an effort to improve their skin: she saw the girls as projects still under way, with movable pieces and errors that could be easily addressed. As an adult, Kate didn't talk to her mother very much anymore, but there were obvious points of crossover between them, places her mother's touch had rubbed off like chalk. She was always exquisitely hydrated, for example. She believed in finding the root of a problem and making swift judgments about how to fix it. Bertie watched her sip from the fountain, mouth turned up into a slight smile. She did have great skin.

"By the way," Bertie said, "aren't we supposed to meet up with that Javier guy at some point?"

"I guess so, yeah, but not till later. He said we could have a late lunch at the upstairs café and then see what we felt like doing from there."

"Won't it be closed?"

Kate stood up from the fountain and shrugged. "Maybe he has, like, the key to the wine fridge."

"What a mysterious gentleman. What a gentleman of quality."

"You're really giving him too much thought."

Bertie knew this was true, but she couldn't help it. She could only remember Javier's face in a hazy way, his skin glowing gold like he'd swallowed a doubloon, with shaggy pirate teeth to match. Since the bombings, it was no longer considered advisable to endure low-level radiation for things like dental X-rays or airport security, and so good teeth had become an important item on the dating checklist. They spoke to a sort of internal stamina, a genetic predisposition to life. Javier's were so yellow, arranged in a jumble, as if he'd always been having too much fun to floss. They were good-times teeth, and these were not good times.

At the cellar bar, Javier had slithered up to them as if from nowhere, filling the empty stool beside Kate and talking to her as though he'd known her for years. Childhoods, injuries, favorite foods: all were discussed. Kate even told him how, after her parents' divorce, her birth father took her to his home in Australia for a month without permission, a technical kidnapping, though she remembered it mostly for the outrageous blue of the ocean. She rarely told anyone this story, but she told it to him. With an arched eyebrow, he invited her to the dance floor, and she accepted, letting him spin her clumsily around and then hold her hand for a little too long on the walk back to their seats. And then he just—stayed. Ignoring Bertie, beaming at Kate. Though it wasn't his indifference Bertie faulted him for so much as his calculation. He'd actually bought more wine for her, sliding Bertie glass after glass of the cheap house red as if he was trying to cure her of something, while simultaneously praising Kate as *naturellement du vin*. Naturally drunk? Was that possibly a compliment?

For her part, Bertie had told him about the boy she kissed once at a concert in eleventh grade, how they'd stood at the top of a hill in the rain, mud clinging to their calves, and she'd thrown her arms over his shoulders and looked into his eyes before leaning in so close they became one beating heart, high up in the storm. The moral of the story being, she left with Kate directly after the kiss and never spoke to that boy again. They always left the boys, in the end.

"Hey, look," said Kate a moment later. "There it is, I think?"

She was pointing around the corner, through a nearby archway. They scooted beneath it and found themselves in an empty, high-ceilinged room with speckled walls and a parquet floor. There was the *Mona Lisa,* positioned as if at the head of a long table, waiting for her guests. To one side of her, there were angels. To the other, a woman fainting into a pair of gentlemen's arms. Kate and Bertie each took an audible breath, then laughed at themselves.

Fuck, Bertie thought. *I might actually love it.*

She felt a twinge deep within herself that she knew could only be relieved by getting her phone out again and taking a picture. Behind a pane of bulletproof glass, the *Mona Lisa* smiled discreetly, looking for all the world like just another skillful copy of herself. This drove Bertie wild—what if it *was* a fake? How would she know? The real version could be in a vault somewhere, too valuable for ordinary eyes. Though, didn't that make this one more real? If it was the one that was seen? She walked the length of the wooden banister that formed a half circle around the glass, taking shots from different angles: high, low, eye-level. A treasure trove of evidence no one would ever want or need. She took a selfie and almost erased it before realizing she looked kind of cute, her hair tumbling down over one eye so she, too, had a mysterious air. From some positions she took three or four variations on the same photo in an attempt to get a perfect version without any glare shimmering off the glass. Each image there, then gone, as Bertie deleted herself with impunity.

Kate pursed her lips. "Why do you do that?" she asked.

"What do you mean?" Bertie crouched down and took a

picture that included half of Kate's face, disapproving in the shadow of the painting.

"I mean." Kate paused. "Can you try just being in a place?"

Bertie had noticed Kate frowning about the photo of the elevators, and the several pictures she'd taken earlier in the morning when they were getting coffee: street shots, children with umbrellas and galoshes. She'd assumed Kate was just tired and in a mood.

"Oh, please, like I'm the only person who posts vacation photos."

"But you're, like, obsessed."

"Everyone is. It's the new human condition."

Kate scoffed.

Admittedly, Bertie spent too much time online. She'd just started at some point, while bored at work, and now it was hard to stop. She would flip through each social media site to see what had happened in the moments she spent on competing platforms, then flip through again, since every second spent in one place was a missed opportunity elsewhere. She took photos of everything she thought people might like, which seemed like a benign public service until she realized how much she depended on the praise. Likes, hearts, stars. Tearing herself away from the internet for this trip had been surprisingly painful, like peeling a suction cup off of her arm. Then peeling off a thousand more.

"Don't be such a dad. Anyway, I use the pictures to draw from, you know that."

Kate looked dismayed. "But then why not carry a sketchbook?"

"I like doing it this way. Can you just drop it?" She didn't need Kate to pester her into keeping a notebook like some goth teenager. She had been to art school. She'd heard all the lectures about drawing from memory versus from life, how geniuses could make a perfect circle every time, and it was just a matter of practice. Even back then, Bertie had preferred working from a static example, though she had hidden it from her teachers and peers, worried that she lacked some vital artistic impulse which showed itself in her shoddy approach. Bertie still worried about that, in fact. More so now that she rarely drew anything for herself at all. Just the dinosaur, which she'd produced so many times it flowed out of her as quickly as air, and as meaninglessly.

She took a deep breath to compose herself.

"Bunny, I'm sorry." Kate poked her arm. "You know it's in my nature to worry about you."

"Well, don't." Bertie took a few more pictures, just to be a bitch. Two of the *Mona Lisa*, and one of a painting of two angry little dogs, cowering. "You're always trying to fix me, but I'm fine."

"I know."

"Okay."

"Okay."

They looked at each other, and Bertie gently reached over and moved a piece of hair off Kate's shoulder, and Kate smiled. Bertie wondered what it would be like to actually be fine, but could no longer really imagine it.

—

The thing that made the world's collapse so hard to parse was the regularity that persisted, in spite of everything. People still had air-conditioning, for example. They paid their bills on their cell phones, and even as various foods were rationed—avocados disappearing when Mexico closed its border with the U.S., coffee and tea in the seasons of storms—motivated citizens were able to use online maps to track where and when truckloads of greenhouse produce were scheduled to arrive, and plan photogenic rituals around them. Tomatoes glistening in a manicured grip. Blackberries staining plump lips. Bertie felt it should be impossible to form such strong new habits and preferences when you might at any time be killed by an IED set up by the freeway, but it was possible. Oh, it was. For the color of polluted sunsets, the necessity of cross-country road trips when all the airlines briefly shut down their commuter routes in the midst of a fuel crisis. Using homegrown squash to make ersatz guacamole, and pretending it was cool instead of necessary. There was a jangling presence of mind that drove everyone forwards, a new ingenuity, which only sometimes curdled into something less photogenic. So that when the cease-fire was announced, and things calmed down enough for air travel to resume and parents to allow their children to apply once more to out-of-state colleges, the calm was almost more unsettling than anything. A silence that could drive you mad. The world waters soothed, as if—as Kate observed to Bertie—some great hand had reached down to turn off the jets in a hot tub. Leaving behind the sensation of water recently boiled, and the shimmering aura of a dial that could, so easily, be turned back up.

—

They left the *Mona Lisa* behind and spent a dissolute half hour among the large French and Italian portraits, with imposing men and women sneering down at them, draped in silk. After that, they walked upstairs to the Dutch Old Masters, through a sea of uneaten feasts, a wall of rabbits hung up and partially skinned. Bertie felt her stomach rumble as they passed by paintings depicting peeled lemons, thick slices of ham, grapes with a wet, unsavory sheen.

She took pictures of all of them.

The day Kate told her she was moving to Los Angeles for a promotion, Bertie had been in a good mood. She'd gotten out of work early, so she'd gone to a bar in their neighborhood, and was eating pretzels in the sunshine when Kate showed up.

Bertie still remembered the quirk of a smile on Kate's lips as she came out onto the patio, the way she'd pulled her sunglasses up over her hair and how pale she'd seemed. They were all pale then, after spending so many nights behind blackout curtains, so many days staying inside and away from the windows, "Just in case," as the news anchors had put it. But this was different, a lack-of-sleep pale, a loss-of-blood look. When she sat down, Bertie passed her a beer and a handful of pretzels, and Kate dunked her fingertip into the beer, covering it with foam before swirling it around and putting it in her mouth.

And then she broke Bertie's heart.

The sun had been going down. *What?* Bertie remembered saying, over and over, genuine in her incomprehension. Kate wouldn't look at her. Bertie thought: *After all we've been through?* She thought: *Don't we more or less belong to each other, now?* Weren't rats on a sinking ship more identifiable by the ship—that is, the vessel of their togetherness—than by the individual rat? But here was Kate, who may as well have been jumping off the spaceship Earth. There was a real chance that, once she left for L.A., it could all start back up. She'd wave goodbye from the window of a cab, and the next day a bomb would drop. They'd never see each other again. But she was still going. "I want to move forwards," was all she would say about it.

Bertie now took a picture of a padded museum bench with a moderately interesting textile print, and another picture of a potted plant that looked kind of like a giraffe, in a way she thought she might later find funny. Kate pretended not to see. She rearranged her skirt, so the zipper sat flush with her spine, and shifted her purse from one shoulder to the other, her smile only slightly strained. It had been a long week, in some ways. A long week of them together every minute, always having to agree what to do next, sharing a bathroom. Kate kept taking Bertie's towel. But still.

"Is a promotion really worth . . ." she began, just as Kate said, "Listen, do you maybe want to . . ." But they were both interrupted by a sound that echoed, suddenly, down the hall. Footsteps and light chatter that they couldn't quite catch, probably because it was in French.

The women exchanged a look. They hadn't seen anyone else since leaving the guard at the museum steps, hours before. No people or even any signs of people: a crumpled piece of paper, say, or a coffee cup left on a ledge: just hall after hall of high ceilings and rococo frames, with the occasional discreet air-conditioning vent cooling the rooms to a steady chill.

They hurried towards the sound as it receded down the long passageway, catching sight of the back of a man's head—but only just, as he turned a corner and disappeared once more.

"Javier!" Kate called. Then she turned to Bertie. "I think that was Javier."

"Really?" Bertie had thought the man looked familiar, too, but in a different way. Then again, she hadn't seen his teeth. *Down, girl,* she told herself. "Well if it was, he didn't hear you. No way Javier would ignore his *belle femme radieuse.*"

"God forbid."

"And heaven forfend."

Kate looked at her sideways. "I just want to say hi, at least."

But try as they did, they couldn't catch up. The faster they went, the more turned around they got, the museum map limp and useless in their hands. A smattering of laughter echoed from the end of a hallway, and they rushed towards it only to find themselves alone in a dark, tomblike room full of female nudes; a room with no exit save for the door they'd just come through, which seemed impossible. They heard someone behind them and turned around to retrace their steps, but none of the rooms they reentered were quite the ones they'd left. The walls were painted different colors, or the light had a new quality, casting longer shadows, or else no shadows at all.

One room was just full of pictures of meat—meat on a hook, meat on the table, meat slabbed so thickly onto the canvas that it seemed ready to drip from the bone.

A few minutes later, Bertie stopped outside a bathroom marked with a lady in a triangle skirt, and found she could no longer continue. She tried picking up her foot and moving it forwards—*Just basic walking!* she told herself—but it felt like lead.

"Listen," she said. "I really need to pee. Maybe let's take a pause here, and then think about leaving for some dinner or something? I'm pretty sure we've blown right past the late-lunch idea."

Kate was surprisingly amenable. "It's true. Now that you mention it, God, I'm starving. When's the last time we ate?"

"Breakfast, I think?"

"That's insane, we're in France. We should be eating every twenty minutes."

Bertie paused. "Where do you think they went?"

"I don't know," Kate said. "I don't even know where we are anymore, exactly."

As it turned out, they were on the second floor, right in front of Poussin's *The Rape of the Sabine Women*, in which everyone was running but no one looked truly distressed. The bodies were all arranged in attitudes of extremity, but the expressions were calm, even placid. Bertie remembered it from school, where it had been the favorite of one of her first-year professors, who had waxed on for ten whole minutes about the play of color on Romulus's tunic. There were actually two copies of *The Rape of the Sabine Women*; the other one was at the Met. Twins, made many years apart, but with the same basic heart.

Her stomach growled, so loud it made her jump.

"Oh, wow," Kate said.

"There's no rationing on red meat in Europe right now, is there?" Bertie asked. "I'm kind of in the mood for a steak." It was their special thing, steak and wine. Not so unusual, but still, theirs. Almost romantic, which was fitting, considering how rarely either of them dated anyone they actually liked.

"No, that's pork. And you're right, we should celebrate." Kate crouched down on the floor and began to thumb through the guidebook they'd been relying on for restaurant advice, in the absence of online reviews.

"Celebrate what?"

"You know. New adventures."

Bertie flinched. "Or old friendships?"

"Oh, come on," said Kate. "Don't be lame. We're about to do all this great new stuff, we're being brave, we got a secret Louvre tour . . ." She trailed off, folding down the corner of a page in the guidebook.

"You are," Bertie said, softly.

"What?"

Was it really possible Kate didn't get what it meant, to say a thing like that? Bertie rubbed her face with her hands. *Shut up*, she told herself. *You'll ruin everything*. But she didn't shut up. "Well, *you're* about to do new stuff. I'm going to be stuck in my same job, with my same commute, drawing that dinosaur until I go blind and stab myself in the eye with a stylus."

"So quit your job."

"It's not that simple."

"It actually is."

"Maybe, but what difference does it make if you're just going to ditch me anyway?"

"What's your problem?" Kate asked. She looked genuinely surprised. "I thought you were happy for me."

"Where did you ever get that idea?"

"I don't know. I guess just from the fact that you *should* be."

"Fuck," Bertie said. Then she turned and walked into the bathroom.

—

Once, on a family trip to Arizona, Bertie had spent all day walking through a river, because she decided it was too hot out to let herself get dry. Her mom and dad, apparently made of sterner stuff, had strolled contentedly on the path above her, but Bertie waded up to her ankles, then to her calves, fighting with every step against the river current. At first it had been gentle enough that she barely noticed it, but the closer they got to their rented camper, the more she felt the water drag her back. Her sandals had no traction, so she kept slipping, twisting her ankle and banging her knee, and fifteen minutes before the end of the hike, she got so frustrated she started to cry. Which her parents declared an *entirely teenage response* to the situation.

Do you always have to make things so hard for yourself, Roberta? her mother had asked, dredging her onto dry land. Never except in moments of annoyance did anybody call her Roberta. *I'm just trying to live my human life*, Bertie had replied. And then both her parents had sighed.

In the bathroom, she peed, furiously. Banged open the stall door so it swung on its hinges, and washed her hands, though it took three tries to find a sink that would register her presence with its motion detectors. In the mirror, Bertie saw she looked insane. Like a Munch painting, or a cartoon dog getting hit on the foot by a hammer and going electric in its dismay. *Why can't you grow up, Roberta?* she wondered. *Why can't you just. Grow. Up?*

"Look," she said, pushing through the swinging bathroom door. "I'm sorry, I'm only being shitty because my stomach is eating itself. Let's go . . ." She stopped. Kate wasn't sitting where she'd been, and with a quick look to the left and right, Bertie saw that she was nowhere. "What the hell, Kate? Where'd you go?"

There was no reply.

Bertie paused, dumbfounded. Had Kate come into the bathroom while she was inside, somehow slipping past without her noticing? She went back in and looked in all the stalls, but they were empty. The hand dryer was still running from when Bertie had turned it on, but it went silent as she stared. Back out in the hall, she walked up and down, peeking into nearby rooms as they branched off the main line. But Kate wasn't anywhere.

Bertie remembered her shouting, "Javier!" Her voice so excited, as if he were a dear friend. There had been a twinkle of desire in the sound, which Bertie had ignored at the time. "That motherfucker," she said quietly, not knowing whether she meant Javier—who must've reappeared—or Kate.

She could picture it so easily. Him coming up from behind her and saying, *Boo!*, then clasping his hand around her wrist. Kate laughing, and letting herself be pulled into a surprise kiss. The two of them running down the hall.

Maybe they'd told themselves they would meet up with Bertie by one of the exits, all three of them walking off into the night for dinner and drinks, as planned. But that wouldn't work. Even if they tried, there were a hundred ways three people could pass each other by in a place like this. All the hidden alcoves, all the sudden abortive ends to visitor loops. The museum itself colluding to keep them hidden. And for what? Just so Kate and Javier could have sex, which either one of them could have had any time, if not with each other, then with someone else, at least equally attractive.

Bertie's eyes got hot, the way they always did just before she began to cry. If she let it happen, it would be an ugly cry, not something poetic and brave. She didn't want to spend the night alone. She didn't speak great French; neither did Kate, but together they'd muddled through the streets, asking people directions and then mashing up a workable translation from their two imperfect understandings. Kate must've known that Bertie would have trouble making it back to the hotel by herself. She didn't have the guidebook. She didn't even have a map.

With a shuddering sigh, Bertie shoved the heels of her hands into her eyes to push back the tears, then picked herself up and looked around until she found a sign marked *Sortie*. She remembered that meant Exit, and she would've known anyway from the icon on the sign, a little genderless body rushing through an open door into nothingness.

The first thing to do was get out of the museum. Then she would figure out what to do next. Paris was just a city; the streets were just streets. With a little effort, she could get herself where she needed to go—so she assumed. So she still, then, believed.

—2—

In the morning, Bertie woke up and saw Kate in her bed by the window, long hair covering most of her face, and she lay there for a while, watching her sleep. Their hotel room was spacious and ornate, with brocade draperies that matched the fabric headboards of each bed. Bright, silken accent pillows had been tossed by each of them onto the floor during the night, and Bertie leaned down to grab one now, placing it behind her head and propping herself upright. She was both relieved and somehow annoyed to see her friend just where she was supposed to be.

Although the hotel wasn't either of their styles, it was centrally located, about a mile from the Louvre, which meant they could sleep in today and still walk there in plenty of time to make the meeting time Javier had suggested. It was also on a quiet one-way street; normally the room, with its quaint balcony view and air of privacy, would have been out of their mutual price range, but with tourism at such an abysmal low, they'd managed to secure a deal.

Anyway, the silliness of the decor felt special. Wrought-iron embellishments at the entrance, gold leaf on the wallpaper, except in a few places where it had been methodically scraped off by some optimistic thief. "We are *en vacances*!" Kate had cried when they arrived, falling back on the window-side bed without first checking which one Bertie wanted. Bertie, who could never relax until she'd snooped a bit, walked around the room peeking in all the drawers and picking up the extraneous doilies that littered every surface. The space smelled of lilac and powder, but not in a sickly way. It was just enough to feel extravagant, as if a vicomtesse had lately been bathing her milky skin in the attached washroom. Finally satisfied, Bertie threw down her bag and sat on the second bed, bouncing once or twice to test the cushioning. "This will do," she'd said.

Now, a warm, honeyed light bathed the room, intermingling with all the purple fabric and the faux Louis XIV chairs. Bertie willed herself out of bed and set to work making two cups of coffee with the fussy coffee pod machine that came standard with the minibar. Once she and Kate were both truly awake, they would probably go down the street for espresso and tarte aux pommes, which had emerged as Kate's favorite Parisian treat. But both of them agreed that a cup of coffee while getting dressed was imperative, quality of the coffee be damned. For months last year, they'd lived without any real coffee at all—you could still get Nescafé with the right ration cards during the blackouts, but fresh beans weren't on any lists of allowable imports—and were now determined to enjoy absolutely every cup that they could.

The American coffee famine began after an enormous hurricane tore through the Gulf of Mexico, destroying much of Houston and becoming, as the newspapers said, "the latest major impediment to trade." The storm lasted more than a week, slamming the Gulf Coast with thirty or forty inches of water and then going back out to sea for a night or two to regain strength before hitting again. Bertie scrolled through the news at the time with a slowly rising sense of horror. At first the looming hurricane didn't garner much coverage—Texas was used to them, and the residents located in its path were ready with sandbags and paraffin lamps, plus enough canned provisions to last them for days. But then it came, and with it, the floods. Each day the photographs were more alarming, with houses torn in half, cars with their lights blinking on underwater, and once or twice a herd of longhorn cattle moving mournfully through a flooded pasture. Thousands of people were evacuated from the Houston area, and quite a few died, but even then, in the first flush of urgency, it seemed like an ordinary form of disaster, the kind that could be fixed with a lot of Red Cross donations and a bit of FEMA elbow grease. This was early in the unrest; people had not yet begun to emigrate away from the flood zones. Few bombs had gone off, and those that had still seemed incidental. No one knew yet, how bad things could get.

It became clear that this storm was different when the natural gas and oil pipelines were shut down due to unsafe conditions and lack of access—after which refineries, too, ceased production. Immediately, gas prices shot up nationwide. People panicked, and hoarded. Blogs and newspapers started counterpointing their photo essays of old women in National Guard rowboats with pictures of long lines at the pumps: fathers leaning idly on the hoods of their cars with red backup gas cans dangling from their fingertips, while their young daughters and sons hung out of the car windows in various states of excruciating boredom. Bertie recognized a new feeling in herself as well: a large-scale nervousness about the future that she would come to know intimately. Things that had always seemed permanent came tumbling down like dominoes. If one storm could knock out the country's access to oil, how vulnerable were they? Where else could they be hit?

The coffeepot beeped, then flooded the first cup. It smelled grainy and watered down, like diner coffee, but in a good way. There were levels of coffee—espresso, pour over, diner sludge, gas station swill—and Bertie had missed each and every kind, with all their internal variations. She sipped her cup, then readied the machine for the next round, adding more water, another pod, a fresh mug. In bed, Kate stirred, making a sound somewhere between "What?" and "Nooo." She pulled a pillow onto her head, and then moments later threw it off again, staring up at the ceiling.

"Oh, here we are," she said, her voice full of sleep. "That's nice. Are you making me breakfast?"

Bertie's shoulders tightened up at the suggestion, though she wasn't sure why. *Are you making me breakfast?* she mimicked silently. "I mean, I'm doing my best."

"You are God's gift," Kate told her. "A gift to the wretched and the woebegone."

"Maybe the woebegone would like to put on some clothes so we could finally go out and get real breakfast?"

"They will certainly try." Kate sat up in bed, and when she saw that Bertie was also in her pajamas, she threw her last remaining pillow at her. "Hey, black kettle, this is the pot speaking."

Bertie surprised herself by turning around and flipping Kate off. "At least I'm out of bed."

"Oh, at least you're . . ." Kate paused and furrowed her brow. "Whatever." They stared at each other in prickly silence. "Am I mad at you?" Kate asked.

Bertie tried to answer, but her mind was blank. What had they done last night? There was something she couldn't quite remember. Perhaps they could blame Javier, at that cellar bar with the kicky music. Had that been just yesterday? It seemed like longer. Inside Bertie, a yawning sense of distance and loss opened up, which was, she assumed, the product of a bad night's sleep.

"I think we're both just mad at ourselves for being hungover," she said at last, and Kate nodded, her face flushed with relief.

"That makes sense."

In a mood of forgiveness, they puttered around, putting on clothes, asking each other's opinion on things. Kate held up a rumpled skirt and said, "Damn, I was going to wear this to the museum, but I guess I wore it yesterday?" And Bertie shrugged.

"Wear it again. Who cares?"

"Um, Paris?"

Bertie laughed. "Probably not."

"I guess you're right," Kate said. But in the end she chose a pair of black pants, clean from the bureau where she'd unpacked her suitcase. Bertie pulled on the same jeans that had apparently been tossed by her bedside the night before, not much caring what the Parisian opinion might be of her taste in denim. But she did take the time to apply a little eyeliner and tie a scarf around her neck, because although she was really too old for it now, she still liked being approved of.

"Okay," said Bertie, as they made their final check of the room before departure. "Remember to bring your umbrella, because— Oh, wait." She peeked out the window. "I guess never mind. It's not raining."

Kate frowned. "That's a first." They'd barely seen the sun since their arrival in Paris. There had been general cloud cover and occasional downpours, not to mention the smoke that sat imperturbably over the city's bombed-out neighborhoods, which expressed itself today as a light haze. Of course, it wasn't especially unusual for the weather to take a turn, and this was arguably a turn for the better, but both women still felt uneasy looking out at the clear blue sky.

Wishing *bon matin* to the friendly clerk at the front desk, Kate and Bertie pushed their way into the sunlight, squinting slightly in the glare.

"What time did Javier say?" Bertie asked.

"Eight forty-five, as the outside limit. So I was thinking we should try for eight-twenty, eight-thirty, just to be safe."

They stopped for coffee and pastries first, Kate predictably choosing her beloved tarte aux pommes but Bertie making a game-time switch and going for a chocolate almond croissant, which dripped filling all over her fingers. Sitting at a street-side table, the women watched the city rise in pleasure all around them, soaking up the early warmth. Beautiful girls in simple shift dresses strolled side by side with interlocked pinkies, and men walked at safe distances behind them, admiring the silhouette. A class of children went past, fifteen or twenty of them holding hands, each one turning and squirming to talk to friends up and down the line. They stopped for hot chocolate at a café across the way, which caused a minor chaos as the teachers tried to keep account of all their disentangled charges. One little girl spilled her drink down the shirt of another, and both cried. A little boy whispered with his friend before pinching a third boy on the bottom, and the two conspirators laughed when they heard the victim's satisfying yelp. Trees lined the street, and cast dappled shadows on the pavement, rippling and shifting in the breeze.

"Why don't we do this every day?" Kate asked with a tranquil look on her face, which was upturned to catch the sun.

"We live in Mountain View, California, darkest heart of Silicon Valley."

"We could do this there."

"No," Bertie said, after some thought. "They closed that one nice outdoor café."

"Oh well, maybe when I'm . . ." Kate glanced over, then trailed off. Bertie knew she had been about to mention Los Angeles, but was happy to pretend otherwise, letting the comment drift into nothingness. Part of what upset Bertie about Kate's move was Kate's attitude about it, the jittery normalcy with which she approached the idea of leaving. As if there were no reason not to do it. As if the world were the same as it had ever been. There was a fire burning in southern California, which had been active for so long that a fringe group applied to put it on the National Register of Historic Places. Their online petition cited a declaration from the artist Jean Cocteau, who, when asked what he would save from his house if it were to catch fire, had replied, *I would save the fire!*

Bertie picked at her croissant, without much appetite. The almond paste left smears on her plate, gluing flakes of pastry all across the table. Kate leaned over the iron railing they were seated beside and rested her chin on her folded arms to watch the children finish off their chocolate. She smiled, and Bertie followed her gaze; the little girl who had been spilled on was licking her shirt with great satisfaction. Bertie suddenly wanted to scream.

"Don't you ever think about it?" Bertie asked Kate.

"About what? Having kids?"

"No. The world, the . . . I don't know. About . . . all the *it* there is these days?"

Kate sat back up. "What? For real? Do you ever *not* think about it?"

She had a look on her face that made Bertie feel bad about her question—bad, but not wrong. She just couldn't shake the feeling that something about Kate had changed since the ceasefire; the air around her had lightened and clarified, whereas Bertie felt her chest was being compressed, all the best oxygen leaking out of it and leaving her gasping for breath. She would be sitting at her desk at work and find her head swimming, auras bursting in front of her eyes, and have to lie back with a cold compress to keep from passing out. And now here was Kate, smiling, gauzy. Flirting with men in underground bars and enjoying the apple-cheeked Parisian youth. Which—wasn't that why they'd come here? She couldn't quite get a grip on her problem, her point.

"Whatever, I'm sorry," Bertie said. "You just sometimes seem so . . . serene."

"Oh, Bertie." Kate's expression changed, quite suddenly. "I wasn't thinking. Of course, it must all be so much worse for you."

"It's fine, I love you, let's not talk about it."

"Okay, let's not."

"Really," Bertie said into her arms, "I'm just still kind of hungover."

"Ha." Kate gave an appreciative laugh. "And here I thought you looked relatively human."

They agreed to have an early night and give themselves a chance to recover before their flight home. They would probably be tired after the Louvre, anyway, since museums had a way of exhausting a person. Bertie suggested that later in the afternoon they could go to another café and sit for an hour or so; Kate could read and she would do some drawing, maybe sketch out a few pages of her neglected graphic novel. She had once spent weeks doing figure studies to teach herself about each character: the young woman protagonist pouting her lips, or twirling her skirt, or leaning in for a closer look at something suspicious. Now, Bertie could barely recall how to draw the woman's face, and she knew it would feel good to practice.

"We're supposed to see Javier, though," Kate pointed out. "For dinner or something? I think there was a bar he said he could open up, for drinks?"

"Well," said Bertie. "It was just an idea."

—

They paid their bill and dropped a few centimes on the table as a tip, but by the time they really got moving it was already eight-fifteen, and they found themselves hurrying through the streets, allowing their usual competitive walking strategy to take hold and push them into a jog. They arrived at the Cour Napoléon at eight-thirty exactly, sprinting past the arch and underneath the horses with their arms raised like stars of track and field, stopping to catch their breath only once they reached the large fountain beside the pyramid. In the unaccustomed heat, the air seemed to shimmer, and Bertie felt herself glowing with sweat. Nearby, a father and his teenage son were tearing pieces off of a stale baguette and feeding them to a crowd of pigeons fluttering and cooing at their feet.

While Kate dug around in her bag looking for a mirror to help spruce up her makeup, Bertie watched a trio of middle-aged women peering at something on top of a nearby tower. They were so focused, it seemed like the object of their interest must be something really striking, but Bertie couldn't figure out what it was. The gargoyles, maybe? Or the architecture? She caught a flash of movement in one of the upstairs windows and decided it must be a trick of the light, a bird or cloud moving in front of the sun. Or perhaps, she thought, there might be a person inside, playing peekaboo with the women in the square. The idea gave her the shivers, and she was glad when Kate snapped her mirror shut and said, "Let's go."

The museum was technically closed to the public on Tuesdays, so there wasn't much of a crowd—just a few Parisians in business attire taking detours on their way to the office, and a couple of tourists waving at their cameras. A young man stood in the shadow of the north wing and looked at his phone, casting occasional glances at the two of them. Bertie tasted something funny and metallic on her tongue, but it wasn't unusual these days to run into a little itinerant air pollution, so she tried not to pay any attention. At the door to the glass pyramid, Kate knocked out a fluent pattern that seemed to echo in Bertie's head, and after affirming they were guests of Javier, they were grudgingly welcomed inside by a short and grumbling female guard. "Pas vous," the guard said, shaking her head at the mother and her small daughter who tried to slip in behind. Then she locked the door and scuttled off, leaving Bertie and Kate to their own devices.

It was a little bit thrilling: the emptiness, and the grand scale of the place. The women sailed down the first flight of steps and found their way into the central wing, passing a set of elevators that seemed to be going up and down of their own accord.

"What do you think about seeing some sculptures?" Kate asked. "I know this place is chock full of da Vinci, but it all seems a little done to death, doesn't it?"

"Yeah," said Bertie. "I kind of agree." She remembered wanting to visit the *Mona Lisa* very much, being excited to get close enough to see something new in that inscrutable expression. But now that the opportunity was in front of her, she found herself oddly uninterested. "Let's look at some of the weird stuff first, anyway."

There was certainly plenty of that, including a marble child strangling a marble goose and, on a pedestal nearby, a nude man vivisecting a pig. Neither of them images Bertie would've chosen to immortalize in stone, but both of which she tried to capture on her phone for later internet commentary. Even offline, Bertie kept a running mental list of things she might say on social media, statements full of hashtags and acronyms that would, out loud, have sounded insane. She liked sharing her every thought with other people—she just liked it—the interconnectivity that was possible in each moment of being alive. Probably it meant, as Kate often warned, that she was becoming a cyborg, but then so was everyone else. No experience was real anymore unless it was photographed and shared; everyone's dreams were full of screens to swipe left or right on. A museum, in particular, cried out to be documented: like a phone, it was a space that made its own context, a zone of curation.

And so Bertie was vexed that her pictures today kept turning out black or blurred despite her careful framing. Shot after shot, try after try. Flipping through her camera roll, she saw a prior string of blanks that she didn't even remember taking.

"Look at this," she said to Kate. She tried shooting a picture of them together, and it turned out as incomprehensible as the rest.

Kate agreed the blacked-out photos were kind of weird, but then said mildly, "You're on that thing way too much anyhow," and Bertie was forced to agree.

They began to wend through the various Egyptian exhibits, paying special attention to the hieroglyphs, and then to a mummy's head, laid out on a cushion. Its face was illuminated with gold leaf, the same as the walls of their hotel, and with a similar sense of having been picked at in times of desperation.

"So spooky," Kate said. "Why in God's name do you think they just have the head?" She lowered her voice. "And do you think that means someone just got the legs? Or, like, the butt?"

Bertie laughed. During the bombings, her conversations with Kate had frequently taken on a hysterical edge—she recalled one day in particular when they'd been looking at the map of new blast sites and she'd commented only, "Kentucky, fried"; and another time when Kate had taken a pencil to a similar image and used it to create a connect-the-dots dick pic. They both dined out on this skill often, keeping people giggling uneasily through times of crisis. Though she did wonder if they'd gotten too good at it. In front of them now, the mummy's flesh was dried tight against the bones, topped with a mop of all-too-human hair. It had been someone, once.

"Uuugh," said Kate. "The eyes follow you wherever you go."

"There are no eyes," Bertie replied.

"Well, the sockets."

"I don't see how—" Bertie started to correct Kate, but something stopped her. "Oh," she said. As she stepped left to right, then right to left, it did appear that the skull's vacant expression turned its interest towards her. With a nervous look at her friend, she knelt slightly, then stood on her tiptoes, walked all the way around the glass case in which the skull was arrayed. She couldn't figure out how it worked. "Curse of the mummy, I guess," she said.

Kate made a face. "I don't like it."

"Well, let me try something." Bertie aimed her phone at the skull and took a picture. It was totally black. "Damn. This, too. But at least you can't say it's looking at you there." And, as a loophole, they both found this stupidly comforting.

– 3 –

After high school, Bertie and Kate lost track of each other for a little while, catching up mainly during semester breaks, and otherwise reduced to hearing about each other's exploits secondhand through parents or mutual acquaintances. Kate had, with some fanfare, gone to a small women's college all the way across the country, making a point of moving to a place her mother had always wished she'd lived herself, so her parents would deem her choice sufficiently ambitious. Bertie, meanwhile, had stayed closer to home, at an art school twenty miles down the highway that had seemed very cool to both of them when they were sixteen, but which turned out to be kind of a comedown from the point of view of her guidance counselor.

"They're not very academically rigorous," the woman had said, hesitant even to send a recommendation. "I don't usually suggest this type of school for a student of your caliber." And she was right, as it happened, though being outside academia was never what bothered Bertie. Her bigger problem turned out to be thinking she should study painting in order to get a solid background in classical technique, and thus missing out on the shoptalk of the cartoon and animation students, many of whom went on to get jobs in movie studios or doing inks for large comics publishers. Bertie didn't know about any of that. She had opinions on the figurative qualities in Picasso, but no sense of which cons—Comic-Con? Adventure Con?—were good places for a beginner to go and try to sell chapbooks or make some industry friends.

She felt the failure of this very keenly: of not having pleased anyone, least of all herself. Not the guidance counselor, who was so insistent on her good GPA, but also not her new professors, who wanted students who actually liked painting, and whose postgrad advice revolved mainly around galleries and agents and the Whitney Biennial, none of which applied to what Bertie wanted to do. Academically, she slipped by without triggering any alarm bells, and even finished a few one-shot comics in her senior year, which she launched online to minimal fanfare. *Rage the Rabbit* was two pages long and featured a bunny defending a ziggurat, wearing a suit of armor; *Sophie the Ghost* and *Elsa Everywhere* were closer to her actual interests, a few pages each of women working with computers and accidentally stepping through doorways in time. But that was the extent of her professional portfolio.

It was only by luck that she ended up with the job she did. During her senior year, she took to dropping by her adviser's office hours rather too often, hoping but not willing to ask that she might actually be *advised*. That poor woman—Bertie saw now what a hopeless case she must have seemed to a prizewinning scholar and landscape painter who didn't really consider animation a fine art. Professor Zwicky gamely asked Bertie about her thoughts on graduate school, but both of them knew she didn't have any, after which there wasn't much to say, and their office hours dwindled. Bertie had already begun making plans to move home and go back to the fancy cheese shop job from her high school days—*At least now I'll be allowed to handle the wines,* she thought grimly—when Zwicky mentioned, in an offhand way, that some tech companies in California had contacted the school about illustrator positions.

"Probably not very up your alley," Zwicky said, taking a sip of the diet soda she always had several cans of on her desk. "It's very reactive work, just doodles and things for the marketing team. And who even knows what these companies really do." There was a warning in her voice, but to Bertie it sounded like heaven. Money, just for drawing things. A preference for cartoonish style. And not enough art world knowledge or cachet to know the difference between various BFA degrees, so that Bertie's specialization in painting would not be looked on unfavorably. As it turned out, the company she applied to mainly sold online advertising, but they also had an entertainment arm, a research and development arm, and a series of philanthropic ventures, all of which needed cheery illustrations. Bertie would learn that this was the favored Silicon Valley business model: doing one thing well, and a hundred other things in the shadows. She was flown down for an interview that involved a drawing test and a long series of questions about how well she worked with others, which, by rights, she should have flunked, given how little she liked group projects. But somehow her desire for approbation—always strongest when it involved being praised for meeting a set of demands she secretly thought were stupid—reared up and brought her through just fine.

"I can't believe it," Zwicky said breathlessly, when she heard about the offer letter. "You'll probably have the highest starting salary in your class." For an art student, it was a dubious compliment, but Bertie was so relieved not to have to live with her parents that she beamed with total pride.

—

Those first years were good for Bertie. She found out that Kate had also moved to the Bay Area, pursuing what turned out to be a failed internship with a local paper and then swiftly moving on to a series of nonprofit roles, in which she flourished. Bertie was perplexed by the change of plans—Kate had always been insistent about writing, and now she seemed not to care about it at all—but unsurprised by the success. She regretted the years they'd spent apart in college, as if some layer or version of Kate had been sanded off and would never return, and she tried to make up for it by being as close as possible now, so she wouldn't miss anything more. Over time they built back up their friendship, first getting coffees and gossiping about old acquaintances and then moving on to drinks and shows which they ignored, preferring to lament their love lives, or else to talk big about the dreams they felt were just on the horizon. Both of them dated a lot, though unsuccessfully, choosing the solace of easy sex over the ontological work of rearranging their lives for relationships. For a while, Bertie lived in the city with a couple of roommates, sharing a three-bedroom apartment in the Mission and reveling in the tacos, the margarita bars, and the large buses her company sent every morning and afternoon to shepherd its employees to and from the office. She often slept against the window on her way back home, but in the mornings, when her thinking was still fresh, she used the commute hours to sketch out narratives for the graphic novel that was then just starting to take shape in her mind.

After a couple of years, Kate began hinting that she should move to the South Bay, with her. Most of the cooler people at Bertie's office were going to Oakland or else sweeping out over the city wherever they could afford to, leaving a film of kombucha bars and yoga studios in their wake. But that was expensive, and Bertie was, in fact, getting tired of the commute, and her roommates. They'd been a good introduction to San Francisco when she first arrived: a young law student who knew the best spots for martinis and a stoner who worked for a competing tech firm; they all went out as a group several times, and for a while it was their habit to drink wine together in the evenings or go to the movies when one of them felt low.

But the camaraderie had worn thin over the years. Angel liked to cook aromatic curries and leave the dishes in the sink for a week, and Jessica smoked all the time, even indoors, claiming that marijuana didn't leave behind an odor. Bertie had initially thought of them as a scrappy sitcom family, pushed together by circumstance into something greater than the sum of its parts, but although mismatched personalities played well on television, in real life it was hard to reconcile living with someone who left their laundry lying all around the house, especially when they claimed it was a choice in the name of efficiency, a "disruption of the domestic space." A few months before the end of their second lease, the roommates stopped even being polite, which at first felt like a new level of sisterliness—the comfortably bitchy level—but which in retrospect Bertie knew had been the beginning of the end.

"What you need is to live with grown-ups," Kate said. "Or at least around grown-ups." They were twenty-five then, and all of

Kate's pronouncements sounded like fact. Part of which was pure confidence, but she was made extra credible by the intensity of their renewed friendship, and by the quiet of the one-bedroom apartment she rented all by herself. It was always clean, if somewhat beige, and full of spices and treats that Kate had collected to please her own taste, which no roommates ever made fun of or stole. One weekend, Bertie came down to the South Bay to stay with her, and they drove around looking at various units coming on the market. It started out as an exercise, but by Sunday afternoon she'd signed a lease; the apartment itself was nothing special, but the complex was small, with a pretty garden, and best of all, it was walking distance from Kate's house. They toasted that evening with champagne, and when Bertie told her roommates, they seemed genuinely happy for her, at least once it was established that she would still pay her share of the final month's rent.

It shocked Bertie a little that she was able to make such a major decision in such a short amount of time, but when she said as much, Kate laughed and told her that it was better than making no choices at all.

—

Unprecedented among her peers, Bertie stayed with the same company for years after she graduated college, and for a long time, she even liked it—a fact she proudly told her mom and dad whenever they talked on the phone. There was a great deal of opportunity for someone like her to stretch and grow, so long as they were willing to put the effort in, and Bertie was. She moved up from sketching other people's concepts to pitching her own in what seemed like a very short time, and soon was producing work from start to finish that the company used in a very public way. There was a thrill to that, seeing something she'd made herself out in the world where anyone could come across it. Her drawings and ideas were part of the company's public image, and that made her feel smart and capable, despite the fact that her name was never attached to anything: it all belonged to the company, not to her, and they all shared the same reflected glow. *It's like communism,* she sometimes said. *Except very, very capitalism.*

In the art world, a few of the people she'd gone to school with were emerging with gallery deals or show-running their own cartoons, but Bertie didn't envy that, at least not most of the time. Some of them crashed and burned, after all, while she was achieving steadily, at her own pace, and living a life several steps above what she'd been taught to expect for a "starving artist." In her spare time, she sketched, then colored with watercolors, and finally inked three pages of her graphic novel, which felt like a momentous achievement. No one besides Kate was allowed to see them, but at least Bertie knew they existed, like a tiny promise she kept locked away. She planned out several more before putting the whole project in a drawer to "marinate," which was where it remained. She told herself she wanted time to digest her ideas, but in point of fact the ideas had begun to dry up, and Bertie was afraid to look too often at the finished pages in case the "ideas" in them started seeming as foolish to her as the ones now swimming around in her head.

You could always start again, she told herself. *If you really needed to.* But given how long it had taken her to begin just once, doing it twice felt impossible, to the point of being sadistic.

Instead, she drew portraits of her friends on bar napkins, and they laughed with the pleasure of recognition, although they also forgot them or accidentally ruined them with cold drinks most of the time. Which was fine. Kate had one of Bertie's real paintings, framed, in her living room, and that fact never failed to make Bertie smile. The two of them were usually enough. They met each other's romantic prospects and dissected them lustily until they disappeared: men with goatees that scratched Bertie's face when they kissed, high achievers and soulful loners, all of them seeming to possess one positive quality that wasn't enough to compensate for their weakness in other areas. They reminisced about old loves, like the boy Bertie ran through the rain to kiss at a concert in high school, whom she'd never actually called afterwards, despite the pleasing shape of his face, the taste of his mouth. *Oh well,* they told each other. *If it was meant to be, it would have been.*

In the lead-up to Bertie's thirtieth birthday—a turn of events that was met with hilarity from all quarters, due to the rhyme of "Bertie turns thirty"—not to mention the option of adding in "dirty"—her parents moved to a small town in upstate New York, wanting, in the first flush of their retirement, to take advantage of being a train ride away from the city's famous theatre scene. With the drought in California spreading all up and down the West Coast, it seemed like a prudent idea as well: heading east to the rivers and the snow, away from all the unrelenting sun and continual wildfires. Seattle wasn't exactly the Mojave, but it was warmer in the summers now, and Bertie got the sense that her parents needed an adventure. There were no grandkids on the horizon, so why not?

You never know why not, before it happens. That's what Bertie realized. Time passes. Slow, then fast. Bit by bit, and then it's gone.

—

She remembered the day Kate had knocked on her door. It was a Saturday, the early morning. She was still in her pajamas and didn't think anything of her friend dropping by, though they didn't have plans. Maybe Kate wanted to go out to breakfast, or drive to Half Moon Bay for a walk. They liked to do things spur of the moment. It was one of the pleasures of living so close. Her face—Kate's face, that is, when Bertie let her in—was white.

"Have you heard anything?" she asked.

"About what?" Bertie didn't subscribe to the paper—no one did—and the only way she would have heard any news that early in the day would have been if she looked at her phone and fell into a social media sinkhole. Which, with an outsized sense of virtue, she had decided against that morning. As Kate stared at her, Bertie was aware of existing in a Schrödinger's moment, between knowing and not knowing—something. Unsettling, but there was a certain calm in it: sensing the storm, like electricity on her skin, while the sun was still shining, the day still serene.

"Jesus. Um." Kate paced around the small living room, which was contiguous with the small kitchen and dining room, running her hand through her hair. "I don't know how to say this. But, um. There's been an accident. Or—an explosion."

"Where?" Bertie asked. "Downtown?" She tried to think if there were any power plants nearby, or natural gas deposits: stuff that might be prone to blowing up. There were oil derricks off the coast in L.A., but not this far north, as far as Bertie knew. Kate was shaking, she noticed. Folding one hand over the other on an impossible mission to keep them still. Bertie hadn't heard anything outside, but that didn't necessarily mean much. Maybe a filling station had caught on fire, or—God forbid—some idiotic, disgruntled man had built a bomb. "Was it at Stanford?"

"Bunny, no. Please." Kate beckoned Bertie over to her own couch and grabbed her hands as they both sat down. "I mean there was something big. In New York."

Her parents had sent a card that looked like a birth announcement, which actually said: *We're having a late-life crisis!* And inside: *We're moving to New York!* Though of course that wasn't technically true. They were moving to Woodstock. Or somewhere near Woodstock, actually: a Catskills town with the stupidly adorable name of Bearville, which Bertie called "Boreville" when she felt like teasing them about their rural turn.

"How big?" Bertie heard herself asking, but suddenly she didn't want to know.

Kate's voice was hoarse. "A lot of things are gone."

"From—you said an accident?"

"They aren't really sure yet. I guess—" She stopped and looked up at the ceiling as if the answer might be there. "I guess some people were saying that, but it's starting to look like maybe not."

"Then what?"

"Like, something that was done on purpose."

Dropping Kate's hands, Bertie ran over to the kitchen table and grabbed her phone. She tried calling her mom, but it went straight to voicemail, so she tried her dad next. It didn't even ring—all she heard was a weird, piercing sound on the other end of the line. A machine sound, but a deranged one, screaming and screaming at Bertie until she started to scream back.

"What's this?" She held up the phone to Kate. When Kate hesitated to take it, Bertie shook it in her face, then pushed it against Kate's ear. "What is it? Is it a disaster signal? I don't understand."

"Babe, I don't know." There were tears in Kate's eyes, tears on her cheeks. She had always liked Bertie's parents. When they were young, Bertie's mom baked bread and let them steal wine from the basement, and sometimes she sat down with them to have a glass, so Bertie's dad would get back from work and find them all together, shooting the breeze. *My women!* he'd say. *Look at these beautiful women!* When her mom made a point, she trailed her fingers through the air, conducting. Slower and slower, the more she drank. "They were probably at home, though, right? I bet the cell tower's just overloaded. That can happen when a lot of people are trying to call at once."

"Why didn't they stay where they were?" Bertie asked. "They were fine where they were. Their complaint was that it got sunny? Too sunny? That's a complaint?"

"I'm sure they're trying to call you right this very minute."

"So you're getting older and you want to make a change. That's fine! But buy a condo. Take up skydiving. Travel."

"They like theatre," Kate said with a shrug, then realized immediately it was the wrong thing to say. "It was—when did they see that weird Finnish production of *Hamlet*? The one with the set that was just a big whale? Wasn't that really recently?"

"Last week sometime," mumbled Bertie.

"So there you go! And that was on Broadway. They wouldn't take the train back that soon, the show tickets are too expensive."

But Bertie didn't believe her.

They spent the morning eating snacks and poring over the news. It came in fits and starts—nothing much for several hours, and then three separate reports in fifteen minutes. Each new headline ratcheted up the tension.

"God, why don't you have a TV?" Kate asked, trying to pull up a video on Bertie's laptop and getting frustrated while it buffered.

"I don't want one. They take up too much space."

"But you watch more TV than anyone I know, you just do it on your tiny computer. You're going to go blind. And this is crazy!" Still, Bertie refused to leave the house, even to go to Kate's apartment, where a TV was available. She felt a magnetism to her own small set of rooms, the last place her mom and dad had seen her and therefore the place they were most likely to picture her, if they tried.

The news was jumbled between the big papers and the major broadcast stations, everyone scooping everyone else, social media losing its collective mind. There were a lot of unsavory comments, too: *What do you expect with that "president" of ours?* and A *wicked life invites disaster, Proverbs 12:26* and the more straightforward *We r all f*cked*. Through it all, Bertie kept trying to reach her parents, but by noon both numbers were yielding the same shrieking pitch, and Bertie had started crying every time she heard it. Something about the sound itself, as well as its meaning; it burrowed its way into her mind and duplicated itself there endlessly, almost religious in its significance. Finally, at eleven p.m., Kate pried the phone out of her fingers and gave her a sleeping pill and put her to bed.

Maybe that was the first day (*Do you ever think about the . . . all the* it?), for Bertie and Kate, at least, when things changed; time passed slowly and then hit a wall. There had been other small disasters after a tempestuous national election, but nothing on quite such a scale. And in the months that followed, everything seemed to increase in speed: floods and fires around the world, skirmishes between citizens and the police, a doomsday cult in Kathmandu that took lethal doses of arsenic in a populous square and terrorized thousands of people with their convulsive deaths. By the time the bombings started in earnest—first in Berlin but then Shanghai and then London and America at large—Bertie had received official word from the state that both her parents had been killed in New York. Apparently they got rush tickets to a musical they'd been wanting to see. She could imagine their glee, her father's whoop of triumph and her mother's more restrained, but still immodest, smile. When she was in high school, they'd never cared much about the theatre, but it came on them like a fever at sixty-five.

– 4 –

"Tell you what," said Bertie as she and Kate crept away from the mummy exhibit. "There are some paintings I want to see. Something a little more temperamentally soothing, pretty portraits."

"In pretty frames?"

"Mais, bien sûr, ma cherie. But of course."

Bertie cast a last look over her shoulder as they left the mummy behind. The nothingness of its eyes was somehow too familiar, a screaming void, an empty phone call, that followed you wherever you went.

—

Bertie and Kate had made plans to buy a house together in the countryside, for when things started to get really bad. Maybe northern California or eastern Washington, which would be cheaper. End of the World House, they would call it. Clapboard siding and a hill behind, for either sunrises or sunsets, depending on the orientation of the land. Grassy fields, but with trees in the distance; you would have to be careful about poison oak and ticks. Inside, light would stream through the windows, bending past gauzy curtains to fall on empty coffee cups and stacks of books. None of the kitchen cabinets would quite close. There would be old furniture, bought for a song at the local flea market or left over from the people who'd lived there before, with blankets tossed over the backs of everything to tamp down the dust.

Of course, things were already bad when they came up with the idea. During the months when bombs were dropping—*the nouveau Blitz,* Kate called it, though that wasn't quite right, since there was never a clear set of allies or enemies, just the shock of walking by a building and seeing it blown to smithereens, a toilet suddenly exposed to the air, an arm uncurled from beneath a cracked block of concrete—Kate and Bertie held slumber parties almost every night. It wasn't an official thing; it just happened. One of them would show up at the other's door with a bottle of whiskey or wine, and they would lie on the floor or on the couch, blankets burrito-ed around their knees and feet, talking and listening to the deafening thuds.

Bertie remembered it all vividly. Kate, making a pillow from her arms and hiding her face when she was scared, which was often. Kate, tugging on her bottom lip when she was thinking. She was rarely aware of doing this, so sometimes Bertie would reach over and grab the lip, too, and Kate would protest by sticking out her tongue and spitting, and they both would laugh. Sometimes the sounds they heard seemed very close by, like the footsteps of a giant who was lifting the roofs off nearby buildings.

Before moving to Seattle, Kate's family had lived in Pittsburgh, where she'd hung out with a straight-edge punk crowd, anti-fascists who loved to thread safety pins into all of their clothing and sometimes their skin. It was the origin story of her glorious purple hair, her alienating taste in music. She'd known a girl there who pierced her own lip on a school bus and got gangrene, and Bertie couldn't help but wonder if this was where Kate's habit came from, the calm reassurance of checking that her own lip was still there. Which, during their dark nights of drinking, listening, waiting, Bertie was also happy to partake in. Kate's lip, still there. Kate, still present and accounted for.

It was a time of continual, self-imposed curfew. The city had designated a few bomb shelters, but no one really seemed to use them, at least not after seeing how poorly built they were: hasty constructions of concrete and sound-dampening foam, meant less as a solution and more as a political prop. As if a rushed public works project could somehow put the world right. Police activity became violent, too. At first everyone went to protests as if they were parties, throwing up peace signs for the camera and lugging around poster board with clever slogans decrying any number of ills, but soon the police caught wind of the fact that these photos were tagged with people's names and locations, and started visiting the photographers and also some of the subjects at home, in the name of "maintaining a peaceful social atmosphere." Around the same time, the whole idea of being part of a whirling mass of humanity on the street stopped seeming appealing and started to seem like a good way to get killed. Brunch became more of a thing again, but it didn't take long for that to feel too public, too, so people made a show of eating at home to "save money" and "make their personal space more enticing."

The thing was, even at home you weren't safe, not really. Lightbulbs had to be unscrewed in the evenings and replaced by candles, which were hidden behind blackout curtains. You had a blackout buddy, and you stuck to that buddy like white on rice. A lot of unexpected romances sprang up, people who had been together by chance when the first bomb dropped and now felt compelled to stay together, keeping each other as talismans against harm. One of Kate's coworkers was engaged to a man who'd been standing behind her in line when they got stuck in an ATM vestibule. The VP of Bertie's division at work was rumored to be sleeping with his kid's nanny, though that particular rumor had actually been around since before the bombs.

And then there was Kate and Bertie. They got good, in those months, at being inside. They leaned into the punch-drunkenness, and often the real drunkenness, of it all, which was a good distraction from restless feelings, though slightly less so from the fear. Together, and for an audience of none, they staged a one-act play wearing masks they'd fashioned out of paper grocery bags, impersonating animals of the jungle: Bertie was tigers, monkeys, snakes, while Kate was panthers and birds of prey. They built six-story houses out of playing cards, and then taught themselves poker. Tried and failed to sleep.

There were times when Bertie couldn't stop crying. She missed her dad, she missed her mom, she wanted to die, too, if they were gone. Her heart was just a shred of a heart; she could feel how bloody it was. She could *feel* it. Kate held her, then. She stroked Bertie's hair until she calmed down, and then used a propane stove to boil water and brew them both mugs of tea, making shadow puppets on the wall behind the blue ring of fire. One time Kate showed up and found Bertie throwing out all of her clothes, claiming to be following the advice of an internet guru and simplifying her life. "It's self-care!" she screamed, as Kate pulled armfuls of sweatshirts and dresses out of garbage bags and threw them back into Bertie's bedroom. "Self-care! Self-care!" If Kate resented being the one to offer this level of oversight, she rarely showed it. Most often they spent their evenings telling each other the plots of old movies as if they were ancient myths, gently correcting each other when any detail came out wrong, as if those stories were tethering them to the world of the living, the lives they had lived.

Then, one evening early in the cease-fire, just a couple of weeks after the peace talks in Norway, Bertie went over to Kate's apartment and found her gone. No answer when she knocked; no answer when, assuming Kate was in the shower, she knocked louder and shouted, "Hey, let me in, jerkface!" Bertie slid to the ground outside Kate's door to wait, and texted, *If you're getting ice cream, I want mint chip please.* Now that electricity was becoming more reliable again, grocery stores were dipping their toes back into the frozen-foods market. She waited. The sun began to go down.

After half an hour, with no Kate and no reply, she left.

Bertie never did find out where she'd been. "Oh, I was out," Kate told her breezily the next day, as if it were no big deal. But after that, the sleepovers tapered off, going down to one or two a week, then one a month, before stopping altogether. Bertie still sometimes sent Kate unaffordable real estate listings that matched their requirements for the End of the World House, going so far as to claim her favorite bedrooms in a few, to which Kate always responded, *LOL*. But it wasn't until she announced her move that Bertie understood the depth of Kate's *LOL*; how much of a joke and a game she perceived their plans to be. They were cold to each other for a while—well, cold didn't quite cover it—but now they were pretending that none of that had happened. Which would work right up until the day Kate drove away, or until Bertie cracked and actually asked her to talk about it, both of which seemed, to Bertie, impossible.

—

As they navigated through the wings of the museum, Kate began to nitpick Bertie's choice of outfit, on the basis that it wouldn't make a good impression on Javier.

"Great feminist credentials," Bertie said brightly. "Telling your best friend to wear shorter skirts. Why not ask me to smile more, too?"

"First of all," said Kate, "you are not wearing a skirt, so telling you to wear a shorter one would be nonsensical. All I said was that maybe the dirtiest jeans you could find were not the absolute best choice when you have plans with a person of influence."

"Oh, he's a person of influence now, is he?"

"He did what he said. We're here, right? So who knows? Maybe he's important."

"Hmm." Bertie observed the gilded walls of the room they were walking through, and the chandelier that veritably dripped from the ceiling. They were beautiful, but that didn't mean Javier was critical to their beauty. Probably a janitor could've snuck them into the museum as easily as a curator or financier—maybe even more so. Bertie realized with some satisfaction that Javier had never specified what his job was. "I like my jeans," she said.

"Well, like away. And second"—it was a personal pet peeve of Kate's when people didn't finish their lists—"you can't call someone anti-feminist just because they say something you find dickish. That's reductive."

"Interesting choice of words."

"I am a writer."

"Really though," Bertie said. "Are you?"

Kate looked at her. Bertie clamped a hand over her mouth, inadvertently mirroring a picture behind her of a child holding back a scream. The question had rolled off her tongue so easily it must have been waiting there for some time. But Bertie hadn't known.

"Wow," Kate said. "Okay."

The women stepped apart and pretended to become very interested in art on opposite sides of the room. They were used to dealing with cold wars: early on in the trip, Kate had pointed out a euro coin on the sidewalk, and when Bertie bent down to grab it, Kate said, "Hey. That was mine." Which Bertie knew was true, but couldn't bring herself to admit. "You just said something out loud," she complained. "That doesn't mean I didn't see it." After that they'd barely spoken to each other for an hour.

Now they stood back-to-back, listening to each other's footsteps to avoid turning around at the same time. Bertie knew she should apologize. She had a strange sense, in fact, that she'd already wanted to apologize to Kate about something—not the euro, something else; a leftover feeling, like a hangover of guilt—but couldn't find the words. They were stuck in her throat, behind a lump of umbrage—a hangover of equally opaque anger.

At the end of the hall, Kate turned, and sniffed, focusing all her energy on a painting of a young martyr, drowned in a river and floating downstream. *Isn't that a little on the nose?* Bertie thought. But she didn't say anything, and when Kate moved into the next room, Bertie shuffled behind her, hands jammed into the pockets of her jeans.

—

She followed her through an apartment museum, and then a central gallery of white marble and bright light. All the while, the back of Kate's head fumed, her hair tossing from one shoulder to the other like the tail of a furious cat. If she had been a cartoon, Bertie would have drawn her with a bubble of steam leaking out of her scalp. And what about herself? She would have made her eyes big. She would've made her mouth small. Beads of sweat pinging off her into the ether.

What Bertie couldn't figure out was whether she was just jealous. That Javier had seen something special in Kate, and decided to bring her here. Which—Bertie wasn't interested in Javier, but she knew how powerful that kind of attention could be. The gravity of the acquisitive eye. She'd seen it all the time at school, during painting critiques and group shows, where consensus always built around a handful of pieces as if by magic. She saw it at work, when angel investors were given tours of the open-floor-plan office. Once one person noticed you, others would follow. It was the whole principle behind a museum, really; the method by which great art was anointed.

Finally, they entered a small circular chamber, carefully tiled with cool stone.

"Oh," said Bertie. Because here they were: the pretty paintings, in pretty frames.

Kate turned to look at her, eyebrows raised.

"It's the Gallery of Apollo," Bertie explained. Then, not wanting to seem too interested, in case Kate was still mad enough to storm out and spite her, she shrugged. "It's supposed to be pretty cool, I guess."

In fact, it was one of the places in the Louvre that Bertie had most wanted to see. The gallery was hung with row after row of portraiture in rococo frames, placed so close together that they looked like LEGO pieces or Tetris tiles. Sun streamed in through the windows, made brighter by the heavy gilding, and Bertie squinted in the glare, trying to see the end of the hall. The guidebook had described the gallery as a small, enclosed space, but apparently that was wrong. It continued, back and back, farther than the eye could see.

Bertie recognized in some of the portraits a face she often tried to affect herself in photographs: bored, but amused. Pretty, but distant. Hopeful that a single sharp gesture would imply a lifetime of thoughtfulness and wit. She pulled out her phone to take a selfie with one of the pictures, but then remembered that it wasn't working.

"For Christ's sake," she mumbled, whacking the phone against her thigh. Which did exactly nothing. She snapped a few shots of the coved ceiling, then deleted them all when they came out as black squares. She thought, *Pics or it didn't happen.* A dumb old joke that had lately taken on the weight of literal truth.

Kate rolled her eyes at Bertie, then turned her attention to a portrait of a nude woman draped over a tiger. Balancing on one foot, she mimicked the pose in something between an arabesque and a pratfall. "Huh," she said with grudging approval. "I could get used to this."

“Well, you might have to,” Bertie said, peering into the distance. “Seems like this room goes on forever.”

She meant it as a joke, but the farther they went, the more Bertie felt an offness to it. There was something slow, almost liquid, about the air in the gallery. A languor that clung to the limbs, as if leaking out of the world of the paintings. Plus, the space was just too big: she was sure the guidebook would have mentioned if such a famous room had been recently renovated.

“Do you think this is at all weird?” Bertie asked.

“Hmm?” said Kate. She was leaning over a glass case of jewelry, bracelets and a small tiara. The gems flashed on her skin, speckling her red, green, blue. “I mean, no?” She paused. “Or, I guess, this whole day has been weird?”

“I don’t know,” said Bertie. “Something about this doesn’t feel right. We should have hit the end of the gallery by now.”

Kate shrugged. “You’re the one who wanted to come here.”

“But why didn’t we see the *Mona Lisa* first?” Bertie asked. “Isn’t that basically Louvre 101?”

“That’s exactly why you didn’t want to do it.”

“No, you didn’t.”

“I sort of did, I just ” Kate trailed off. “Look, to be honest, you’re being kind of a lot today. Can’t we just enjoy this?”

Once, Bertie and Kate had gone car camping along the edge of a cold California lake and watched lightning strike the mountains behind them, frigid with awe. They’d jumped into the water naked, their hearts nearly stopping in the glacial melt, and it was only later that they’d realized the storm could’ve turned at any moment and struck the waves and burned them up. *Anything is possible,* Bertie had thought, then. *Even that.*

Now, she rubbed her hands over her face, and began to say, "Well, sorry—" when a sound came from nearby, like rats shuffling through newspapers. Kate straightened out of her crouch.

"Shut up," she said.

"I'm *sorry*, I just—"

"No." Kate turned and raised her eyebrows, then motioned down the hall. "Shut up, I think I heard something."

"I don't think—" Bertie began, but she was interrupted again, this time by a peal of laughter echoing down the hall. The women froze. Then, without even looking at each other, they took off towards it at a run.

The sound—a mixture of hilarity, conversation, and scuffing feet—seemed to travel around as they tried to catch up to it: it would be ahead and then to the side; it would inexplicably seem to be coming from behind the walls. A figure darted across the gallery in front of them and gave Bertie a White Rabbit feeling—*I'm late, I'm late, I'm late,* she thought. *For a very important . . . what?* It was almost embarrassing to realize that other people had been in the museum all this time, as if Bertie and Kate had been lounging at home in their underwear and looked outside to see a neighbor watching them through the window.

Bertie stopped short. "Kate, wait a minute, there's something wrong here." But Kate kept going.

"Javier!" she said with delight. "I think I saw him."

"Wait, though. Just for one second. Please?"

Kate waved her off and disappeared around the corner. Bertie sighed and ran after her, but she wasn't around the corner, either, and soon thereafter Bertie came to a staircase, branching out in two different directions. One towards an exit, and one going who knows where. Both were empty.

"Goddamnit, Kate," she said. She sat down, heavily, on a step.

As a child, Bertie had learned to stay still when she got lost and give people a chance to track her down. It always worked in the grocery store, where a clerk would eventually spot her eating grapes and plant her up front with the cashiers, calling her name out over the intercom until her mom came to collect her. It had worked with her dad once, too, when Bertie pooped out in the middle of a hike, and her father had gotten half a mile away before he realized she was no longer following him. All afternoon he'd been threatening to leave her behind to be eaten by bears if she didn't hustle. "Too bad I'll never see you again!" he declared, as he finally walked off. "Too bad about the bears!" But he must have assumed she was still behind him, because it took him almost fifteen minutes to turn around and sprint back to her. When he found her, huddled under a tree making elf houses with pinecones and twigs, he'd swept her up into his arms and called her a little shit, before taking them both out for ice cream.

But would Kate come back? Bertie wasn't sure.

Five minutes passed. Then ten. Bertie thought about how Kate had been so certain she'd seen Javier off in the distance. How she'd hurried towards him, with a luminous smile. It was true that Kate had always been a master of the French exit. She was friendly, but she hated saying goodbye. *Where did Kate go?* people were always asking at the end of the party. The hosts, the guests, the hangers-on. *Why didn't she say anything? Is she coming back? Is she gone?*

Usually, though, she at least told Bertie. She would whisper in her ear and then vanish with a wink. Sometimes they'd hold hands and flee together, laughing with the windows down as they drove home through darkened streets. They always checked in with each other before making drastic moves—Kate letting Bertie vet her eye makeup before she took the long stroll across the bar to hit on someone, Bertie allowing Kate to put her hair up and spray it into place. A pinch of the elbow, a squeeze of the hand: they had a language of care that kept them intact when the whole world was falling to pieces around them. And if that was gone, then what did Bertie have? Who would hold her together?

Twenty minutes. Bertie looked around herself at the marble stairs, the arching ceilings. *You're being kind of a lot today,* Kate had told her. And she felt like a lot. She felt like everything, spilling out of every pore.

The hallways were silent. Wherever she'd been headed, for whatever reason, Kate was gone. Bertie waited five more minutes, and then she left, too.

—5—

To get out of the Louvre, Bertie discovered, you had to walk through a high-end mall, a hidden passage of haute couture that was no less disconcerting now for being empty and closed, bathed in shadows, than it might have been lit up. *Look at you,* the headless models seemed to say. *What a shame to be you.* Their clothes so clean, their bodies pared down to fashion essentials, without hands or feet, without faces or minds. When the door shut behind her, she felt the *clink* of the lock in her bones, the same way she had when she and Kate arrived at the museum that morning—the only difference being that now she was stuck outside instead of in. And now she was alone.

She'd been ejected into the Tuileries, and around her, pedestrians huddled together as they walked under shared umbrellas, tête-very much à-tête. It was raining again. Bertie shivered as her jacket began to adhere itself to her skin, and she decided to find a bar and get as drunk as possible.

After that, things got blurry. She kept thinking she was being followed through the gardens, but whenever she whipped around, there was no one there. Chestnut trees loomed above her, as colors and shapes pressed in from the sides, the sense of cold hands reaching out from the shadows, until eventually Bertie found her way to the street. Then what? When she tried to think back, it was difficult, like walking against the wind. She might have ended up a few blocks from her hotel, strolling over the Seine and past Saint-Sulpice, or maybe she crossed the river in a cab; there was that pressure of windows and walls, the heat blasting in her face and then disappearing, lightening some load; maybe euros from her wallet, maybe the stress of finding her way alone. Then she was at a bar full of American expats: lamplight spilling onto the sidewalk, people smoking under the awning, everyone speaking English, so familiar it warmed her from the outside in.

—

Her memories were hazy and multiple, overlaying one another until she forced them together and made them stay. Bertie drank a glass of red wine, very fast, and then ordered a whiskey. Kate had abandoned her, and here she was. So much for their quiet evening of reading. So much for the end of their grand tour. All her life she'd followed the rules, getting A's on her report card and landing a job that brought in cash. She'd walked the straight and narrow path as if in a game of Candy Land, collecting gumdrop after gumdrop, with the occasional licorice twist. She'd been nice to Kate, almost all the time. And this was what happened. Being nice got you this.

But maybe the path hadn't been so straight. Half the whiskey, now, was gone. Maybe there had been many ways to look at herself from the very beginning, which didn't line so neatly up. Her bar stool, she realized, could spin around, and she spun it now, smiling at the boy seated next to her, to whom she realized she had been talking for some time, describing her confusing evening and telling him, *To hell with Kate.*

"Who ditches their best friend on *vacation*?" she asked, slurring just slightly, tilting her chin onto her shoulder to maintain eye contact as she twirled. "For a *man*. Who *does* that?" The boy shook his head and frowned, leaning his elbows on the sticky bar. He couldn't have been more than twenty-four, and he wasn't much of a conversationalist. But he was listening to her, and maybe that was enough. He bought her another well whiskey on the rocks and got the bartender to give them a red basket full of salted pretzels; according to the flag patch sewn onto his backpack, he was Australian, though who could say. "Wrong bar for Aussies," Bertie said conspiratorially. "But don't worry, I won't tell."

She took a sip of her drink. "Do you know," she said. "I mean, have you noticed, that the world is ending?" The boy just gaped. Bertie nodded, feeling sage. "And even though the world is, like, over, people still want everything to be normal? People still want to do a . . . a *juice cleanse*?" As she leaned forwards to emphasize "juice cleanse," the boy leaned back in astonishment, though it was unclear to Bertie if he was reacting to all that immoderate living, or to the fact that Bertie had elbowed over the pretzels, knocking them all across his lap. "I just want to, like, shake their shoulders and say, guys, there's no Florida anymore! The KKK has ahold of Mississippi!"

"The what?" asked the boy, saying his first words to Bertie, or possibly even his very first words of all time. The air shimmered around them.

"The racists! With the hoods!"

To which the boy said nothing but did adopt a look of grim understanding. He was definitely Australian. He had that accent, like biting a lemon with every word, and he was bronzed all over from surf and sun. Bertie wanted to tell him that the world was not to be relied upon, that the things you trusted would sneak up and sink their teeth into you when you least expected it, but he had so many freckles, and they were so cute, and she kept getting distracted and trying to touch them. Which was harder than it should have been, because he kept looking around for the dropped pretzels, putting them, one by one, back in their basket. Then he started to eat them. The boy was wearing a probably ironic t-shirt, screen-printed with the words G'DAY! (Or was that one word? Did it count as a compound if it was technically just misspeaking?) She wanted to say again that life as they knew it was over, that friends were not friends and safety was an illusion, but even through the alcoholic fog, she knew how maudlin that would sound. So she bent over and kissed the boy instead, hard on the mouth, and he accepted it with the same gallantry he'd accepted everything, except perhaps the spilling of the pretzels.

They made out for a little while in the bathroom, which was wood-paneled, and covered with scratched-on graffiti. It felt good at first: his warm chest, the uneducated roving of his hands. Bertie hitched her T-shirt up, bringing his palms in contact with her skin, and the boy responded by unzipping his pants, an idea about which Bertie shared his enthusiasm; around them the words of past occupants screamed in all caps, entreating them to CALL ZOE SHE'S A BITCH, and announcing EIFFEL TOWER!! JOIE DE VIVRE!!! And Bertie considered, *Why not joie? Given vivre?* Why not live just a little bit?

She made a sudden turn and banged her head against the stall door, cartoon stars emerging before her eyes as cartoon birds tweeted above her (or maybe she was imagining those?), and she simultaneously smacked her elbow into the empty toilet paper dispenser. The boy took this opportunity to put his hands on both of her breasts, and with her funny bone zinging electric within her, she chased him away, catching just enough relief on his face to be furious at him. Because how dare he, after all, think he knew better than she did how embarrassing this all was.

—

Those rules she'd followed. What good had they done her? What good did they do anyone? Her parents had been supposed to live until a very old age. They had both stopped eating red meat and avoided everything unsavory on the internet. They liked Clark Gable movies, and ingenious new productions of *Fiddler on the Roof* that made use of found objects for the prop list and offered costume styling somewhere between David Bowie and the board game Settlers of Catan.

They did everything right. And if life was indeed a game of Candy Land, then they had fallen into a molasses swamp, one of those random calamities that games were full of, if you made the wrong roll of the dice. It sounded cute, but it wasn't: you'd drown in molasses, a painful death. The sticky substance would pour down your throat and fill your lungs like sweet pneumonia, taking with it even the dignity of a final breath.

—

Somehow (somehow?) Bertie ended up back at the hotel. The boy was gone. Without closing the curtains, but also without turning on the lights, she took off all her clothes and got under the covers naked, still grumbling to herself about the burned-up fields in Kansas, and about how Venice was finally, for good and ever, sinking into the sea. (Although this last was mostly conjecture based on satellite imagery, since Italy was one of the few European Union countries that hadn't yet opened back up its borders. Otherwise, Bertie and Kate might have gone to the Cinque Terre in order to sunbathe by the sea. Their choices would've been different. Their path, forked.) The world was unwell. But was anyone talking about it? No. Not enough. They were quietly renovating fancy museums and sneaking around to have sex with dubious Frenchmen.

As she closed her eyes, Bertie felt her anger melt into a vast and hollow fear, familiar from childhood and bad hangovers. The sense of tipping over into a void, standing at the edge of a cliff and leaning past the guardrail a little too far. Or, more specifically, of lying flat and still in bed as the room spun around her. She fell asleep with a heater breathing onto her face, troubling her hair, too tired to move out of the way. Alcohol burning off her in a fever, and leaving nothing behind except a smell of acid sweet.

—

In her dreams, she and Kate ended up at the museum again; she was wearing the same dirty jeans, but every time, Kate had on a different outfit, each one nicer than the last. There was the time that the floor was covered in several inches of water, so their feet got cold and blistery as they wandered through the wings. The time the *Venus de Milo* had grown new arms, and they couldn't agree if it was even the right statue, despite the label on the wall.

The time they saw Javier walking through a door marked *Staff Only/Passage Interdit* and banged to be let in, though he never seemed to hear. Kate wore a black silk blouse with puff sleeves, a crepe dress with gold sundials all over it, a pair of shoes that were hot pink with two-inch soles which made her look like a delivery girl for a demigod, blessed with feet that could go the distance.

In one dream, Kate woke up in bed and sniffed the air as she threw off the covers. She said to Bertie: "Do you ever think to yourself, *My body smells like a roast chicken, and I just* love *it*?"

They didn't feel like dreams. Instead they felt real. The walk down the curving staircase to the hotel lobby; the breakfasts, all different but also the same. A crumb stuck to the lip, a bitter coffee ground lingering on the tongue. But it also felt real when Bertie woke up three different times in three different dream places, always having to pee. *You're awake,* she told herself, straining against her bladder. *This time you're really awake.* But she never was till the last possible moment, when she ran to the bathroom and was finally relieved.

Periodically, as she tossed and turned, Bertie became convinced she heard breathing and that there was someone else in the room. But when she looked, the other bed was empty, the corners tucked tight. All night, moonlight spilled through the window onto Kate's pillow, and no matter how many times Bertie checked, it remained pristine.

–6–

In the morning, Bertie leapt up in the middle of a nightmare, stunned to find her breasts were on full display, and certain the hotel room was under attack. Stopping only to pull on a T-shirt and a pair of shorts, she dropped to the ground and looked under the bed, then ran to the door to peer out of the peephole, only to find that nothing was there. The hall was empty, except for the room service trays left out for collection by the morning staff. And although the trays were, in fact, disgusting—derelict with plates and beer; flatware covered with ketchup and eggs; french fries, which the menu called *pommes frites*—they were not ominous per se.

She tiptoed back to bed and hid under the blanket. Her hands were shaking. When did she ever sleep naked? Certainly not when Kate was around. They had an unspoken agreement not to act as though they shared one body, since they so often seemed to share one mind. Although they might visit a Korean spa together and steam in the nude, when they were having private time at home they didn't even change into pajamas without first retreating to separate rooms.

Under the covers, Bertie felt ill. Was she hungover? Probably. She certainly felt gross enough, as though the film of tacky spit on her tongue were also being exuded all over her body, sliming her skin and bunching her hair into greasy locks around her face.

She made a tiny opening in her blanket fort and saw that Kate was still fast asleep, her chest rising and falling, one arm flung off into space while the other was bent beneath her head. She didn't like to be woken up before she was ready, at least not on vacation, and so even though Bertie really could have used the company, she let her snore.

The purple walls looked especially purple this morning. *Dear God*, Bertie thought, were they really going to go to the Louvre today? She felt like hiding in a movie theatre and watching an American blockbuster dubbed into French. The salty popcorn would be good, too. Maybe she could convince Kate to drop the whole museum idea, though of course she herself had been just as excited when Javier suggested it. What an unpleasant man. He kept feeding Bertie wine, so much wine; it was his fault she felt this way.

She crept out of bed and dragged herself to the shower. A godsend: though what could possibly have happened the night before to make her feel so dirty? She had a vague recollection of a bathroom, someone's tongue. A man peering at her over his shoulder, ringing the illegible bell of memory. She and Kate were staying in Paris until the next day (weren't they? A part of Bertie wasn't so sure, but it seemed to be the same part that had taken off her shirt and pants while she slept, so Bertie ignored it), and yet she already had the end-of-trip feeling of having overstayed her welcome. Bertie let the hot water burn her skin, and scrubbed herself twice with the milk-and-honey-and-violet soap that the hotel trucked in from the fields of Provence. Then she got out and defogged the mirror with her hand, brushing her hair until it was stringy and neat, with a sharp center part.

She would make coffee. She would put on clean underpants. It would all be okay, and they would have a lovely time, after eating tartes aux pommes. This seemed like a convincing order of events, but for some reason Bertie was still jumpy when she walked back out into the bedroom, wrapped up in a hotel towel. Digging around on the floor for her bra, she knocked a glass coaster off the bedside table, which thudded harmlessly to the floor and spooked her as badly as if it had shattered.

"Is it over?" Kate turned and moaned, half asleep. Then she opened her eyes and stared at Bertie, whites as big as dinner plates. "Oh, there you are. I thought I'd lost you."

"I think you're maybe still dreaming," Bertie said.

Kate nodded and ran a hand over her face, smudging it left and right and then smacking her own cheek. "Can we have coffee?" she asked. "Is that still a thing?"

"It's still a thing."

"Thank God."

"And amen, and everything."

As Kate slowly poured herself out of bed, Bertie fussed with the coffee pod machine, almost forgetting to put water into the back and catching herself at the last moment before probably burning the plastic thingamajig to bits.

"Oh, Lord," said Kate. She was inspecting herself in the mirror, pulling her hair from side to side and sucking in her cheeks. "Why do I feel like death?"

"I think we must've really tied one on last night."

"Ugh, who says that? 'Tied one on'? Are you my dad?"

"Well, you know what I mean." Bertie thrust a cup of coffee into Kate's hands. "Here. Drink this and be nice again."

"I'm always nice. It's my one flaw: I'm much too nice."

With coffee in hand, the two of them sat in grim silence, sipping. Finally, Kate looked over at Bertie and asked, "Did you make me mad last night?"

"I honestly can't remember," said Bertie. "But I kind of wanted to ask you the same thing."

"That's weird. Because I kind of feel mad, but I'm not mad, you know? There's nothing to be mad about."

"Then I forgive you," said Bertie. And Kate rolled her eyes and replied, "Well, thanks." Bertie didn't really feel mad anymore, anyway. She mostly felt scared, though she could find no more reason for her fear than for Kate's anger.

At last, Kate finished her coffee and jumped in the shower; she always complained that Bertie used up the hot water, but she had the skill of taking very short showers anyway, claiming or perhaps bragging that she'd been educated in the ways of the perpetual California drought. Today, though, she lingered in the bathroom. Bertie had time to file her nails with the crappy hotel amenities nail file, and even to tighten a button on her white shirt with the crappy hotel sewing kit. She was busy admiring her handiwork when Kate came out, and the fluorescent light above the sink illuminated how terrible and obviously lavender the thread she'd chosen actually was.

"I thought you'd died in there," Bertie said.

"Just about," Kate agreed. "I almost fell back asleep."

"Maybe—" Bertie hesitated. "What do you think about the idea of skipping the museum? See a movie? I mean, we're both pretty wiped, and how do we even know that guy wasn't just pulling our leg?"

"No, come on," said Kate. Her hair was puffy and smooth from the blow dryer. "He promised. We promised. We're supposed to have lunch with him at noon, and he said he would bring sandwiches."

Bertie's heart sank, though she tried to hide it. Kate really seemed to like Javier, although she couldn't for the life of her figure out why. "French sandwiches or, like, peanut butter?"

"Baguettes. Ham and tomato and cheese. Maybe pesto. Something extremely unhealthy."

And since this did in fact sound quite good, Bertie allowed herself to be dragged from the room by Kate's insistent tide. Neither of them remembered to check the weather, so neither grabbed an umbrella; the doorman offered them one from the hotel's stash as they walked out the door, but it was so heavy, the women decided it would be better to let their coats get damp than to lug something as large as a broadsword all around the museum.

—

It was a fresh day, light and alert despite the rain. On the street, women wore smart jackets with the belts tied around their waists instead of being buckled; they were still in high-heeled shoes, though some had admitted the mild defeat of high-heeled boots. Men wore suit jackets, and seemed to repel the weather with their state of mind. Kate and Bertie ran down the block to their favorite café, where there were no inside tables available, so they stood at the bar. Both ordered espresso and tartes aux pommes, though in retrospect Bertie wished she'd gotten something else. An almond croissant, an egg sandwich; it was a bad habit of hers to order with Kate out of nervousness about her own rotten French. Not for the first time, she regretted her failure to study up before they arrived and refresh what she remembered from high school: a few more useful phrases, some vocabulary, maybe just a whiff of grammar. 'Où est la salle de bains' only got a person so far. Kate insisted she was doing well, but Bertie wasn't sure she believed her.

"I kind of like this city in the rain," Kate said. She leaned against the bar and picked at her tarte, eating it slowly so they could maintain their claim on the space. Around them, the café grew more and more crowded, and as people streamed in, Kate and Bertie made a sport of watching their glasses fog up. Large round lenses made the wearers look like cartoon robots, with console elements instead of organs. Small ones made them look like ghosts.

They ate silently, and each ordered a second espresso, earning a withering look from a pair of businessmen waiting nearby to take their place. Across the street, a line of schoolchildren in yellow slickers entered a different café, and through the misty window you could see them throw off their coats and begin to run around, probably screaming. Kate made a quick nod towards the businessmen with her chin.

"What do you think they'd say," she asked, "if they knew we were going to get a private viewing of their precious Louvre today? What did Javier call it?"

"Oh, right. The crown jewel of French culture?"

"I think it might have been the crown jewel of culture, period."

"Well, either way, those guys wouldn't like it. They would

consider our vulgar American ways a blight on the landscape of their sophistication."

"Which is possibly true."

"Oh, it's definitely true," said Bertie. She had noticed that, even in the midst of a global crisis, Americans became indignant whenever international news turned away from them. Other countries could be blown to kingdom come and it was a distant tragedy, but in America, even a brief reluctance to thrive was something that could not be borne, a state of affairs so despicable that it required twenty-four-hour news coverage and analysis. Perhaps it wasn't only for safety that so many nations had closed their borders and gone into a media blackout; maybe everyone just finally got sick of them. So much wound licking: it did get gross.

"Still," she said, "better us than them."

In the distance, smoke rose from a neighborhood on the outskirts of the city; one of the less fashionable arrondissements which had been taken over by Algerian, Syrian, and Italian immigrants after the beginning of the recent crises. Bertie hadn't heard about any new bombing taking place—in fact, the news in the past few days had been so ordinary, so mundane, that she couldn't quite remember any of it—but the smoke could've come from something previously undetonated, a non-nuclear mortar that dug its way into a crumbling building and waited. If so, they'd know soon enough: it would show up on a TV screen, or a passerby's phone, some shrieking app.

For now, though, there was still the possibility that it was a campfire in someone's backyard, or a grill on which some man or woman was cooking a bloody morning steak. In the café across the street, one child grabbed a croissant from another and stuffed the whole thing into her mouth. Maybe, at the end of the world, there was no value greater than hunger; no reason greater than your own desire. Did she believe that? No. Yes. Maybe.

Kate took her hand and squeezed it.

"Oh, hi," Bertie said. And they got up to walk over to the museum.

– 7 –

The courtyard was almost empty; the museum was closed. A man and a woman fed bread to a flock of industrious pigeons, and occasionally the pigeons would feel some hazard in the air and fly off to roost on the heads of the horses cast in bronze at the top of the arch. Water still flowed through the fountain, though God knew why; there were water shortages in many European cities, and although this water was probably recirculated through the fountain again and again, some percentage of it must have evaporated with every spray, only to be replenished from Paris's meager reservoirs. In the Bay Area, all the fountains had stood empty for more than a year, or else had been turned into desert planters, filled with a mixture of sand and loam.

The women ran into the Cour Napoléon in the nick of time, their hair pasted around their ears from the rain, but their hearts triumphant. The hangover they'd both woken up with was wearing off, too.

"Sweet shivering Jesus," said Bertie. "I hope they actually let us in."

"Don't worry," said Kate. "There's a secret knock. It's very James Bond."

They hurried towards the large glass pyramid, past a glowering group of men, one of whom—his nose long, his hair lank—stepped into Bertie's path so his shoulder rammed hers, then shouted after her, "Regardez òu vous allez, putain!"

"Et ta mère, asshole!" she screamed.

"Whoa," said Kate. "Where'd you learn that?"

Bertie rubbed her shoulder. The air smelled like nickels. "Well. My boss wasn't very excited I was going on this trip, but when I told him I'd already bought the tickets, he taught me how to say three things, and that was the third one."

"Okay, I know the bathroom thing is the second one, but what was first?"

"Je ne comprends pas le français. Which I don't, very much."

"Useful." Kate nodded in appreciation. "Covers pretty much all of the essentials in life."

"Except food," said Bertie. "And for that, there is pointing."

Almost before they knocked on the door, a small woman in a guard outfit propped it open for them with her foot. "Avec Javier?" she asked, and Kate agreed. "Ah, uh, oui." They slipped by. The guard glared past them to a father and daughter who were trying to follow Bertie and Kate into the bright, glassine entryway of the Louvre, and slammed the door in their faces. She locked it, pointedly, then scuttled off.

"God," said Kate. "Do you feel like we just got locked *in*?"

"I mean, technically, we did," Bertie replied.

"Helpful."

"Yeah . . ." Bertie indicated the glass all around them. "But I bet there are plenty of heavy things in here we could throw through a window if we really needed to."

They wandered down the steps, down the hall, idling between the wings; Bertie kept glancing over her shoulder and noticed Kate doing the same, even though there was nothing there. A distant crash made both women jump, but afterwards the room went quiet, and they laughed at themselves, nervously.

It was a beautiful museum. Everywhere they looked, the walls were plush with images, colors, so much so that the paintings seemed about to spring to life. And some of the statues, too, if you looked closely at them, appeared to breathe—just subtly—in and out, until you were forced to look away lest one of them break character and scratch its nose. Javier had promised that the magic of an empty Louvre was the way it allowed you to look at all the art unimpeded; but somehow it felt like the other way around.

"Just a reminder," Bertie said, leaning her chin on Kate's shoulder, "I wanted to go to a movie today."

"In Soviet Russia," Kate murmured, "movie watches you."

Rolling her eyes, Bertie turned to walk farther into the Denon Wing, but she miscalculated her step and accidentally backed into a sign directing viewers to the *Mona Lisa;* as it brushed her arm, she shrieked.

"Jesus," said Kate.

"Sorry." Bertie put one hand over her heart, steadying the wobbly sign with the other. "Sorry. Let's just—um, let's see something pretty."

"Or sharp."

"Or heavy."

"Preferably all of those things at once."

They continued down the hall with a new sense of purpose, collecting a list of objects that could be used in case of emergency to inflict blunt-force trauma on the windows—small sculptures thrown, large sculptures pushed, and the cache of armor

Bertie was fairly sure existed somewhere, pulled off its display to be worn and wielded while jumping free—and when the list was sufficiently long, they checked how soon it would be lunchtime. Not soon enough.

"Should we just hang out for a couple of hours next to *Winged Victory*?" asked Bertie. "We could lie down on the floor and worship her, while also napping. Or—whoa." She ducked. "What the hell?" A bird had flown right past her head.

"Was that a pigeon?" asked Kate. They could hear the bird's wings whisk the air up near the ceiling as it flitted in and out of sight, silken feathers beating madly against the plaster.

"No, it was like, a sparrow maybe, or—hey!" Another one veered between the women; this time its boomerang shape revealed it as a swallow. The birds darted up and down, skimming just over the floor and then swooping back towards the crown molding. They started chattering to each other, too, making a sound that was less a song and more an animated form of Morse code. Bertie thought of the parakeet she'd had as a child, a small blue-and-green creature who'd been caught by a cat when she took it outside to hop in the grass. Before that, it had talked to itself—or maybe to Bertie—for hours, twittering and clicking, occasionally interrupting its own running commentary with a scream. Several times it had vomited millet onto her hand, and her father told her this was a parakeet's highest gesture of friendship: sharing.

"Oh my God, this is wild," said Kate. "They must've come in with us."

"Aren't they endangered?" Bertie watched the birds disappear down the hallway, hair prickling up on the back of her neck. An ineloquent longing overtook her. "What are they doing here?"

"Maybe we found the last ones."

"Or they found us."

"Yeah, or maybe they live here," Kate suggested.

"And what, pick up snacks in the café?"

"They transmute fruit paintings into live fruit." Kate gestured to a picture beside them, in which a king's table had been rendered in oils, replete with grapes and melon and ham. A monkey stood over the food with a proprietary grimace on his face, and—Bertie noticed, with a jolt—he was, in fact, waving off a bird as it dove towards a pile of strawberries with the grim purpose of a tiny bombardier.

It almost had the feeling of a message—something Bertie had been searching for, with no success, ever since her parents died. But before she could get a closer look, Bertie realized Kate was already halfway down the hall, and ran to catch up with her, footsteps clattering through the empty, soundless space.

—

For a while, the pair of them had shared a good group of friends in the Bay Area, who they used to see almost every weekend. South Bay friends crashing on couches up in the city, and city friends coming south to escape their hangovers and drive down to Santa Cruz to watch the roller coasters from the boardwalk; everyone occasionally sleeping with everyone else. They took coffee and salami sandwiches to the redwoods for hikes that either went too long, making everyone grumpy, or were abandoned preemptively, with the would-be hikers sitting twenty feet off trail in too-big boots, smoking pot and looking at the sky through the treetops. They wandered around downtown and ended up in dive-y bars, including a Mexican place with a mariachi band and extra-strong margaritas, which felt magical when they stumbled inside, but ended up closing the next weekend for massive health code violations.

There had been months, even years, that passed this way. Bertie would go to work all week, slowly coming to understand which of her outfits did not constitute business attire (a sheer T-shirt that showed her bra under harsh fluorescent lighting, for instance, or a skirt that rode up a little too high when she climbed the glass stairs to the micro kitchen) and adjusting for it with a cardigan she kept at her desk for emergencies. She finished projects, and let others fall by the wayside after they lost buy-in from key stakeholders, developing an uncanny sense for which ones would end up this way, then carefully calibrating the effort she put into them so she'd look proactive and diligent while in fact spending up to two hours each day reading webcomics on her computer. She grew expert at flicking between browser tabs when someone walked up behind her, even though everyone else was fucking around too, scouring the internet for the names of their respective friends and frenemies. It was considered polite to pretend.

On Fridays she took a weekend bag to the office and caught a ride to the Caltrain station in time to make the five-thirty northbound to the city. You could drink on the train, so Bertie often swiped a couple of beers from the office TGIF party to share with whomever she rode up with: alcohol on public transit felt illicit even though it wasn't, people smiling together as they sipped, like so many kids up past their bedtime. It took time for Bertie to get tired of all this performative drinking, and even more time for people to stop smiling at one another. A suspicion that set in slowly, and then tightened its grip till they all had white knuckles.

There was a period in which all Bertie and Kate's Jewish friends moved to Israel, which turned out to be a mistake but seemed pretty reasonable at the time. Their Black friends were the first to stop making north-south pilgrimages across the Bay, not wanting to draw attention to themselves with open containers; Bertie remembered getting indignant on their behalf, and then sort of forgetting about it. Because what could she do? The mood had changed by that point, anyway. It was before the major bombing campaigns, but in retrospect the signs of disaster were already there. Like when the fascistic Mississippi mayor tried to secede his town from the union, or when the last summer ice melted in the Arctic, and a beloved British nature documentarian committed suicide. Everyone started to hunker down. They were busy with work, and some people had begun having families, too, so they stayed home with their kids on the weekends, which made sense. People evaporated, though only by about fifty percent: they still existed as texts and likes and shares. Like ghosts, showing up at a séance by way of knocking over your teacup.

At a certain point, it came to feel like Bertie and Kate mainly had each other. Everyone else disappeared, or disappointed. After breaking up with a particularly appalling online date, Bertie decided it would be okay if all she had, at the end of the world, was Kate. She was, after all, the only person besides her own parents who Bertie had ever really been able to rely on.

"Look," Kate said, excited. "An elevator! We're lazy. Let's take it to the next floor up." The elevator had opened right in front of them, empty. Beside it, several others were in the process of ascending or descending, the numbered lights above them flickering signs of their progress between the levels.

"But *Winged Victory*," Bertie said. "It's in the middle of the staircase right over there. So famous."

"I'll be honest," Kate said. "I don't care."

"Well, then I'll meet you up there. I want to look."

"Fine by me. See you in moments, Bun."

Bertie watched the doors close across Kate's tight smile of satisfaction, noticing for the first time the dark smudges beneath her eyes, the tired air that hung around her. Maybe she really did need a rest. They were both worn out, of course. But Kate usually wore enough makeup to disguise it.

—

As it turned out, *Winged Victory* was just a statue, and Bertie got bored of pretending to be inspired by it after less than a minute. *Well, never mind*, she told herself. Not wanting Kate to know how quickly she'd lost interest, she killed a bit of time running up and down the steps, and hoping the laws of interval training would decree this exercise sufficient to offset all her recent days of sitting around, gorging on bread and wine.

This had been her and Kate's plan many years ago, after high school but before college—the bread and wine part, that is, not the exercise. They'd wanted to come to Europe for the summer and take trains and pretend not to be American for a while, but as it turned out, neither of them could afford to do so. Instead, in their last few months at home, they went swimming in several too-cold lakes, and took a car-camping trip that ended when Kate told a ghost story by the campfire that kept them both awake all night; they lay in their tent, hearing the wind whistle against the nylon rainfly, and listening to the delicate crunch of footsteps around them that were probably deer or possibly just raccoons, but could have belonged to a murderer. The air had been so sweet then. Unburnt.

They had tried to re-create the event years later, in California, but got stuck in a lightning storm. Bertie flicked the memory away, perturbed somehow by its familiarity.

That final summer before college, Kate had worked as a secret shopper for a chain of local grocery stores, testing their responses to her presence and questions behind the safe cloak of anonymity. Once, while driving home from a sting, she got a flat tire and called Bertie from a pay phone—not to pick her up but to come keep her company while she figured out how to change it. She gave the name of the intersection, and since GPS wasn't common then, Bertie had to look it up on a map. She brought Diet Cokes, and after Kate successfully jacked the car up, each of them loosened two of the nuts on the tire. They were so proud of themselves, and then so scared that they wouldn't tighten the nuts enough on the spare, and it would go bouncing out across the street as soon as Kate pulled into traffic. But it didn't—she was fine. They were both fine. Before they finished, a couple of guys in a truck had offered to help them, and they were close enough to done that they could calmly and happily decline.

That summer had been full of what seemed to them like everything. Everything there was to share. Dinner with each other's families, or else dinner adjacent to each other's families, while watching TV marathons. Getting roommate information for college, and making snap judgments together based on names and zip codes and lists of alien-sounding hobbies. Sneaking wine in Bertie's kitchen from a bottle her mom kept on top of the fridge, until her mom came home and sighed and said, "You know that's cooking wine, right? I've told you the good bottles are downstairs." After Kate left for school, Bertie sent her an email, hoping it would help her settle in, and it took a few days for Kate to respond. By the time she did, Bertie was moving into the dorms herself, and she didn't reply for half a week. It was, she thought, how friendships ended. By tiny cuts. The inability to sit together on a lawn somewhere and eat Popsicles, laughing about nothing in particular. They had gotten so lucky, later, when they ended back up in the same place.

Bertie finally made her way upstairs to the correct bank of elevators, but Kate wasn't there. She should've arrived faster than Bertie, that having been the whole point of the elevator, but Bertie reasoned she'd probably walked down the hall to the bathroom, so she waited, looking out the window onto the square below. There it all was again in miniature: tourists taking pictures, children chasing the pigeons so they flew up in large clouds of snapping feathers and then landed again a few feet away. Three women, about the age that Bertie's mom had been when she died, were huddled together directly below the window, admiring the architecture. After a moment they spotted her, bodies exclaiming their surprise, and Bertie waved at them, causing a surge of what looked like laughter and then three happy waves in reply. Another figure, smaller and more distant, also looked up, and Bertie got a creepy feeling, so she ducked away. They probably shouldn't be letting a lot of people see them in here; she didn't particularly like Javier, but she didn't want to get him in trouble. Not when it might get her in trouble, too.

Still no Kate. Bertie took out her phone—momentarily thinking of texting, but then remembering that wouldn't work—and tried to take a picture, but it came out black. Maybe the lighting was bad. She leaned against the wall between the windows and closed her eyes, put her pointer finger in the soft spot between them, which she'd been taught in yoga class as a way of balancing her chakra, or whatever. When she opened them, an elevator dinged its arrival, and out walked a man in a red gingham shirt and blue jeans. He had brown hair, brushed to the side in an attempt to ward off a minor bald spot, and the kind of baby face that white guys in their thirties seemed especially prone to.

"Hi, Bert," he said, and took her hand. "Sorry, I went down a couple of floors first by accident, and I think I was in a basement? Then I figured it out. God, this place is huge."

"Okay, dummy." She heard the words leaving her mouth, but they smeared the air around her slightly. He was—who? She knew who he was. He was Dylan, her boyfriend, who hated Bob Dylan, because everyone assumed he'd have to love him. He worked as a personal assistant at another large tech firm, and was surprisingly sanguine in his role running errands and making connections for someone more important than he was, though it meant that at home he was loath to run errands of any kind. A big fan of efficiency: apps to order food to your house, apps to tell you the nearest beer bar. Bertie hadn't thought she would ever get him to go on a trip with her overseas, because he wanted to explore America first, and never even really got around to that, though when he was drunk, he did like to talk about a road trip he once took with his friends to Zion. He only agreed to come to Paris after a bomb scare very close to his apartment: a sort of carpe diem thing, Bertie thought.

She remembered the moment, after weeks of dating, when they both realized they'd actually kissed once in high school, at a summer concert in the park. How they'd laughed, thinking about her muddy shoes sliding on the grass, his teenage lips crushed against her own. It was so unlikely: they'd been two people, in that place and time, and now here they were again. Dylan hadn't even grown up in Seattle, he'd just been in town for a visit. For years, Bertie had misremembered his name as Devon.

Spotting the bathroom sign, Dylan indicated towards it with his head. "I kinda have to pee, do you mind?"

"Fine, fine," said Bertie. "I mean, we should wait for Kate to catch up, anyway."

"Who?"

"Um, Kate? You know. She—" Bertie stopped. He was looking at her so strangely. And of course. "Uh, nothing. Never mind." Maybe Kate was right behind them. She was just around the corner, surely. Dylan was being weird, but he was always weird. That was part of his charm. "You know Kate, though."

"Babe, you have so many friends, I can't keep track."

"No, I don't." Bertie frowned and kicked his shin. "I basically just have Kate and you." Now she remembered: Kate was going to come on this trip if Dylan couldn't. That was right, wasn't it?

"Well, you would know." Dylan held up his hands, one still gripping hers, all mea culpa, and they went to the bathrooms and then strolled past the Renaissance, the Middle Ages, towards a fancy apartment suite that once belonged to Napoléon III.

It had taken Bertie years to get her feet underneath her, dating-wise. In college, she fell hard for several boys, but never ended up doing more with them than making out or having brief and alien sex. She remembered the first one she'd let put his hands inside her underwear—not just under her bra, but below the belt, where he went to work on a kind of questing, desperate touching that had embarrassed her even at the time. He had dark hair and his family lived on an island in the Puget Sound. He liked Andy Warhol so much—so much—that she should've known his relationship to originality might be suspect. He always wanted to re-create all the sex he'd seen in movies with her, there in the dorm beds, but he lacked the technical skill.

That was Henry. After him there'd been Lincoln, too tall and just not nice. There was a painter from Chesapeake Bay, and an animator who drunkenly explained one night that women couldn't be cartoonists because they didn't have the guts to make ugly art, and that he didn't mean any offense, but Bertie could take herself as an example, since here she was painting watercolors of mountains and flowers, even though that hadn't been her plan. She despised herself so much for going home with him that night that later she drew a horrible picture of him jerking off and talking about gender essentialism, and pasted photocopies up around the school. She didn't sign it, though, so she worried for years afterwards that maybe she did lack guts after all.

After college, there were so many dates met in dark bars, always less handsome by the light of day. Some were men who worked in finance—Bertie later thought back to them and wondered which, if any, had amassed enough power to be culpable for the stock market crash, and whether any had gone to jail. None had been good kissers, which made her suspect they were all sociopaths—and some were just clunky. Clunky humans. One a bus driver, one a barista (*Is it baristo, for men?* Bertie had asked, which had ended the date when he didn't get that it was a joke and adopted a look of deep concern), one a corporate consultant specializing in streamlined communication channels, who couldn't keep up even a minimum of polite dinnertime conversation.

But Dylan was different, wasn't he? They'd met—or re-met, technically—about a year ago, at a tech conference afterparty hosted by Bertie's company in downtown San Francisco, one of those huge and obnoxious parades of wealth and camaraderie that they threw from time to time. There were acrobats hanging from ribbons and doing sky dancing, and a full-size human replica of a funny TV scene from the 1950s, with a housewife slipping over and over again in a tub of Jell-O, her mouth turned down in comic woe. Costumed servers slid through the crowd with plates of thematic appetizers and cocktails; the theme was Time, and it was adhered to very loosely, but near the unfortunate TV housewife, there were meatloaf bites and mashed-potato shooters as well as unlimited glasses of nice Shiraz, so that was where Bertie and Dylan were both camped out. When he told her where he worked, she squinted at him.

"You're not supposed to be here, are you? It's a private party."

"Well . . ." He laughed in a way that made charming wrinkles by the sides of his eyes. Bertie was just starting to find laugh lines attractive then, and his were exquisite. He looked so familiar, though she couldn't think why. "They let a few of us sneak through every time." As it turned out, his boss, a C-level executive, had been invited to mingle with the founders of Bertie's company on the ersatz grassy knoll in the middle of the party, which had been fenced off to avoid the danger of anyone mingling above their pay grade. Bertie was curious about what part of Time the grassy knoll was meant to represent, since she and Dylan were already hanging out in the Wistful Past. Perhaps it was for pre–climate change nostalgia? Farming culture? Ancient Picts building mounds for their dead? Or else, more likely, it had just looked nice to the event designer—*a timeless tableau,* she would have pitched it—who also probably had back-channel access to high-grade rollaway sod.

They bantered for an hour or two, getting increasingly Shiraz-drunk, and then somehow Dylan convinced her to dance to the combo electronica/string band that was set up in a section of the Future. He'd been wearing the same shirt he was wearing now, in the museum; it seemed like he was always wearing that shirt, but when Bertie accused him of having multiples, he denied it, and she'd never been able to find any extras in his closet. What had he packed for this trip? There must be other shirts in his bag. She could dig through it when they got back to the hotel.

Bertie had gotten tired of the conference around ten-thirty, by which time the dancing was general across all the periods of Time, and showed no signs of letting up. She was very drunk, which was nice. She put her arms around Dylan's neck and pressed her cheek against his cheek, whispering that it was late and she was going to go home; he already knew by then that she lived in the South Bay and had a long car ride ahead of her, while he lived in the Mission, not far from her old apartment and less than twenty minutes from the party. Feeling the buzz of his evening stubble against her skin, she smiled and slid away to figure out if there were still shuttle buses running, or if she'd have to call a car. But then he was beside her, winding his fingers through hers and saying it would be silly for her to go all that way when his place was so close. They made out in the cab, a little too much, and by the next morning, when she crept out of bed to catch her old shuttle to work, it all felt good and familiar.

But how . . . had they gotten here? She had convinced him to come to Paris, which was incredibly romantic, of course. But who had brought them to the Louvre? Something about the circumstances were hazy and fuzzed over, and even though this moment felt exactly as good as she might have hoped it would feel, with Dylan's arm slung low around her waist and the warmth of his body leaking into her own, Bertie still felt she was owed some kind of explanation. There was no one with them; they were alone in Napoléon's absurd apartments, where even the fireplace was gold, and the furniture was all a deep satin red, and an oddly familiar pair of birds was painted onto the ceiling. Dylan had no particular interest in art, and though he'd majored in history in college—a state school, but a Cal-system state school, so pretty good—now he mostly read tech books and watched TV shows set in outer space. Still, he seemed moved by their surroundings: he kept reaching out, as if to touch a curtain or chair, and then dodging back at the very last moment, giving Bertie a wicked grin. He kept checking in on her from the corner of his eye, making sure she was still there, though where would she go? They'd been dating for almost a year, and she wanted to keep doing so.

She pulled him closer then, so he'd behave, and slipped her hand between two of his shirt buttons, pressing her fingertips into the hair on his belly and onto the skin surrounding his navel.

"Oh, hi," he said, and she felt funny to hear him phrase it that way, but she let her hand linger, and let him lean towards her face, pausing for just a moment with their lips almost brushing and their breath intermingling before closing the space between them with a kiss. And another kiss.

From there, matters rapidly progressed. There was an old circular couch in the exhibit area, and Bertie would've liked to lie down on it, but Dylan told her no. He had a nervous look on his face that Bertie thought must be either fear of museum authorities or some unfamiliar form of desire; certainly his palms were warm as he led her away from the velvet ropes and towards a nearby table lined with clocks, which seemed to Bertie a less comfortable choice and frankly more dangerous for the art. Though she supposed, well, fluids? So maybe he was right. There were still questions blinking in the background of her mind: about their presence in this place, the not-quite-there reasoning behind it, and something about Kate. Kate something. But what? It was hard to focus while unbuttoning Dylan's shirt and revealing his chest, just a little bit doughy from the free IPA in a fridge near his office that was always being replenished by the food services people. And when he reached down to unzip her jeans, going slowly on purpose, laughing quietly at the way she bucked against his hands, all issues of substance flew out of her mind.

—

When Kate and Bertie were juniors in high school, Kate had cornered Bertie by her locker one morning and said, "Bunny, I did it. I finally did it." She was glowing with pride, and Bertie's heart sank, because "it" could only be one thing. Kate had a new boyfriend then, one who was known for getting around—the kind of boy that girls told each other they might try to date when he was free, as if he were a flavor of ice cream, available to anyone at the right price. Kate had been dying to lose her virginity, which she saw as a burden and a liability, and though Bertie was nowhere near ready for sex, she found herself kind of jealous that Kate was. They talked about it as though they were on the same page, swapping crushes and desires, but Bertie saw in that moment how quickly she could be left behind, made into a witness for her friend's changing life, while her own remained too dull for comment.

Kate at this point clarified that she'd just given the boy a blow job, and in her relief, Bertie blurted out the first thing that came to mind. "Was it gross?"

"Well, kind of. But also kind of hot." Kate looked evenly into the middle distance, which at that moment contained several senior girls hanging a poster for the prom. "It's hard to explain."

"Oh, really? I guess it could be kind of *hard* to talk about."

"I *firmly* believe that's true," Kate said.

"I mean, I wouldn't want you to get ad*dict*ed to doing it."

"No, that would be a sticky situation."

They laughed, and Bertie felt somewhat less terrified, even as she wondered what it tasted like, and how briskly Kate had brushed her teeth afterwards. Later, in the years after college, Kate would sometimes also date women, and if anything, Bertie found this more confusing. By that point in her life she'd learned how not to flirt with her friends' boyfriends, but the first time Kate brought a girl out for drinks, Bertie was in such a frenzy to be cool about it that she ended up overcompensating and tying a cherry stem into a knot with her tongue in an effort to impress her.

In all the periods of their closeness, Kate and Bertie had talked openly about sex, and it was a relief to Bertie, when they began hanging out again as adults, to be able to take part in those conversations without feeling she was leaving something important out, i.e., her total lack of experience and lack of qualification to participate. But Kate treated her exactly the same way she always had when she was young and virginal, and Bertie wasn't sure if that was a relief or a disappointment.

"You know," she said once, over two-for-one-Tuesday margaritas, "I never had sex in high school. Not at all."

"Yeah, obviously," Kate replied. "I mean, who would you have been having sex with? You wouldn't date anyone." She looked wistful for a moment. "Maybe I should've shared Ben. That's what a really loving friend would've done."

"Ugh, no, the 'sticky situation' guy? That would've been too incestuous."

"I don't know. I think it would've been kind of sweet. We could both have gotten it out of the way so easily."

"You're being gross."

"Yes, I am." Kate sipped her margarita with great gusto, then held up two fingers to the bartender, ordering another round for them both. "But only out of love for you."

—

In the museum, Bertie and Dylan built to their usual sexual climax, but now at a castle in Paris, under the drum of a light Parisian rain. Bertie couldn't help but think what a good story this would make to tell Kate, how the eighteenth-century table burned into her forearms as Dylan pressed against her, kissing her neck. *Ridiculous,* she told herself. *Who does this?* Bertie almost whacked one of the clocks with her elbow, but Dylan pulled her back just in time, then picked her up and swooped her down to the ground in one great, gallant motion. The floor was uncomfortable, but it made for an exciting change of view, and he managed not to bonk her head.

"We probably shouldn't be doing this," Bertie said, still nervous from her near-miss with the clock.

"We," Dylan countered, "should actually never do anything else." Which was a nice enough sentiment that Bertie bit his ear.

He kissed her, and adjusted her body beneath him as if she were light as anything, light as air. After a final few breathless seconds, he lay down beside her and they looked in opposite directions, admiring the dustless parquet, while their heartbeats slowed back down to normal. Bertie found it all somehow familiar: not the sex, per se, but the heightened emotion, the physical hunger, hair on her arms standing up in surprise. As if the weather had changed, the sun going behind a cloud and the temperature dropping. Maybe this was what love felt like. A cold, sharp wind. Maybe this was a beautiful moment that would live on inside her forever. Watershed, like a celestial event.

"You know what?" she said to Dylan. "I think I love you."

Without looking at her, he reached up, frowning, and scratched the underside of the table with his thumbnail. "Hmm," he said. His face slightly pained. Was it possible he hadn't heard her?

"Hey," she said.

"Yeah?"

"I said, I love you."

He opened his mouth as if to speak, but then didn't, and instead put a hand over his eyes, pinching something back. Maybe tears? Were they good ones, or bad, though? Dylan's cheeks were still pink from exertion, as was his chest, which was splotchy and mottled in a way Bertie usually found endearing. He got ticklish after sex; she could reach out right now and run her fingertips over his thighs and he'd giggle, girlish, the pink rising even higher. Maybe if she did that, everything would be okay again; she was about to. But when he took his hand away, his expression was empty.

"Actually," he told her, "you said you thought you loved me. Not quite the same."

"Oh, for God's sake." Could he really be this obtuse? She had thought she was done with boys who acted terrible on purpose. They were a disease you caught in high school, that you treated with antibiotics and tough love. Or with bad sex, and then a sudden infusion of good sex, tender bites on your shoulder in the dark. "You don't have to be a shit. Just say thank you or something." Maybe he was trying to be funny. He did that a lot.

But his face kept changing, softening, then turning cold again. "Whatever," he said. "It's not like it matters." Then he didn't say anything for a while.

Bertie was dumbfounded. They were on vacation in France, kissing under a table. Why wouldn't that matter? She supposed the state of the world did put a general pall on romance, but in some ways, that made everything feel more urgent to her, not less.

The first time she took Dylan to meet Kate, he . . . *Wait*, she thought. Hadn't he claimed he didn't know who Kate was? That wasn't possible. She could remember their meeting. She could see it in her head. They were at an outdoor table at a barbecue place, where the oilcloth was the same checkered red as Dylan's perpetual shirt. Tree branches hung over their table, and sticky leaves occasionally fell down on their hair; at some point a spider dropped onto Kate's arm, and she shrieked until Bertie picked it up with one of the leaves and moved it to the ground behind them. They got cold beers, chicken wings, a big mound of pulled pork that they attacked first with plastic forks and then with their fingers, piling it up on points of toast that bore grill lines and a smoky flavor.

Kate had regaled Dylan with stories about Bertie as a teenager, to fill out his picture of her beyond that one, fated kiss: the time she got a black eye playing softball and refused to participate in gym for a year; the many times during their period of outspoken vegetarian-ness when they'd snuck downtown together to eat cashew chicken in a Chinese restaurant with gigantic booths, calling it "secret Chinese" with great seriousness, as if anyone cared to break their code. He'd laughed, and rubbed Bertie's back with his palm, talking about the terrible things his boss had asked him to do, like write an email to the boss's ex-girlfriend at ten p.m. on a Friday or pick up a specific lunch that required waiting in a forty-minute line in Oakland in the rain, and somehow getting it back to the office before it got cold. Bertie made fun of both of them, kissed both of them on the cheek, held hands with Dylan under the table, but occasionally pressed Kate's toe with her own so she'd know Bertie still loved her, too, so much.

Each detail was clear and precise, right down to the flavor of barbecue sauce on Bertie's fork, a touch of plastic beneath the sweet bite of the vinegar that came to her while she nibbled on the tines. The only thing that she couldn't bring to mind was Dylan's face, and the harder she tried, the less he showed up. She could see his body—or some soft, male body, anyway, topped with a tuft of dark, male hair. But where his features should've been there was just an indistinct, white blur.

An oval. A faded space, as if voided out by a gum eraser. She blinked. He was there, in front of her, on the museum floor, but she couldn't bring him back into focus at the restaurant. He fell apart, into shapes and lines. It reminded her of designing cartoon characters, before she decided what kind of people they'd be: laying out bodies on grids or graph paper, without specific noses or eyebrows or smiles.

The room buzzed unpleasantly—or was that her brain? She pressed her fingertips into her temples, just to make sure her own face was still there.

Dylan turned over and saw her alarm, then rolled on top of her in a push-up shape.

"Wait a minute. Bertie?" He stared into her eyes as if trying to see through them. She imagined him tapping on the glass at an aquarium, trying to get the attention of some indifferent shark. Or maybe he was the shark, tapping from the other side. "Are you really there?"

"I'm." She put her hands over her eyes. "My head is. It's."

He lit up with an unexpected smile. "Let me guess," he said. "You feel like crap. Sort of shaky, sort of confused?" But how would he know that? He bent down, resting his knees between her legs. His breath didn't have any odor. What had they eaten for breakfast? Didn't they have coffee, at least? No, that was her and Kate. But wait, that was impossible. Kate wasn't here. "Wow," he concluded. "You feel it. This is really happening."

As she looked at Dylan, Bertie's brain kept fritzing out—making word salad at the sight of him, hymn, hmm. She remembered now that it was actually Kate who'd brought a new guy—to meet Bertie!—at the barbecue restaurant. His name had been Alan, and he was Korean American, a software engineer with a severe haircut and about ten times more money than he needed, so he treated them all to dinner. Afterwards she and Kate had decided that Kate should ghost him, because he was too strange. He played the fiddle, and he'd actually brought his fiddle with him. He was nervous they'd drop pork on it, so he kept asking to switch seats. Maybe that was where Bertie had gotten the idea for the meetup with Dylan? But why would she have chosen a restaurant with such dubious connotations for men?

"You don't play the fiddle, right?" she asked.

He scratched his head. "You mean the violin."

"Some people say fiddle." Alan had assured them that this was the case, even though, as he also insisted, he could play Bach concertos, too. He just chose to embrace a more folksy style, though this claim didn't pair well with his outrageously expensive watch, a Patek Philippe that Bertie recognized from ads she'd seen in *Vogue*. Men on sailboats with their sons. Crew cuts. Sweaters. "What kind of watch do you have?" she asked. But Dylan wasn't wearing one. He leaned down and licked her nose.

"You taste inconstant," he said. "Did you know that? Human inconstancy has a strong flavor." He was getting sort of hyper, glowing with a sense of private fun. "I remember it. When it was me, I could taste it all the time. Like metal in my mouth."

"I don't like this," she told him. "Let me up."

"No."

"Please."

He squinted at her. "No." Then, more thoughtfully: "Trust me, it's for your own good."

This wasn't like him. Was it? He was weird, but not usually mean. Where was Dylan? Wait, no, where was Kate? Where was anyone Bertie recognized? She rolled, knocking Dylan-Someone's arm away, and jumped up. She started breathing rapidly, in tiny bursts. Everywhere, the furniture was gilded, and Bertie felt the momentary disorientation of a person waking up in the wrong bed. Dizzy, a little sick. Had she ever been to Dylan's apartment and looked at his clothes, or was he always in the same shirt because it was the only shirt he owned? Did he own anything? What did his couch look like? Did he have an Xbox? Didn't all men have Xboxes?

Bertie realized her pants were unzipped, and she zipped them up, blushing.

"Look, I'm telling you, you need to calm down. You're going to make yourself crazy." Dylan lay on his back, arms under his head, legs propped. Pants open. Concerned, maybe, but not enough. He appraised her with the same look he used while trying to decide if he liked the nose on a glass of wine. Sitting on the tiny patio outside her apartment, a bottle between them, and the sunset stuck at just the right level that both of them had to squint in the light. They'd once gone camping at a state park, and when Bertie picked up a log for the fire, there'd been a tarantula beneath it, and Dylan had cried out, melodically, "Tah-ran-tu-laaaa!" They had done these things. She knew. She remembered.

"If you're calm, it will be much easier," Dylan told her, gently now.

Bertie shook her head, tears streaming down her cheeks. She backed away from him towards the door, but he watched her closely, and with a gasp Bertie fell, right on her ass, with a bump. Tripped over a ripple in the carpet and began scrabbling backwards, crabwise. "What's happening?" she asked.

"I'm not going to explain until you try to chill out," he said. "I know what you're like when you're upset. Anything I say will sound like bullshit to you." And he was right about that, at least. She looked at him, his messy hair pressed up on either side like a pair of horns.

"Am I damned?" Bertie asked, in a fit of desperation.

"Well, no. I think then you'd be in hell."

Which wasn't a statement that merited response. The scenes she remembered with Dylan were intermixed with other images, other facts. She and Kate had been arguing about Kate's move to Los Angeles. Hadn't they? They'd been having an important conversation, right here in the museum, but—when? Bertie could call to mind the heat rising in her face, the indignation bubbling through her stomach. Counting items off on her fingers in order to make a point, and then pausing to appreciate a Rembrandt, that beautiful, thickly textured oil portrait of a carcass of beef.

"What is this?" Bertie asked. She was almost to the door. "Really."

"This is the Louvre." He smiled. "The crown jewel of culture."

"I mean what are you. What are you doing. To me."

"Is that what you think?" Dylan asked. "That it's my fault?"

He paused, looking thoughtful. "Without me, it could've been so much worse."

A few more feet. Once Bertie got out of the room, she could run, and Dylan would never catch her. He was too out of shape. She kept telling him to go to the gym, or get an exercise bike, take yoga, something, but he didn't listen. He never listened. Had no good sense.

"Most people never realize," he said. "They do the same things over and over, and it doesn't even occur to them. The feeling of déjà vu, the way it's all just a little bit off. But you did. You are."

He looked impressed. "Maybe you'll still forget, next time. But I have to hope this means something. Just me being here with you. It's exciting."

This is crazy, Bertie thought. *He's my boyfriend*. He was the same as ever; he had to be. A pudgy emotional illiterate who made good eggs, with pico de gallo and a bit of sour cream. A sudden instinct for order took over her mind, and she sat down cross-legged, folding her hands in her lap. She would not run away. She would stay right here, and Dylan would see she was being reasonable. She put an *ah-ha* expression on her face. He would approve of this, and then he'd be nice. The decision made her feel better, immediately calm.

"I'm sorry," she said evenly, watching him from what felt like a safe distance. "I shouldn't have put all that on you, the 'I love you' stuff. Whatever. Who needs labels, right? We're here, in Paris. Let's just have fun."

"Ah," said Dylan. He paused, then sat up and zipped his pants, tucked his gingham shirt back in. Reached up a hand

and smoothed his hair, which seemed to Bertie to get somewhat darker, shimmering into a new shade. Though of course that was also crazy. "We're in the bargaining stage now, are we? I remember that, too. Though frankly I think I spent more time in self-pity." He winced with the recollection of it—whatever, whomever, he'd bargained with.

"Please stop being an ass. It's not funny anymore."

"Sorry." He made another face. "I'm having a hard time figuring out how to be around you right now." Standing up, he did a circle around the round couch, which Bertie still thought would've been a better place to lie down. "Am I supposed to talk to the Bertie who doesn't know what's going on? Or the Bertie, deep down, who does?"

What? Bertie thought. She felt something slowly sliding out of her, being pinched free like a bit of toothpaste from a tube. She considered how, after going to the bathroom, or having your period, or throwing up, there was simply less inside you. But you only lost the things you didn't want or need. This was different. Her mind was being squashed, all the thoughts and emotions dripping away till there was nothing left. The blood drained out of her face, too, leaving her cold and unsteady.

Dylan kept going. "I mean, is it easier on you if I pretend you've never been here before? Never lived through this day? It doesn't seem easier to me. And who knows how much time we have before it happens again. How did you bring me here? Or did I bring you? We need to talk about this."

In high school the two of them had kissed on a hillside. It was dark in that Seattle way, where there was some sort of orange light behind the clouds. Rain falling, mud sliding, a hundred teenagers running back towards their cars, which were full of heat and steam. He'd been skinnier then, and so had she. They wore the slender bodies of youth. But they hadn't spoken again after that. Not for years. She hadn't seen him until today. Except she had. Yes and no. Kate and not. Paris, France, and the end of the world. She and Kate had wanted to come here, to the Louvre. She and Kate had wanted to see the things everyone else saw, too, but with their own eyes. That was how art, how anything, became immortal. Becoming a still point in the universe, around which endless bodies revolved.

When Bertie spoke, her voice was hoarse. "What day is it?" she asked. "Is it still Tuesday?"

"Of course it's Tuesday. The museum is open six days a week, so this must be the day it's not."

With wobbling knees, she stood up, then dusted her hands on the back of her jeans. Could she still run? The room was spinning, but she suspected the spin was actually coming from inside her.

"Just tell me," she said. "How could it still be Tuesday? It was Tuesday yesterday, wasn't it? I met . . ." she trailed off. "An Australian? So shouldn't it be Wednesday? Or even Thursday? I sort of remember it being Tuesday before."

"Kind of," Dylan said, looking uneasy. Wait. Did he know about the Australian? That would be embarrassing. It was like a bad dream. "I mean, more precisely, it's never just Tuesday, or Wednesday. There is no then or now. There are lots of Tuesdays happening all the time, and some that will never happen."

Bertie let out a nervous laugh. The air felt cold and tight, like it was squeezing her. "Okay," she said. "Great. I see."

“Do you, though?” Dylan frowned, the skin between his eyebrows wrinkling ever so slightly.

The air smelled tinny, and she remembered the courtyard outside being the same. Maybe she was dead, and this was her comeuppance for some wickedness she’d done in life. Time wasted on the internet, pouring clickbait articles into her brain, or stealing money from her mom’s purse in childhood and hiding the crumpled bills beneath her pillow. That time she kissed a married man at a bar—a coworker who didn’t last much longer at the company, or, presumably, with his wife.

“Bertie,” Dylan said. “I know you don’t understand everything yet. But you understand something, and that’s a big deal.” He paused, then went on, tentative now. “I have an idea. It could help us both.”

“Please leave me alone,” she said. She was trembling. From top to bottom, from stomach to stern. In a cartoon, she wouldn’t even have eyes anymore; she’d have spirals where eyes ought to be, or black pinpoints. Little sideways triangles indicating eyelids squeezed shut. “Please. Just let me go.”

“You want to get out of here,” he said. “I get that.”

“Please,” she said. “Yes, please.”

“Well, I can make that happen,” Dylan said. “But it’s a risk. It might not go quite the way you’re expecting.”

She opened her eyes and looked at him.

He snapped his fingers.

— 8 —

The first thing Bertie noticed when she woke up was that her mouth was full of cotton. No. Not real cotton. Terrible, red wine cotton. Post-facto sugary alcohol cotton. A coating on her tongue, and the roof of her mouth, lining every one of her teeth.

"Ugh," she said, rolling onto her back and speaking to the ceiling. "I think my eyeballs are hungover."

The hotel room was quiet. Street sounds leaked in through the window, but only friendly ones, a soft *Bonjour!* and a tap on a car horn. Conversation too far away to make out with any texture, the words drifting up towards her like music, the meaning all tonal, in the rise and fall.

Bertie rolled over to face the wall, as if that might fix her, and hugged one of the bed's many decorative pillows to her chest. Purple raw silk, with violet tassels. It did not fix her. The tighter she squeezed, the faster her breath came, until she was quietly hyperventilating, lungs compressed to flat discs in her chest. She must've had a really bad dream, in addition to the alcohol nausea. In ninth grade, she'd dreamed that she killed her soccer coach, shooting him in the chest on the school's shared soccer/football field, and that afterwards a teammate's mother had walked up to her and said, "No one will ever love you now." She had woken up gasping so hard she'd burped a mouthful of vomit, forcing herself to swallow it again instead of puking on the sheets.

Coffee, Bertie thought. *There is such a thing as coffee.* The idea of it brought her back into her body, along with a couple of shuddering sighs. She threw down the pillow and pressed her hands into her eyes, wiping away the sleep that remained there, and probably a good smear of eyeliner, too, since she couldn't remember washing her face the night before. Must've fallen into bed like the dead, though she did apparently find the time to put on an old t-shirt for pajamas.

"Hey," she said over her shoulder, hauling herself into a seated position. "Time to wake up." But the second bed was empty, the comforter pulled tight at the corners. There was a stack of clothes in the middle, a pair of jeans and a long-sleeved shirt, which someone had apparently failed to put away in a drawer.

"Kate?" she said.

When there was no reply, Bertie went about the business of making coffee. She half expected to find Kate in the bathroom, humming and brushing her hair in the mirror, making that slight pursed-lips face she put on when assessing her appearance. But the sink was unoccupied, as were the toilet and the shower, which was the kind with a long silver hose you had to try and prop above you in the bathtub. Bertie filled two mugs with water and went back into the main room, where a man was sitting on the edge of Bertie's bed in his underwear, stretching.

"Morning, Bert," he said.

Bertie screamed, and dropped a mug, which bounced off her baby toe before spilling all over the carpet.

"Goddamnit!" she said. She ran to the bathroom for a towel, which she threw over the expanding puddle. "Oh my God, Dylan, you scared me. I think I dreamed that I was here with Kate?"

"Oh yeah?"

"She was sleeping in that bed." Bertie indicated with her now-free hand, then bent down to assess the damage to her foot. The toe was already blushing an angry red. "Which, where would we even put our spare clothes if the bed was in use? Into the dresser?" She snorted. "Hardly." And then: "You aren't ever going to unpack, are you?"

"Are you judging my homemaking this early in the morning?" Dylan asked. "Without even feeding me first?"

"Hey, if the shoe fits." Bertie frowned. "I hope mine still do. This is starting to swell."

"You'll be fine."

He gave her a kiss on the cheek as he passed, closing the door to the bathroom but then peeing so loudly she could still hear it. Why did men always pee so loud? she wondered. A demonstration of virility? Bertie masked the sound by pouring water in the coffee machine and humming a little tune. She winced, putting weight onto her foot—and also, a more internal wince, her heart still clenched up from the mysterious dream. But soon the pain faded, and she found herself bobbing back and forth, half dancing. Here she was, in Paris with her boyfriend. The pod machine burbled and started to brew, and when Dylan re-emerged, he slapped his belly rhythmically in time with Bertie's humming, getting a good sound where he'd gone to fat.

Something about him looked different. But what? It was strange, Bertie thought, the way a person could change overnight.

Or over a long period of time, but by such small degrees that you didn't notice until it was too late.

"Buddy, you need a gym membership," Bertie told him. A joke, sort of, which Dylan took in stride. *I just worry about you*, she told him sometimes, though he always shrugged it off and said, *Well, don't.*

"There's a gym in my office. I'm not going to spend money on something I could get for free."

"Yeah, but do you want to be on a treadmill next to your CFO?"

Dylan cupped his stomach tenderly. "Obviously not."

"Okay, well, get dressed. We need to hurry if we're going to make the museum."

"Right." He looked at her from the corner of his eye. "I'm on it."

Deftly, he slid on his jeans and buttoned up a gingham shirt.

"That shirt? Really?" Bertie asked. The image of it prickled against her vision. He wore it too much. She always said so.

"What's wrong with this?" Dylan pressed his hands to his chest, tugged the hem, inspected the buttons. "It's my favorite shirt."

And what was wrong with it, really?

They looked at each other. A silence fell. But then Bertie shook her head and smiled.

"Nothing," she said. "Drink your coffee, then let's go eat croissants."

—

The morning was crisp. They stopped at a café for espresso and breakfast: a chocolate croissant for Dylan and a mini quiche lorraine for Bertie, who said she'd been eating too many sweets. Having gotten a bit of a late start, they hurried through the food, and Bertie noticed Dylan was acting extra squirrelly, checking the time and pushing her to finish faster, which was strange, since he didn't usually care that much about punctuality when he was away from work. Anyway, he was also being sweet. He kept picking up her hand and kissing the back of it, pressing it against his cheek.

"So we're going . . . to the Louvre," he said as Bertie polished off her espresso.

"Yep."

"And you're sure." He tapped his fingers on the table, one-two-three-four-five.

"I am." Bertie squinted at him. "Do you not want to?"

"No, I do. Very much. I just wanted to make sure that you did, too."

"No place I'd rather be."

"Well okay then."

"All right."

"We're in Paris, after all."

"We sure are."

There was another moment of silent assessment between them, and then Bertie signaled for the bill, asking in better French than she remembered being able to speak. Dylan's French was quite good, too—superior, in fact, since he'd taken it all the way through college, and had, prior to the onset of the bombings, occasionally tagged along with his boss to Montreal on business, impressing all the Québécois. Even his accent was pleasant, the intonation falling to the back of his throat in a way that made him sound like he was on the verge of cynical laughter; because of this, Bertie usually let him handle the restaurant chitchat, but today it came to her so easily.

They arrived in the Cour Napoléon with several minutes to spare, and Dylan insisted on walking around the square and looking at the busts that lined the palace exterior, though Bertie would've preferred to go right in. There wasn't much in the way of a crowd, but everyone seemed watchful that morning. Whispering behind hands, standing a bit too close. A man with gray hair pushed past Bertie with a cough of disapproval, and soon after, a mother and daughter began throwing bread crumbs—less at the pigeons that gathered around them and more at Bertie and Dylan's feet.

"Come on," she said, tugging Dylan's elbow. "We don't want to be late."

"For what?" he asked, but Bertie didn't reply.

In fact, she wasn't sure herself: she just knew they had to hurry now. She had the strange sensation that she was stepping into a set of footprints, following them like tracks in sand. She also wanted to bury her face in Dylan's neck, stop them right here, forever, in this happy moment. But there wasn't time. At the pyramid door, Bertie knocked three times, then twice, then three times again, as Dylan looked on with interest, and a security guard came to let them in, frowning at the young couple who peered in after them with a hopeful, jealous expression.

"Allez, allez," the guard said before locking the door and scuttling off. The museum was so quiet, it made you want to drop something, just to hear the object shatter, as baby Bertie had, according to her mom, dropped cups and spoons from the perch of her high chair, over and over again, delighting in the sound. It was cold, too. Bertie's skin froze, shrunk a little, then loosened up when met with an unpleasant breath of warmth; she turned around and found Dylan behind her, exhaling pointedly onto her neck.

"Hey," she said. "Quit it."

"Okay Bunny." He gave a rueful smile. "Just wanted to keep the blood flowing."

They walked down the glass staircase and wandered into one of the museum's three wings—the Denon Wing, which Bertie remembered from looking up the floor plan online. There was no one else there; that seemed weird, didn't it? The museum was obviously closed.

Hushed halls and noise-dampening velvet benches. The tallest ceilings were all covered in milky angels, fleeing sin, or else demons crawling out of the sea, spewing gremlins and general pestilence.

Bertie stopped. Something felt wrong.

"Wait," she said. "What did you call me?"

"Sorry?"

"Just now. What did you say?"

Dylan perched on the edge of a bench, in front of a monk's portrait; a monk or, perhaps, a saint. Bertie could never tell the difference. They all had that round bald spot, the same Friar Tuck robes. A kind of uniform, she thought, not unlike Dylan's stupid shirt. He cocked his head to the side, as if preparing to absolve her of wrongdoing.

"I'm sure I called you Bert."

"No, you didn't."

"But that's what I always call you."

"Yes!" Bertie pointed at him, feeling a wave of vindication. He did it in line at the grocery store, asking her to run back into the aisles and get a tub of chocolate-covered pretzels. Walking down the street after dinner in the city, full of tacos, holding her hand. In bed, lazy after sex. "Yes. You do always call me Bert."

He scratched his ear. "So I don't see the problem."

"The problem is, you didn't say Bert."

"What did I say, then?"

"You said Bunny."

"But why would I call you that?"

A good question.

There was a hole in Bertie's chest. Inside, she and Kate were crammed into desks in a high school classroom, leaning over Bertie's hand and the little blue sketch of a rabbit she'd drawn there with her contraband ballpoint pen. A bit of blood was dripping from Kate's nose, down onto her lip.

Dylan leaned towards her with interest. "Eh?" he prodded.

"I don't know."

"Why do you think?"

"I said I don't know."

He raised his eyebrows. "And you really can't guess?"

She felt dizzy, strange. All morning, things had been a bit off, and now the strangeness closed around her, like she was being vacuum packed. The air being sucked from her lungs, tucking tight around her ribs, her gentle rolls of waistband fat, her feet within her shoes. There was a large window in the room, hung with an enormous, gauzy curtain that blew in a nonexistent wind.

Why had they come to the Louvre? There must have been

a reason, but she couldn't remember what it was. Why did she keep imagining Kate in Paris, ogling a pair of gendarmes in police blue as they rollerbladed down the Champs-Élysées? Dylan nibbled on his cuticles as he waited for her answer. He'd never called her Bunny before.

She seemed to remember walking into a bar with Kate, a fancy one, maybe in the Ritz. Mirrors everywhere. They'd gone to the bathroom, where Kate had found a Givenchy lipstick left behind on the sink. The brand had recently been discontinued, the animal proteins no longer available to make those rich shades, with their scent of powder and rendered fat. This one was used, but when Kate rolled it up, most of the tube was still there, so she took it back to the bar and borrowed a butter knife to lop off the top (*For hygiene,* she said) before placing the lipstick in her purse. Bertie had stared at the discarded end where Kate left it on a napkin, glistening like a wad of gum. In front of her, now, Dylan licked his lips, his tongue red and moist, upsettingly familiar.

"I . . ." she said. "No."

"No, you won't guess?"

Bertie shook her head, not quite sure what she was refusing, but suddenly, solemnly afraid. "No, no, no." She started backing away, her hands searching the space behind her, her eyes stuck on Dylan, who kept eating away at his nails.

The first weekend they were officially dating, he'd made the optimistic gesture of suggesting they drive to Half Moon Bay and rent a room at a B&B. Or, well, the app version of a B&B, some widow's old abandoned beach apartment, complete with doilies and a bag of mediocre local coffee beans. Bertie had taken the train to the city and Dylan had picked her up at the station in a car he'd rented on his phone; it was a car-share service, where you could borrow someone's keys in exchange for a full gas tank and a surcharge. When he saw her, his eyes lit up. "Sorry about the, um, aroma," he'd said. Indeed, the old sedan smelled like cigarettes covered up with air freshener, but it was otherwise clean and ran just fine. They dropped their things at the apartment before heading out on a stroll, still a little nervous and careful with each other, lapsing periodically into charged moments of silence.

Bertie had always loved the beach at Half Moon Bay, which felt like a place where anything could happen. She'd been making visits there since she moved to California, whenever she needed to get away from her real life. Cliffs rose above the sand, and the park was often shrouded in mist: clouds clung to everything, including the water, the driftwood, the people. An undelineated section of the beach was set aside for nudists, and as Bertie and Dylan walked along the tideline, silently negotiating whether or not to hold hands, they saw an old man climb out of an orange nylon tent wearing nothing but a baseball cap. His body was riddled with pouches and lines, plus little, surprising sprigs of hair. He waved at them, and they waved back.

"How does that man look so comfortable?" Dylan asked, and Bertie cuffed his ear.

"Prude!"

"No, I just—" He gestured to his button-down shirt. "I'm cold!"

As it turned out, Dylan had never been to Half Moon Bay before, and hadn't heeded Bertie's warnings about dressing in layers. He was shivering, his skin going blue at the edges.

"You moron," Bertie said, affectionately. "I told you to bring a sweater."

"Well, I didn't."

"Don't you have, like, a jacket?"

"Don't need one." He grabbed her around the waist and hugged her close. "I can just drape you over my shoulders. A Bert-skin coat."

"Ew." Bertie wrinkled her nose. "Murdery."

"Oh," said Dylan. "I'll show you murder."

He dropped her, and raised his arms in front of him like a child's vision of Frankenstein, lumbering and snapping his teeth. *What a horrible thing to say*, Bertie thought, but instead of telling him so, she shrieked and slapped his outstretched hands, then took off down the beach. He chased her, both of them laughing and hopping over pockets of ocean trash.

They had coffee and ice cream at a small café; later they had dinner in town, handmade ravioli for her, and for him, linguine with clams. Bertie kept thinking, *Maybe this, maybe this could be really good*, as she looked at Dylan's flush-mottled cheeks, the pink tip of his nose. Yes, there had been that moment, when the words "I'll show you murder" hadn't sounded quite so funny. But it had passed. The flat look in his eyes, the low intonation—it was all gone so quickly that Bertie found it easy to convince herself she'd just made it up.

—

Now, she bumped against a wall in the Louvre as she backed away from him, trying to look casual while also getting space to think.

You're imagining things, Bertie told herself. But what was she imagining? Not the empty, inexplicable museum, and not the expression on Dylan's face, which was curious and strangely eager. Other memories of Paris drifted through her mind, like the memories of dreams. Things that couldn't have happened, but did happen, to her. Kate smiling at a line of children who walked, hand in hand, into a café. A dark bar, full of cigarette smoke and a jazz band, where Bertie got bored and tore a napkin into tiny pieces while she waited for her friend to stop flirting with a man whose teeth were yellow Chiclets.

"Oh, good," Dylan said. He exhaled in relief. "Last time it took longer than this."

"Longer?"

"Of course, I was pushing things this time around. I wanted to make sure it wasn't a fluke, the way that you woke up, before. God, that was scary."

"Who are you?" Bertie asked. "Where's Dylan?"

Which made him frown. "I know this is hard for you. But we're here now. We should make the best of it."

"We're . . . what?" Here in the Louvre. Here in Paris. In the here and now. Was that what he meant?

"We started over." Dylan was using his soothing voice. The one he reserved for when Bertie was hungry or mad. "Time is supposed to be an arrow, but it's acting like more of a loop. It's been happening to me for a while. But now you're here, too. Which—I know I should be sorry. But from my point of view, it's a real improvement."

He looked, for a moment, worn and thirsty, like a shipwreck victim sighting a plane. She could see days, months, years on his face. Then she blinked and it was gone.

"Umm." She turned her head to the side, trying to find some equilibrium. The room was spinning. This had to be a bad joke. "I think you're being kind of a dick."

"Bertie," he said. "Sweetie. I'm not. I just thought it would be easier if we started the day from the beginning, so you could get your feet back under you." He brushed a strand of hair behind her ear, and she shivered. "I've gotten better at riding out the changes. But I've had kind of a lot of practice."

Dylan's hand lingered on her neck, his thumb gently resting on her skin. "This is the first time anyone else has figured out what was happening during a loop. Let alone twice. I had a feeling, when I saw you in the courtyard. I just didn't know what it meant."

"Oh," Bertie replied.

A slight rain. A young man with no jacket, as a thin crowd flowed past the women walking with purpose towards the museum. Had not some part of her already realized? Sensed him there?

Another impossible memory: Dylan, on top of her, in a golden room, his shirt open, his hair askew. His fingers, snapping, and the world going black. She had loved him, then. But when had it been? Where had it happened? He breathed, now, right into her nose, and part of her wanted to kiss him, and stop this absurd conversation. To pull him close and feel the warmth of his chest on her chest, the way he sometimes pressed his thighs right into hers as if lining up two paper dolls.

"I thought," Dylan said, "if we came back here, we could re-create the circumstances that brought us together. Anyway, I wasn't going to take any chances. It's you, Bert. You and me."

He smiled at her, his eyes like specks of dry ice. Somehow cold and hot at once. Bertie held out a hand to touch his cheek, which was the most familiar thing in the world to her, or so she'd thought a minute ago. Then she shoved him with all her might, and when he stumbled back, she ran.

—

Down the hallway, down the staircase—Bertie told herself to just keep going. Past the Renaissance and down through Mesopotamia, past some truly enormous portraits that seemed all to be pointing their fingers at her in blame. There was, on one single wall, an angry Virgin Mary, an angry Christ Child, and a furious, reproachful John the Baptist. *Damned,* she imagined them saying. *You're damned!*

She needed to get out. She needed to be on the street, to run back to the hotel, and try to call the United States Embassy. Not that she could possibly explain what had happened, but saying she'd been attacked by an unstable man ought to be enough for the police. As she dodged through the exhibits, Bertie couldn't escape the feeling that she was running around in circles—or not in circles, exactly, but on a pre-described path, the narrative arc of a video game. The kind where, every time you died, you started again, from the same place.

That, she thought. *I've seen that, and that.* Each statue, each painting, each smart juxtaposition. The *Mona Lisa,* the *Venus de Milo, Winged Victory of Samothrace.* They were the pieces you'd choose to highlight if you wanted your audience to recognize them and feel smart. The greatest hits. A mummy and a virgin martyr.

Time is a loop, Dylan had told her. But that was crazy. He was crazy.

"Hi," he said now, stepping out from around a corner, having apparently found a shortcut. Bertie stopped hard, skidding on the marble floor, and fell to the ground. "Oh jeez!" he exclaimed, as she cracked her knees against the tile and tumbled forwards onto her hands, rolling over and coming to rest on her back, staring at the high ceiling. In no time at all, Dylan was there, offering his hand. "Sorry, sorry, that keeps happening!"

"Where's Kate?" she asked. She ignored his hand.

"I can't tell you that."

"Can't?" Bertie asked. "Or won't?"

"What difference does it make?"

"Kind of a lot, actually."

"Well, let's try living in the middle space."

She covered her eyes instead of replying, and Dylan exhaled noisily. "I told you before, it's easier if you relax while things are still coming back to you. Maybe take a couple deep breaths." But Bertie didn't want to relax.

"You stole her. You took her away. This is some kind of horrible trick."

"It isn't! Bert—"

"Fuck. You," she said.

"I just." Dylan pressed his mouth into a line. "Bertie, I've been where you are, okay? And I'm trying to help you, I swear. Don't you see? This is all happening to me, too."

"*You're* happening to me."

"But." He crouched down and pressed his thumb into her arm, making a small but painful indentation. "I had to get here.

To happen." Bertie twitched her shoulder, and then her whole body away from his hand, but Dylan looked up at the ceiling as if gathering his thoughts there.

"Do you know," he said, "I can't even remember, anymore, how it started for me? I know I was at work. My boss was listening to records. And then I woke up in my bed at home, and somehow it was the same morning all over again. But what exactly happened? I think about that a lot. Was it the music? Did I get struck by lightning? Did someone take out a cosmic hit on me?"

Bertie lay there, heart pounding, and felt a flash of hot and cold. The familiar motion of dragging oneself out of sleep into . . . this. *Morning, Bert.* Their first day in Paris, she and Dylan had gone to see Foucault's Pendulum in the high arch of the Panthéon, and then lounged on a curvaceous wooden bench outside, eating tarte au citron from a cardboard to-go box. The bench was shaped like a wave, and they'd snuggled together and watched a sea of students come and go from a nearby university, trying not to fall asleep despite having flown all night—or day, depending on your perspective—to get there.

She shivered now, as she had then, pressing her hands into her cheeks to stop her teeth from chattering. But she felt so incredibly awake. Kate had always been afraid of getting stuck somewhere, and Bertie had laughed at her. *How could you possibly be stuck?* she'd asked. *If you don't like it, just pick up your things and go.*

Dylan frowned into the distance. "I never knew when I was going to start a day over again. Or a week, or a month. You'd think it would always start in the same place, like a movie with a beginning and end. But it didn't. It was jumpy. Scary. I would always begin by not knowing, and then these memories would leak into my head. Sometimes they went so far back—it was like I was living a different life completely."

He looked at her. "So, you see, it could be worse. It actually would be worse without me. At least I know how to control when and where we start. You have the benefit of my experience."

"Oh?" said Bertie. "Is that what you'd call it? What I have?"

"Yes, I would." Dylan held out a hand, again, to help her up, and Bertie, after a brief hesitation, took it. What else could she do? He'd always known how to wait for his moment. At the party where they met, he'd followed her patiently, with a plate of meatloaf, until she finally turned to him and smiled.

"Tell me something," she said.

"All right," he agreed. "If I can."

"It is all gone?"

"All what?"

She paused, and chewed on her lip as she considered. "The stuff that came before?"

Dylan tilted his head. "Does it feel gone?" he asked.

"No." Everything felt, in fact, more present than ever. The look on Kate's face when she had something funny and mean to say, the weight of her on Bertie's couch when they propped Bertie's laptop up on the table for a movie night, as long as there was no blackout in effect. Bertie thought: *I am outside my life.* But not all the way out. Like she'd stepped away from a party, onto a balcony for a breath of fresh air, and could still hear the muted sounds inside.

"I think," Dylan said, "for us, things are never gone, exactly.

They don't disappear, they get added, in layers. At least memories do."

"Added how, though?" Bertie asked. "Added why?"

Dylan squeezed her fingers, thinking. And then, to her surprise, he let go and told her.

– 9 –

He began by suggesting she imagine a snowy field. A snowy anything, but a field would do. Not on a clear day, but while it was snowing, so each flake cut its own urgent path through the air before coming to rest.

What was the snow? Was it each flake, or was it the field?

Was that a trick question? she wanted to know. Some kind of bullshit?

No, he said.

—

He asked: What do you remember, and she said she remembered waking up at the hotel, and drinking coffee and wandering the streets until the cobblestones cramped up her feet and she had to sit down and have a café crème. She remembered sitting across the table from Kate and raising her eyebrows as they both ordered illicit foie gras, and eating crispy pigeon in a creepy-cute restaurant decorated with clowns. She remembered before, making pancakes with Kate at her apartment in Mountain View, after a sleepless night when the bombs came so close they thought they would be hit—thought, at one point, that they had been hit, as a shockwave traveled through their bodies, coming in through the feet and leaving through the fingers, tightening their muscles like an electric fence. The pancakes were grainy, and came from a mix that Bertie had found in her cupboards the day she moved in: an If You Lived Here, You'd Be Home By Now kind of gift from the company that managed her building.

She remembered a period in which Dylan had ordered takeout from the same delivery app every night for a month, always getting the same eggrolls and broccoli beef, delivered by the exact same guy. Bertie thought it was gross to be so consistent, and finally persuaded him to break up his routine by spending the night with her in the South Bay, sleeping over at her apartment. He ended up staying the whole weekend, only returning home on Monday night after work. At which point, the delivery guy showed up with an order that Dylan hadn't placed and asked if he was okay.

That's sweet, kind of, Bertie had said when he texted to tell her. *He thought you were dead!!* But it turned out it wasn't the guy who was worried at all; it was the app. Its algorithm had taken note of Dylan's ordering habits and placed an alert on his account when he varied from them so intensely. The free delivery was less of a gesture and more of a wellness check—the second they'd done—after which, according to the delivery guy, Dylan's push alerts from the app would have increased obscenely had he not shown back up. *Repetition can be important,* he'd told her, and she'd sent back a crying-laughing emoji and the words *I guess!*

Bertie remembered sobbing on Kate's shoulder when her parents died. She remembered telling Dylan about it on an early date, the way he'd closed his eyes as he listened to her describe the tone of the emergency response siren, and how at first she'd been afraid that his closed eyes meant the story was too much, and that he was getting ready to disappear back into whatever casual sex his phone could concoct for him, as so many men had before. But he didn't. Instead he opened his eyes and took Bertie into his arms and whispered comforts into her hair, and he stayed. He held her, and he stayed. So she remembered both of them as people who, in that time, she could not have lived without.

Which one was real? Dylan asked her, and she wanted to say, The one with Kate. The one that was true before you showed up and inserted yourself where you didn't belong. But then he said, So you'd give the other one up? And she had to admit that she would not.

The thing was, both lives were hers now. Both were her. Which was, according to Dylan, the point. The snow on the ground rising up to meet the snow in the sky until they were one, building upon on each other in endless layers. Small additions, coming together into something big.

—

Even when the day started over again, pieces of the old one were left over in the back of Bertie's mind. Changing her, by degrees. Adding love, or hate, like muscle memory. Not so much a revision of the truth as a subliminal suggestion of it. Most people weren't aware they were living their lives over and over again, but they could still be nudged by the repetitions. That had been Dylan's plan when he saw Kate and Bertie in the courtyard, in fact: to peel them apart one day at a time, until he could fit himself in where Kate had been. Not forever, just for a while. A lost weekend, with a lost love.

In Soviet Russia, Bertie said softly, the truth revises you.

Exactly, Dylan agreed.

But, he insisted after a moment's reflection, he hadn't known Kate would actually disappear.

– 10 –

"Look," Dylan said. "I thought it would be straightforward. Normal. From your point of view, anyway. I would wait until you'd gotten so annoyed with Kate that, one morning, I could come up and say hi, and you would be happy to see me." He put on a face of mock surprise, holding up his hands in a friendly pantomime. "Like, '*Oh my gosh! Is your name Bertie? Funny story, but I think we've met . . .*'"

"But that's not what happened," Bertie said.

"No," Dylan agreed. "I don't know exactly why it went the way it did. Usually the loops are self-contained: it proceeds the way it starts. I've never just been . . . drawn in that way. All I can think is that I wanted it so badly, it just happened."

He kept his eyes trained on his feet, like a toddler mid-reprimand. "You know, I meant what I said, about our memories. I don't think they go away. But they do . . . accumulate. They keep coming and coming, every time you start over. Until one day you look up and you can't tell what came first." He frowned. "I've been doing this for so long, and I've lost things. Pieces of myself. Like, I can remember a hundred versions of a day I spent in San Francisco buying sandwiches for my boss, but the early things, the places I don't go back to, those are harder."

It was true that he'd never been one to talk about the past, not his family, his childhood, school. Their relationship had existed almost entirely in the present tense, except for a single day they'd shared, before, their teenage bodies in the rain.

"But you remembered me," Bertie said.

"Yeah," Dylan agreed. "And that's kind of the point. You were the first thing I was sure about in so long." His face was disarming, his hand, as he scratched his cheek, familiar. With a smattering of blond hairs on the back and some uncomfortably dry skin at the knuckles. But that familiarity was not real, apparently. Or it was, the way a mirage was real. It's there, but it's not.

"Wait," Bertie said. "So why do I remember *you*? Not in high school, I mean, but now. I know things about you." The way light fell in his kitchen on Sunday mornings. The pressure of his fingers, tugging gently on her hair. "About us."

"Starting a loop," Dylan said thoughtfully. "It's not just about time. It's about possibility."

"Meaning?"

"You go back, but in a way, you go sideways. The memories you have, they don't just come from what you do in the loop itself. They come from the world in which that loop is possible. We wouldn't be here, together, in Paris, if we didn't have a life together. So we did."

"But that's—" Bertie stopped, and leaned against a nearby wall.

"Impossible?" Dylan asked. He tilted his head towards her, and she remembered unwillingly what it was like to kiss him, how he assembled and disassembled in her mouth like a piece of candy cracked in two, the flavor forever refreshing her memory of the glorious whole. He was the same as always. Also not.

"You know," he said, "for a while I thought maybe that my boss made all this happen to me. Some weird tech billionaire experiment. Live forever, stay young." He wrinkled his nose. "I couldn't figure out how he pulled it off. But it would definitely be in character for him to have tested something dangerous and stupid on me first."

"How sad for you," Bertie said, her eyes narrowed.

"I'm not asking you to feel bad." Dylan shrugged. "I'm just trying to explain."

Bertie snorted. "But you're so pure and good? You came to Paris, and you found me, and you think we're going to live happily ever after?"

"I mean." Dylan fiddled with a string on the cuff of his shirt. "I don't know."

"You keep trying to tell me that my being here is all a big accident," she pressed. "But it isn't, is it? This is exactly what you wanted. *'I saw you and I knew, Bert.'* Those are your words." Her whole body was hot, now, boiling mercury, but she couldn't stop. "Did you really think that it would be nice for me? That I'd be grateful to be part of this? Just because we made out when we were sixteen?"

She leaned in close to his face. He seemed so wounded. "Did you think I'd believe that you fell in love at first sight, and you've been doing all this for my benefit?"

"Well. Not your benefit, exactly." Dylan made his face calm again, and the heat in Bertie's body abruptly cooled. He had insisted he wasn't responsible. But who else could be? Who else would want any of this?

"What does that mean?" she asked.

"What if," he said, "someone wanted to keep you apart from Kate? What if I heard them say so, and decided to help? Since it fit my plans anyway, it could be two for one. A selfish deed plus a good one."

Bertie froze. "No."

It couldn't be, and yet it made sense. The sublimated alterations of each loop, or whatever, moving them further and further apart. Making them angry with each other, abandon each other, again and again. But who would wish for such a thing?

"No," she said again, trying to force her voice calm. "If you could change things that way, you'd, I don't know, do world peace. Un-burn the rainforest. I mean, yeah. Why don't you fix the rainforest?" Her voice went up into a register of desperation.

"It's not like that," Dylan said. "I can't just do whatever I want. I can sometimes—do some things. Like starting us over: it's kind of like getting a record to skip. And once you've done that, you can maybe scratch the record, change superficial things. But you can't decide what was recorded."

Bertie closed her eyes and leaned back against the wall, between two paintings of the sky. Like being between two windows, both equally closed to her. She reached out to touch the frame to her left, but curled her fingers back at the last moment: some inborn need to follow the rules was still hard coded in her. Even now.

"She was always going to leave you," Dylan said, softly. "I just made it happen a little faster." Then, with some concession, "A little different."

To which Bertie didn't bother with a reply.

The hall around them was quiet. For a moment Dylan looked

like he might be about to say more—then, from some ways off, there came a squeak. Shoe on tile, a mislaid step. Dylan's attention flicked towards it, and his eyebrows went up.

"What the hell," Dylan said. "*He's* not supposed to be here now."

"Who?" Bertie spun to the side and saw a dark form, about a hundred feet away. Slick hair, furtive posture. An open mouth glowing yellow, and then shutting emphatically as the figure scuttled away. Javier. Of course, Javier.

"Oh my God," she said.

Javier, who always showed up where he was least wanted. Always beaming psychopathically, much like Dylan when he walked off the elevator with his bright come-hither smile. The two of them, always smiling. The both. *Who would wish such a thing?* "Oh, shit."

"Bertie," Dylan said, warningly. She glanced at him, and then took off, knowing perfectly well he'd follow along behind her.

—

Javier was idling outside a doorway as Bertie sprinted towards him. He was looking at something in his hands, which she couldn't see. Maybe a phone, maybe it could call the police, since hers wasn't getting any service. Maybe she could steal it and call the police on *him*, since he and Dylan were clearly in some kind of cahoots. Talk to a pair of pretty girls in a bar and then trap them inside your funhouse: that had to be an arrestable offense, even in France. He probably had Kate tied up to a chair, stuck in some subbasement. Bertie had woken up with one man; it stood to reason that Kate had woken up with the other.

Had he and Kate even kissed? Bertie wasn't sure anymore. The bar had smelled of sweat and tobacco, the men had all smelled of shoe polish and alcohol. While Kate batted her eyes at Javier, Bertie could easily have stood up and danced with someone else, an old Frenchman who might have twirled her around the room and pressed her against one of the stone walls so he could run his hand up her skirt and feel her relatively youthful legs. Why hadn't she? That's why they were there, not to police each other but to have a good time. Not to cock-block; to facilitate, and laugh about it after. Even still. There was a magnetism about Javier, which tasted bitter on Bertie's tongue. He made her feel like her hard drive was about to be wiped, like she better not leave anything valuable in his presence, unattended. And what was more valuable than Kate?

She was almost there. She could see the rumples in Javier's well-cut suit now. His hand on a knob, a bead of sweat on his cheek. He'd started all this, she was sure. Which meant he could stop it.

"Hey," she called out. "Wait!"

She ran towards him, but he didn't wait. In one step, Javier disappeared behind the door, and a lock clicked into place behind him, so when Bertie finally skidded to a halt, all she could do was pound her fists and rage.

"Asshole," she shouted, kicking the door so hard she scuffed the paint. But he was gone. Dylan, now beside her, clucked sympathetically, and Bertie kicked the door again, activating the bruise on her toe where she'd dropped the coffee mug only that morning; a lifetime ago. "Ow," she said, dragging out the word and then following it to the ground, where she eased onto her butt and leaned her back against the wall.

"Bert," said Dylan. "Let me help you. How can I help?"

She glared at him. "Is helping me really your priority?"

"Would you believe I just want to do something nice?" he asked. "You've been so sad. It's starting to bum me out."

Bertie sighed.

"That was my chance." She gestured behind her to the impassive door. "He's been here every time: he must know where she is. I could've caught him, and I blew it." She could feel the speed draining out of her limbs, her thighs beginning to cramp up.

"You have a lot of faith in your own abilities. I kind of admire that."

"So how are you going to cheer me up? I hope that wasn't it."

"I was thinking." Dylan slid down beside her, close enough that their knees and shoulders touched. Was it possible he really loved her? No. She pushed the thought away. His little pot belly bumped against his thighs. "I could open the door."

"You . . . what?"

"If it really means that much to you, why not? It would be pretty simple. A record scratch. And I told you, I *like* to help."

Bertie narrowed her eyes and tried to spot the exact moment when his expression would crack open into a mean-spirited smile. *Got you!* he'd say. *Are you really that stupid?* But he seemed sincere, jutting out his lower lip.

"What's the catch?" she asked, as her heart rate increased ever so slightly.

"How do you mean?"

"I mean, what's in it for you? You wouldn't do it if it didn't fit with your plans."

"Hmm," he said. "Point taken."

"And?" she said. "So?"

"Here's the thing." He flicked his knee and scratched at his pants leg, the back of his nails scraping against the ridges of denim. He muttered to himself: The thing, the thing is. "You're right. When I first saw you in the courtyard, I wasn't in love with you. Not really. I was surprised, and happy to get back a part of myself that I thought I'd lost."

"This is a bad pep talk," Bertie said.

"Just listen to me. Ugh." Dylan lifted his hands and dragged them down his face in a simulacrum of Munch's *The Scream*, or maybe more like the horrified emoji, which was itself quite pointedly *Scream*-like. Bertie had done a version of this for the dinosaur character at work, whose arms were so short that only the tips of his claws touched his cheeks as he collapsed into horror. She'd been quite proud of that one. A remote feeling now: her pride in her work. "My point is, I wasn't in love with you *at first*, but then we were thrown back together, again and again. And what we did, what we felt, that became real. For me as much as for you." He bumped her shoulder lightly with his. "*Truth revises you*, remember? We lived together, through that. Both of us."

"No." Bertie flushed. "You never wanted to leave your place."

"I mean, of course, if you want to be incredibly literal, I wasn't going to let go of a rent-controlled apartment in the Mission to move into your seventies South Bay prefab. Sorry."

"I could bike to work."

"But you never did."

"You wouldn't even say that you loved me."

"I didn't want to rush things!" Dylan looked flustered. "That's not the point! I'm just saying, it took me a little while, too, but you grew on me. And when we started the day over again this morning, it only made things more . . ." He stopped and shook his head. "I don't know. More."

"So." Bertie frowned. "Wait. I don't get it. What does that have to do with Javier?"

"You want me to open the door and find him. You want to have your little talk, ask him about Kate. Right?"

A thin film of perspiration formed on the top of Bertie's lip; she licked it off, and it came right back. She thought about putting her hands on Javier's shoulders and shaking him until the truth came out. His golden skin would bruise well, all that purple and green mixing in with his tan. Not that she would really hurt him, just—she would make him understand.

Dylan was waiting. A small voice inside her said, *There must be a reason he's willing to do this.* But she ignored it.

"Yes," she said. "Absolutely."

"Well, first I want something from you. As you guessed. I want—" He stopped.

"What?" And then he looked at her and she could see it in his face.

"Oh my God," she said. "You want me."

Dylan blushed. It was unsettling on him, which was weird considering how accustomed Bertie was to his habitual postcoital flushing, his pale potato of a body. She'd seen him warm and pink from the shower, chilly and goose-pimpled on any number of California beaches. Happy to see her, surprised to see her, drunk on the couch. This was different. It crept up his neck like a sickness.

"I want the whole thing. That would be the deal. We go

back, and we live our lives for one more year. Who knows," he said. "If it goes well, maybe we can just stay there. Or wherever we want to go."

"A year? No way." She thought of Javier behind the door. How he could disappear any moment. "I need this now."

"The time would pass for you and me, but it wouldn't pass here. I've told you, it doesn't work the way you think."

"So, what, when we're done, the whole thing would disappear?"

"Not that, either. This is your choice. But once you choose it, it tends to stick, in my experience."

Bertie felt cold. "I can't pretend that well. You want me to be your girlfriend?"

"Oh my God no," Dylan laughed, with visible pain. "I wouldn't make you pretend. Are you kidding me? You'd run away first chance you got." He paused. "But yes to the girlfriend part." He tucked his hands under his knees, nervously tapping his feet up and down on the floor. "It would be like it was here. At the start, you wouldn't be aware of anything. It might sort of dawn on you over the course of a few months, but by then we'd be in it."

"In it," Bertie repeated. "You think I'm going to fall in love?"

"You already did once. I'm pretty sure you will again. And when it happens, you'll see. It's real. This thing between us. It was meant to be."

"Fuck," she said, softly.

He pressed his shoulder into hers. Their bodies so close together, they were almost one continuous form. "It won't be so bad."

"It will. It is."

"Maybe," he said. "But what choice do you have?"

And she had no choice at all.

Part Two

–11–

Bertie's eyes hurt as she opened them. Too dry. She'd left the space heater on all night again, and now her lips were chapped and her eyeballs shriveled, the glass of water on her nightstand slightly dusty and lukewarm. Lately the apartment complex had been turning off the central heat and air to conserve gas, and Bertie had to remember—she beat her forehead lightly: *Remember!*—to shut off her space heater before going to sleep, or else she was going to burn the whole place down. Around her, the air warbled like the inside of an oven, and she snuggled under the covers in her private swamp, not quite ready to get up and admit she needed to take a shower before venturing out into polite society.

Wasn't there something else she was supposed to remember? Something important? Well, maybe, but she couldn't. Bertie groaned, and let it go. Her morning thoughts were frequently on the darker side, given as she was to holding over the remnants of forgotten dreams.

She did perk up a bit when she noticed the neat stack of clothes on the dresser. Thank God: at least she'd laid out her outfit before getting into bed. She had to go to that party tonight, a "non-mandatory" work event, and the insouciance of tech-world fashion always took some effort to parse. *We're morally superior to vanity*, her clothes needed to say, *but also very rich*. There would be executives there in hoodie sweatshirts worth twenty-five hundred dollars apiece, and since Bertie literally couldn't afford to be so casual, she needed some polish to compensate. Weird that she couldn't remember picking out this particular ensemble—skinny black jeans, motorcycle boots, thin black sweater with the one not-too-noticeable snag—but that didn't matter so much as long as it could transition seamlessly from day to night. Maybe add a smidge of lipstick and re-up the eyeliner at five p.m. to scare her coworkers into thinking she was rock and roll. None of them had ever seen her as a teenager, with flowers in her hair and stars in her eyes, so it could work.

Testing her own strength, Bertie dangled one leg out from under the covers, curling back her toes when they touched the low-shag carpet that filled her apartment, beigely. When she moved in, she'd been excited about escaping the grind of her commute, but sometimes she did miss the city's hardwood floors; moving to the South Bay had been a choice she made in haste and could never take back now, not with rents the way they were. Oh well. The carpet fibers were crisp and warm. Steeling herself, Bertie hopped out of bed and unplugged the heater on her way to the bathroom, watching its hellish glow deflate as she perspired into the morning.

—

Running around and getting ready—eyeliner at the bathroom mirror, pulling her eyelids back to achieve a cleaner line; mug of coffee at the sink in the kitchen, dripping onto her pants, but hey, what else were black pants for?—Bertie lifted into a surprisingly good mood. The air, now that she was up and about, felt less sludgy. Her skin was fresh and clean from the shower, her hair twisted up in a towel. She released it, letting the wet strands tumble down onto her shoulders and hoping that the distant sea air would scrunch them into legible curls. The morning was never so hard once she woke up into it: as her head cleared, the world became familiar again.

By eight-forty-five she was in her car and on the way to work, honking only twice at people who tried to merge into her in the slow crawl of South Bay tech traffic, everyone funneling dismally into the same three-mile radius. Police leaned on their motorcycles at every corner, doing nothing. Their ubiquity was a recent development. No one was speeding, and few of the officers even had radar guns: they just watched you. For what? Unclear. But you got used to it. At the office, Bertie slouched through the kitchen on the way to her desk, grabbing more coffee in one of the office's wasteful cardboard cups, with an even-more-wasteful-but-necessary disposable heat sleeve, as well as a yogurt and a banana. One tiny packet of almonds for later, or maybe for now. Grocery stores these days were a revolving door of missing items and embargoed fruit, but the micro kitchens never changed. Stepping into one gave her a rush of guilty relief, a simultaneous crash and high, that came from being touched by money. Bertie hadn't bought breakfast food in years; tampons, too. She used to sometimes joke, on the phone with her mom, that she could never quit her job because they subsidized her femininity in a way society refused to do. "Do you know how much tampons cost?" she'd fume. "It's like a woman tax." *Yes, dear*, her mom would say, almost certainly rolling her eyes.

She's dead, Bertie's mind chimed in at the smallest thought of her mother. *Dead, dead, dead.* Sometimes she wished she could know the things she knew a little less. A group of coworkers buzzed around the corner, and Bertie dodged them.

Everyone was acting weird in anticipation of being drunk together that evening. They were—what was the word? Twitterpated. Overcaffeinated, which Bertie had to admit was a condition she shared. Her work friend Danzy ran by her desk and said, "Meeting! Ten minutes!"

"What?" Bertie pushed back her chair, trying to catch Danzy by the wrist before she disappeared. "What meeting?"

"With those new contractors. They want to put our heads together about story lines for the campaign, or something. They want to, um, caucus. Or circle back to some things they put pins in. You know. The usual."

"Oh God. And I was having such a good day."

"Du courage," Danzy told her. "The revolution will surely be video conferenced."

Their employer, an advertising behemoth with an ever-expanding portfolio of tech-world priorities, was known to the public mainly for its dinosaur mascot and benign goodwill, despite the fact that the company quietly maintained a workforce that was fifty percent contractors, without benefits or job security. Bertie had, thank God, been hired before this policy became general, but she was always surprised to find out how many of her coworkers were prey to it. Danzy was full-time, but their junior designer, Ruby, was contingent, as were four of the marketing project managers. Their manager, Hiro—actually the head of his department—had also been quite happily contingent, until he discovered he would be required, for tax purposes, to take six unpaid months off every two years, and agitated to upper management to get himself reclassified.

Mostly, Bertie's sympathies lay with the contractors, because their positions were so uncertain, but some of them had such bad personalities that, in Bertie's lower moments, she wondered if they deserved what they got. Especially the off-site contractors, forever video conferencing in from their home offices or kitchen tables. Instead of getting any work done, they spent their time making pointed comments about not being able to visit the cafeteria, and sighing loudly whenever anyone mentioned an employee-only on-site perk. It wasn't even that they were wrong, it was that they were annoying. *If they really wanted to, they could change their situation*, Bertie caught herself thinking sometimes. *And an occasional smile never hurt anyone.* She knew she was being gross, but she couldn't help it.

Good mood ruined, Bertie flicked through her email, trying to finish her free yogurt quickly so as not to rub it in anyone's face. According to the chirpy calendar invite, both the contractors coming to her meeting with Danzy were copywriters on loan from a third-party marketing firm, and in addition to having overinflated egos—"Did you know Earl called himself a living master class?" Danzy had mentioned, a few days before. "He didn't even say in what"—they were pretty weird. The youngish woman, named Susan, always showed up to video chats in a bathrobe—every time a different bathrobe—and spent a lot of time monologuing about her dog's medical history. She had a hungry look, the mien of a street urchin from 1835, despite her very reasonably sized apartment. Earl lived in Milpitas, in a small house with an evidently enormous family, who were around him always. If nothing else, they were all but guaranteed to waste ten minutes at the top of the meeting talking about their sad desk lunches. Or sad kitchen table lunches, as the case may be.

"Hi, guys," Susan said, breezing in front of her computer's camera as Bertie and Danzy got settled in the conference room. "Thanks so much for making the time."

She sat down and put her fingertips to her face, massaging her cheekbones, and Bertie and Danzy smiled patiently, waiting for her to continue. "Before we get started, can I just ask, if you notice me getting some kind of facial paralysis during this conversation, can you call 911?"

"Sorry, what?"

"You ate the beans, huh?" asked Earl, whose own video screen had popped up in the interim of Susan's massage. A small child ran into and then out of view behind him, as Earl swatted ineffectually at them.

"They were chickpeas. But yes, I made hummus. Let's be honest, I probably dented the can myself."

"Uh, guys?" Danzy interjected. "That sounds, uh, serious. Mind filling us in?"

"Oh, it's nothing," said Susan, waving a hand. "Just, I have this ridiculous fear that if I ever eat food from a dented tin can, I'm going to get botulism. Because you know, the bacteria can affect the integrity of aluminum, or something."

"I think it's the other way around," said Bertie. "The botulism gets in because the can has a hole."

"Anyway," Susan went on, casting ice-eyes at Bertie's

correction. "This morning I only *had* a dented can, and I had to make *something,* because you know some of us do have to provide for ourselves."

"Been there!" said Earl.

"So I'm just asking," Susan purred. "For you to keep an eye out. Just in case."

"Well," said Danzy. "Safety first, of course."

"I have my phone right here," Bertie agreed, holding it up. "First sign of trouble."

"I really appreciate it. Okay, then. Let's talk small business. We're sticking with brick-and-mortar, yes? Because it's easier to illustrate?" Susan smiled through the word *easier,* but Bertie and Danzy both knew better than to react.

The rest of the meeting, though tense, was productive, with no visible signs of botulism, and when they finally logged off, Bertie pushed back her rolling chair and let out an *oof.*

Standing up to unplug her laptop, Danzy said, "Remember the time she told us her dog had died on the operating table and had to be resuscitated?"

"Wasn't that our first meeting?"

"I think so. And I mean. Traumatic, for sure."

"But then she asked us if we had on-campus vet services, and basically didn't believe us when we said no."

"We do have a company doctor," Danzy conceded.

"Chickpeas *are* beans," Bertie said. "They're garbanzo beans."

"No, I think they're legumes."

"Legumes aren't beans?"

"It's a square-versus-rectangle thing. Beans are legumes, but not necessarily the other way around."

"Why are we talking about this?"

"Because it beats doing twenty design options for a small business marketing campaign that probably won't see the light of day?"

"Let's go to the micro kitchen and get some chips," suggested Bertie. "And string cheese. And an apple." She touched her own cheekbones, lightly. "Now *my* face feels weird."

"Mine, too. I think we both need more coffee."

They spent a few minutes clicking around on their laptops in the relative silence of the kitchen, blowing on their coffee until it turned the corner from too hot to undrinkable. The transformation was instantaneous: if you stopped paying attention, you could miss whatever brief window there was between burning and bitter cold. Tepid. Tepid was the window. Bertie asked Danzy if she was going to the party that night, knowing that she was. Everyone was. It would be catered by six different chefs, and none of the contractors were invited unless they got plus-one'd by a full-time employee, which made Bertie feel even guiltier about how much she disliked Susan and Earl.

"Are you bringing anyone?" Danzy asked. "Whatever happened to your friend who was moving here, what was her name?"

"Oh," said Bertie. "Kate. Yeah. I think she got a job in L.A. instead, so it didn't come together."

"Bummer. She was fun."

"I guess so. Kind of my bitchiest friend, though, truth be told."

"There but for the grace of God go I," Danzy said, one eyebrow raised.

"You're not bitchy. You just have good taste."

"Well thanks. Hey, speaking of, did you bring a change of clothes for the party? Or are you wearing . . . that?"

At which point Bertie scowled and said she was going back to her desk to mock up some examples of the company dinosaur running various local businesses, ranging from a pizza restaurant to an auto body shop. She also drew a tailor dinosaur with a tape measure wound all around its body, which she knew would be rejected despite its obvious charm for making the business owner look incompetent.

As the day passed, Bertie was swept along by the familiar feeling of having done everything before. When she walked into meetings, she knew how they would go, who would be obnoxious, who quietly helpful. When she handed in sketches, she knew with an uncanny clarity which ones would be passed over and which selected for further review—she kept wanting to point to the inevitable final images and mouth, *Let's see a few more versions of that one*, but she held herself back so as not to seem difficult to her colleagues. The news, online, was a steady march of sameness, too, even in its shocking reveals: a corrupt politician run out of office by an online mob had the same face, it seemed to Bertie, as a man who'd experienced identical treatment the week before. She had once sworn she'd never stop being moved by all the terrible headlines, but there were so many of them, they became normal no matter what you did—the sensation of struggling against bad normalcy as familiar to Bertie, now, as breathing.

She thought about Susan's unfortunate dog, who had so many health problems. Despite being dismissive about it to Danzy, she actually remembered the story about his near-death experience quite well, in part because she'd heard it before deciding just how much Susan sucked. Sometimes the dog, whose name was Herb, wandered into the path of Susan's laptop camera in the middle of a meeting, and Bertie felt a rush of affection for him. He was a stern creature. Instead of barking, he let out occasional requests for attention that fell somewhere between a howl and a yelp. He lay down and stared at the computer, as if staring at Bertie, or into time itself.

"He was such a goofy puppy before it happened," Susan said once. "Honestly, you'd never know it. I called him Mr. Showboat."

But who wouldn't be changed by something like that? Bertie wondered. Who or what could possibly come back from the other side unaltered? His eyes seemed ready to pierce through the veil, and he walked with a small but visible limp. Susan claimed that Herb wouldn't have been aware of his own short death; he'd been under general anesthesia at the time, having his teeth cleaned by the vet. But Bertie thought the evidence was clear. He remembered. He couldn't not remember, on a cellular level, if nothing else. The lights in his body had been turned all the way down and then, in a flash, flicked back up. It made her shiver to think about it.

At four-thirty she stopped pretending to work and read a few movie reviews online, before moving on to snarky blog posts. A woman was cataloging her return to the land in weekly stories, explaining that the bombs and the electrical storms were God's way of telling mankind that they'd been living beyond their means. The woman sewed her clothes by hand and was farming sweet potatoes and corn; she had four goats. She said that she wanted her blog posts to serve as a guidebook for the others who would inevitably follow her example when the power grid shut down, and Bertie wondered if the woman had thought this model all the way through. Was she picturing people printing each post out, hand-binding them with a needle and thread? Still, Bertie enjoyed the stories in the same way she enjoyed reading grisly recitations of true crime: for the spectacle, and to help herself ward off the belief that the same darkness was sweeping towards her, too.

"Hey," said Danzy at five-fifteen. She was arm in arm with Ruby, who she'd promised to bring to the party as her plus-one. "Shuttle buses are starting to run up to the city. You coming?"

"Oh shit, yes." Bertie flipped open her phone and turned the camera on herself as a mirror, checking to see if her eyelids were sweating: a new and fairly embarrassing habit of her body. They were. She wiped them with the tip of a finger.

"Come on, you're beautiful. You can do the rest on the ride up." Easy for Danzy to say; Danzy had changed into a dark blue skirt and wrapped her hair in a gold cloth. She had charcoal gray eyeshadow winging up towards her temples, and her mouth was a hot-pink, kissable bow. To achieve anything half so good, Bertie knew she'd have to spend at least half an hour alone in the bathroom, making delicate flicks of the wrist. Mascara. Mascara. Eyeliner. Powder. But Bertie also knew the traffic would be hell, and she'd have more than enough time to clean her face with Ruby's makeup wipes and apply lipstick on the bus. Which was probably fine. She hesitated for a second; did she even want to go to this party? All day she'd been barreling towards it as if there were no way out, but really, would anyone even care if she just went home and put on sweats and ordered in? She could even call Kate, find out what had happened there. But Danzy was already pulling her up. "You're not crapping out now. We're all in this."

Yes, we're already in it, Bertie thought. And she let herself be dragged to the bus.

—

As a general rule, Bertie liked beautiful things. Not just in an art school way—in fact, she was less than sure she liked beautiful art, at least for its own sake—but day to day. Which was the real reason she couldn't quit her job. She was a fan of luxury, all the comfort that money could buy, and how it could soften the world around you. It had never been the plan, this comfort: not coming from her thrift-store childhood, and not in college, where everyone was competitively abject in both circumstance and aesthetic. But here she was. When she put on a brand-new T-shirt, she felt like a fresh chapter of her life was beginning, like she had just erased the tentative pencil lines around her soul. Buying a bra was a practically religious experience, not that she got to do it very much anymore, with prices going up and materials disappearing. But she supposed that plenitude did not necessarily make a ritual more ecstatic.

The few times she'd traveled for work, Bertie had taken deep pleasure in the hotel rooms they booked for her, always mid-range to upscale, clean and tasteful, with a few decent wines on the room service menu. The soap was packaged, as was the nail file, and the water cups were wrapped in plastic, as if everything in the facility had been run through an autoclave and had to be kept in sterile condition. Lying on her hotel bed—perfectly flat, with the sheets pulled taut and the comforter smoothed in geometric precision—Bertie felt she could've been on a spaceship headed to Mars, appreciating the voyage's carefully selected accoutrements. Everything with a purpose, nothing out of place. There were never any bright colors in these rooms, as if they didn't trust business travelers to be surrounded by anything other than white or beige without getting frisky. But still, Bertie saw the beauty in them. They were high-cost ventures. The linens were nice, and the shampoo came from local, ethically sourced materials. *That,* she sometimes said to an invisible interlocutor, when asked why she was such a loyal employee. *I could never afford that, or that.* At which the interlocutor, whoever they were, would frown.

The party was less beautiful than it was opulent, but Bertie appreciated that, too, since at least it leaned into its ridiculous aesthetic. Where else in her life was she going to walk into a tent and be surrounded by ribbon dancers hanging from the ceiling? They were all wearing animal masks, and the tent was full of jungle plants. A subtle waitstaff paced through the room with meat skewers and shots of soju, which Bertie declined. She had learned not to take the first refreshment offered at a company party, no matter how tempting; there was always something she wanted more in the next room, on the next tray. She just had to stay sober enough to find it.

"This is a little offensive," Danzy murmured in her ear, leaning her chin on Bertie's shoulder.

"How so? For the tiger community?"

"No, it's, like, primitivist. All the performers are Black. Did you not notice that?"

"Oh," Bertie said. She had not noticed. "Ew. Let's get out of here."

"At last." Danzy grabbed Ruby, who had apparently not yet learned how to handle her liquor at these functions. She was soju-flushed and smiling. Then again, she was also twenty-three, so her plan was probably to seek variety and not perfection, quantity over quality. Function, not form. Her hangovers were probably less bad, too.

They wandered through a few more staging areas, reading short explanatory plaques; the theme of the party was Time, and while the jungle room was a pre-human epoch—"Sure," said Danzy. "Pre-human. Mm-hmm"—there was also a farm-to-table garden where you could pick purple carrots from a dusting of soil, and a Timelessness tent that Bertie was afraid to eat from, even though she was pretty sure it was illegal to dose your employees with LSD for the sake of frivolity. They were playing Jimi Hendrix and projecting a light show onto the ceiling, so it seemed safer not to risk it.

She lost track of Danzy and Ruby when the pair of them insisted on trying all the flavors of astronaut ice cream in a space-age hallway; Bertie thought one was enough and wandered away to surreptitiously revisit the ribbon dancers while Danzy was distracted. By the time she got back, they were gone. It was that kind of party. She kept running into old colleagues from disbanded teams, catching up briefly on long-dead projects and then disattaching just as quickly. A couple of hours in, she was finally hungry enough to commit to a food theme, and had stopped to pick up meatloaf bites and white wine when she noticed a nearby hill, fenced off and populated with politely mingling glitterati. They always kept the VIPs away from the regulars at these things, but they usually did a better job of disguising it.

From the inside, a well-dressed man, clearly drunk, was leaning against the fence to talk with someone—less well-dressed but still a man—who was on the same side as Bertie. The drunk one saw her looking at them and gestured that she should join. She made a *Who, me?* face, but was happy enough to oblige, at least for the length of time it took her to finish the meatloaf.

"Here, I bet she gets it," the drunk man said. "You've heard of Rocket Limited, right?"

"Uh, sure," said Bertie. "Shuttles to outer space, right?"

"Well it *was*." The man threw up his hands. "Before everything went to *shit* and so on."

"Didn't their rocket blow up, too?"

"Yes!" He turned to the less drunk man. "See, I said she would get it."

The less drunk man shrugged. In fact, he might have been completely un-drunk; Bertie was getting tipsy now, so she felt that she could tell. An un-drunk radar. Sobriety sensitivity. He stood beside her, pinching the stem of his wineglass a little too tight and trying to keep his face composed. She thought if she listened carefully she'd be able to hear him grit his teeth, or count down from ten in his head. *It's fine in five, four, three, two.* He was round-cheeked like a baby, a white guy with brown, thinning hair and not such a great shirt, but it was okay. She wasn't sure what she had against gingham anyhow.

"I was an early investor," the drunk man went on. "I put in, like, ten mil. Because I believe in dreaming big, you see?"

"No half measures," Bertie agreed, taking a large gulp of wine. "So, um, why . . . ?"

"Are we talking about this? Right!" The drunk man pointed

at her as if she were his favorite student, definitely headed for an A or A-plus. Her favorite place to be. "We are *talking* about how I almost *died*."

"Whoa, heavy." Bertie took a step back.

"I know, right?"

"Everyone is almost dying these days," Bertie said, and the drunk man nodded as if he knew just what she was talking about. He was kind of cute. Maybe? Or at least he was interesting. His companion did not seem to agree.

"Except," said the companion, crisply. "You didn't die, did you, Ron?"

"No, because my wife is a genius."

"I bet she is," Bertie said. Damn, a wife. But still. She gave the non-drunk guy a bit of side-eye, hoping he would shut up long enough for her to get the actual story from the drunk one. Maybe she couldn't sleep with a married man, but she could at least do him the honor of listening to him. The day had been a roller coaster. She woke up that morning in a room as hot as hell itself, and—

"Hey!" Bertie looked up, surprised at herself. "I almost died this morning, too! I left my space heater on all night." *Space!* she thought. But she wasn't drunk enough, yet, to comment on the linguistic synchronicity between rockets, outer space, space heaters, mortal coils.

"Sure, whatever. Sucks." The drunk man clearly didn't care for being interrupted when listening to his own voice was still an option. "My point is, I invested ten. Million. Dollars. And so of course I was supposed to go up with the first launch. But my wife, she had a seat, too, and she wouldn't go. She said I never listen to her! She said it was a stupid thing to do. So I thought, I'll show her, and I sold our seats and used the Bitcoin to take us on a vacation to Mykonos. And while we were there, the damn thing blew up on the launch pad. So, like, now I can't do anything without asking her first."

"You mean she won't let you?" Bertie asked.

"No." His gaze wavered and took on a haunted quality. Figures moving behind curtains. Whispers in the dark. "I mean, I could've died," he said. "If I'd made one choice differently, I could have really, truly died, and I would have." The more he repeated the words, the more genuinely upset he sounded, as if he'd stepped through a door and was dying right that minute, in front of them. But Bertie was turned off by his refusal to find common ground with her space heater story, and could no longer work herself up to a climax of sympathy or attraction. She turned to the non-drunk man and willed herself closer to sobriety instead.

"So," she asked, "what foolhardy ventures have you embarked on lately?"

"Oh, you're talking to me now?" said the man in the gingham shirt. Looking at him more closely, Bertie saw his face was smooth and pink. It had the glow of health, misused, which she found relatable. He gestured to her white wine. "If so, I guess let's go get another one of those? I need to catch up."

"You DO." Bertie marched ahead of him towards the drinks table, calling him after her with a glance.

The drunk man took a few steps back and walked away up the hill of wealth, still shaking his head. "Could've *died*," Bertie heard him say, one last time, in a voice that insisted on the inevitability of every death, even hers. But she and the gingham man were already receding towards the meatloaf and the wine, situated in the nostalgic American past.

"I'm Bertie," she told him. He turned, and took her by the shoulders, looking her up and down.

"Just like I remembered," he said.

Bertie laughed. "What's that supposed to mean?"

"I'm Dylan."

"Like Bob Dylan?"

"God, no. I mean, technically yes, but please never say that again."

"Okay." Bertie laughed again, a giddy sort of up-bubbling in her throat. Reverse champagne. She felt she already knew something about this Dylan person. Something good. As he procured them both more wine, she reached out and felt his bicep through the thin, warm, cotton of his shirt.

"Oh, Bertie," he said.

"What?" She took her hand away from his arm. "Sorry. Was that weird?"

"No." He smiled, a little sadly. Or maybe she was inventing the sadness. Here they were, at the world's most ridiculous party, flirting. Flirting! Right? She was bad at knowing when that was happening, but he took a step closer, which seemed like a good sign. "Just the opposite," he said. "Somehow it's completely familiar."

—

In the weeks that followed, Bertie would frequently hold his hand, bite his ear, touch whatever she wanted to touch. She learned that the drunk man at the party was Dylan's boss, a venture capitalist who'd been brought on board as the CTO of a large social networking company. He was helping them branch out into news publishing, instead of just dissemination, starting with the acquisition of a TV network, a paper, and a video-focused production team, all of which now coexisted uncomfortably beneath the company's umbrella. He also—according to Dylan, at least—didn't do very much actual work. Instead, he went to business lunches that lasted for hours, and came back to the office drunk, putting loud jazz on his turntable. People ten desks away could feel the drum fades rumbling through their feet, though no one dared say anything about it, since he could buy and sell each of them several times. Plus, to be fair, he had many of his best ideas drunk.

Miles Davis blaring, Dylan would be called into his boss's office to take notes on all the possible directions their division could take five or ten years down the line. They were alternate universes, pointing north, south, east, west. They were sometimes so detailed as to include the births of the man's future children, and different timelines gave those children different names, and allowed for different variant sets. Girl, girl, boy. Boy, girl, girl. It was as if, Dylan said, his boss could see the future in different colors, like a bird navigating a thousand-mile migration based on magnetic fields in the sky. He never talked like this when he was sober; his right mind made him risk-averse. He had to be sloshed, lying on his office couch while Dylan sat nearby, scribbling dictation in a psychiatrist fashion, asking *What next?* and *How did that make you feel?*

"Does he remember me?" Bertie asked Dylan once, while

they lay together in his bed. She was comfortable in the bed by now, having seen it through two separate sheet changes and laundry days; this was his third and final set. "That we met, I mean?"

"Oh, yes," said Dylan. "You were in one of those alternate timelines."

"Oh, really? Like I was his girlfriend? I thought he was cute."

"Ew," Dylan replied. "No, not quite. I mean, he didn't say, so actually, I bet, that too. But the thing was, he bought art from you. You were signed on to one of his networks to develop cartoons. I must've mentioned you were an artist."

Bertie found this fascinating, that she could figure into a whole, if theoretical, future after one small cameo in real life. She was also impressed by how much Dylan knew about his company's priorities, by virtue of such a close and personal relationship with his boss's thinking. She herself, she realized, knew very little about what her company actually did; she knew when the dinosaur needed to be sketched as the ambassador for a global health initiative, or when he was "partnering" with schools all around the country to help get kids "roaring to read." She did not, however, know what devices they planned to make, or what direction their experimental division was tilted: AI? VR? AR? Would they make a robot that could augment reality virtually? Or a virtually augmented but also real robot? She would only know when they gave the robot a name and personality and asked her to send it on a best-friends tour with the dinosaur.

What went on behind closed doors at the business park? Bertie could really only imagine. There were rumored plans of a floating city of server farms being designed for the Indian Ocean.

Phones that would fit on a contact lens, or that could be sent into the bloodstream with a child's regularly scheduled vaccines. Most of it, she would remain unaware of forever, or until it was litigated in the press. There being no limit on the company's wealth, there was also no limit on its ambitions. No one was content to do one thing well anymore. They all wanted to do everything. Disseminate enough ideas to the public that they would never reach their mortal end. Just keep replicating in different conversations until the universe itself stuttered out.

While discussing his boss, Dylan brought up the space travel company, Rocket Limited, and asked if she knew anything about her own company's forays into similar technology.

"We have a rocket?" Bertie asked. It was surprising, but also not. She knew they held a patent on a form of human cloning. The company liked to hedge its bets.

"I just hope it doesn't blow up and take you with it," Dylan said, picking up her hand and nibbling the knuckles, down to the wrist. "That's the only reason I mentioned it."

"Well, don't worry. I doubt I'd be invited on board. I didn't even know it existed."

"Maybe they'll do a lottery, though. It would be good optics: let your peons travel to space."

"Unless they died."

"Right, sure. But can you imagine?"

And actually, she could imagine: she felt it in that very moment as he kissed her sternum, her belly, her thigh. It was vertiginous. Not only the thought that she might be on a rocket, but that she in fact was slipping off one, the way a person might slide from the back of a galloping horse without a saddle. Lying naked in bed, with Dylan wrapping himself around her leg, tickling her neck, and whispering dirty things in her ear, she felt like she was indeed falling from a very great height. Or, rather, about to fall. Clinging with her fingertips and feeling each of them lose its grip, one after the other after the other, until there was nothing left.

She supposed her company was investing in rockets because someone at the top of the hierarchy was dreaming of moving humanity into space, terraforming Mars or reaching Titan, living in the shadow of Saturn's rings. Escaping their fate at the very last minute, as the ice caps gave up and released their final deadly dose of methane into the atmosphere. She understood, but she also thought: Why isn't anyone trying to fix it? Why isn't the initiative some kind of cooling mechanism, an enormous air conditioner or ozone re-layering? An artificial coral reef, a massive replanting of the rainforest, an end to submarine vibrations that destroy the inner ears of whales. After she and Dylan had exhausted themselves, she turned to the wall in his room and fell asleep, dreaming of the dinosaur in a white lab coat and goggles, mixing chemicals into the night. She dreamed of him, coming up with some formula and shouting EUREKA! in a spiky scream balloon, inventing some method of saving humanity from the fate that he and his brethren had suffered, all those millennia ago.

– 12 –

It had been a long time, or maybe it had been forever, since Bertie had fallen into a relationship in quite this way. At work, she doodled Dylan's name onto notepads, surrounded by pictures of flowers and stars, and she scrolled through his social media accounts so often that she knew each time he posted something, often within minutes. If he wrote about the two of them, she texted him her reply instead of answering online, and he would then post something new, meant just for her, so their conversation was public and private, visible and invisible, thrilling.

Already he seemed to her like a love story, not that she would've put it to him in quite those words. But the moment they touched at the party, she had melted into him like butter, her attraction so strong it felt preordained. She could hardly believe she'd almost skipped the party altogether. *Can you imagine?* she asked herself, laughing as she massaged her most expensive shampoo into her hair in the shower, knowing he would shortly lean in and smell it, and probably smile.

When she was a teenager, she got crushes on boys, but these had rarely panned out into anything definitive. Most often they existed completely in her head, and as a result she was so uncomfortable the first time she actually made out with someone—junior year of high school, a guy named George, at a party after drinking two rum and Cokes—that she got the full-body shakes as soon as his hand reached up to her breast, which the boy took as a better sign than he should have of his personal efficacy.

Her real teenage crushes had been on girls: not romantically but well—okay, not sexually? Not very sexually. Her friendships, unlike her relationships with boys, had anniversaries and inside jokes, beginnings and endings so specific she could pin them not just to the day, but the hour. Her friend Kate, for example: the big love of her late high school life, who she'd met at school at the beginning of her freshman year, in Honors English. Kate had been seated by the wall, and kept picking at one of the posters there, ripping off small pieces, her hair purple, her boots old Dr. Martens that she wore until they were seniors, when she inexplicably switched them out for skinny black wedge heels purchased for her by her mom. English class wasn't when they became friends, but it was where they met, and Bertie remembered the look of Kate's hair in the late-morning sunshine midwinter, when the light was always dim and even, but somehow the hair was shockingly bright. A hothouse flower, a party balloon drifting near the sidewalk over dirty snow. She and Kate had lost touch during college, so when Bertie thought of her now, it was the same way she thought about books she'd read over and over as a girl, and then never again once she crossed the invisible line into adolescence.

Bertie sometimes daydreamed about what it would have been like if Kate had actually moved to the Bay Area, but she didn't, so the specifics of their friendship had begun to fade, along with most of the details from high school, in the absence of anyone to discuss them with.

Dylan was her only crush now, despite his ordinary hair, and she leaned towards him as continuously as if he were the sun. It was the prerogative of adulthood, it turned out, to become infatuated with people you could actually kiss, could, in fact, touch and possess, even make a life with. Some urgency had left the notions of marriage and children, given the general state of the world, but Dylan had reawakened them, to a certain degree. Bertie already had a drawer in his dresser, the second one from the top, plus a section of his closet for the days when she had a morning meeting and needed to hang up a nice shirt. He had a drawer in her dresser, too, the middle one in the smaller chest. She would've given him something more substantial, but he never seemed to bring that many extra clothes to her apartment, and most of the time all he kept in it was socks and underwear, which she figured was at least hygienic. At night, when they read or watched movies on the couch, he rested his legs on top of her legs until she couldn't take it anymore and had to admit to being squished, at which point her legs went on top of his legs, about which he never complained. She caught him studying her from the corner of his eye, as if he was sketching her into being. Adding fine lines, the hint of a smile, making her turn her head just so to look out the window. A few times she'd tried drawing him, but he never came out looking realistic without the addition of some accessory, like a pair of sunglasses, or a cap that shaded half his face. When she tried taking photos of them together, the shots always turned out glitchy and black, or else with Dylan smeared by motion, as if he were never quite in one place.

—

One Sunday afternoon, while browsing his bookshelf—paltry, masculine, but not illiterate—she found a childhood photo of him stuck between *Gravity's Rainbow* and *Infinite Jest,* and gasped at her instant sense of recognition. Was this what it was like, also, to have a child? To simply know them? She couldn't tell where the picture had been taken—maybe an orchard, or the edge of a forest, a mile from the sea? There was grass and the implication of sky; there were leaves but no branches; there was maybe mist—and he claimed not to remember. But she could see him in that small prototype of a face, the cheesy grin that masked both true happiness and the obvious annoyance he felt at being photographed.

His hair, which was thinner now despite still covering almost all of his head, had been curly and towhead blond; he could've been a figurine of a baby angel. Dimple cheeks, apple breath. Bertie felt her face grow warm as she looked at the only evidence she'd ever seen that he truly existed before he walked into her life. She wasn't sure if she liked it, or wanted to burn it. "Weird," he said, leaning over her shoulder. "I wonder where that came from." He didn't seem to find it strange that he remembered so little from before high school, as if it were only natural for the present to comfortably efface the past. But it gave Bertie a peculiar feeling.

In compulsive response, she showed him a slew of pictures from her own childhood, long since scanned into the computer and uploaded to the cloud, thanks to a mania for online genealogy that had gripped her mother in her last year of life. Bertie's pictures, unlike Dylan's, were all connected to a thick web of stories, like the summer her family had rented a rundown cottage in eastern Washington—*shit on a shingle*, her dad had called it, though he rented it again a few summers later, time having softened his perceptions with its sweetheart lenses—and she spent hours combing through the yard catching grasshoppers, which she kept in glass jars. One of the grasshoppers was named Lovey, because he was dusty white like a dove, and young Bertie spent a full day of vacation assembling his habitat, carefully arraying the jar with grass and twigs, flowers and leaves, before tipping him in from her loosely cupped hand. What she forgot to do, as it turned out, was put adequate holes in the lid, so Lovey's palatial accommodations smothered him—first into a sweet docility that led Bertie to believe they would be friends forever, and shortly thereafter, unto death.

(*I just can't stand the idea of being trapped*, she remembered someone saying. But who? She supposed a lot of people felt that way. When she mentioned it to Dylan, he seemed intrigued, then skittish, and she couldn't figure out who'd said it, anyway, so she dropped the issue.)

Sometimes she told Dylan stories from her childhood as they were falling asleep, running her fingernails over his shoulders. He breathed so deeply, then, it was nice to talk to him, and to imagine he was absorbing parts of her, important parts, along with the oxygen.

"God, I hope I'm not boring you," she said on one such night, as he began to lightly snore. Her bedside lamp was on so she could read, but the bulb was old and kind of yellow, and the room was sepia-toned.

"No, I like this story," he replied. So she kept telling it, even after he was obviously sleeping. How her mother hadn't liked dogs or cats or birds or any animal, really—certainly not the doomed grasshoppers—but one day a husky with bright blue eyes had shown up in their driveway, and her mother had practically lain down on the ground to embrace it. Like a queen in a fairy tale, who marries a wolf. When she spoke about her parents, Bertie couldn't stop her voice from catching, but Dylan didn't seem to notice or mind. "S'a nice story," he murmured in the moments before he drifted away. "S'nice."

She could never really relax in his presence until she knew he was happy, and so the words were a balm to her soul—unaccustomed as she was to this manic desire to satisfy anyone but herself. As "S'nice" became just "Sssss," she turned to her book, a French graphic novel she'd owned for two years and was finally trying to read. In the margins, she wrote out her translations of tricky passages, surprised by her ability to absorb the meaning of so much, when she hadn't really studied the language since high school; not since her friendship with Kate. She also duplicated some of the more interesting images in pencil: a car in the moonlight, a scene through a building's skylight, with books and records scattered around between people, reading on the floor. She started drawing her own ideas, too, the way a landscape might extend beyond the given page, following a train around the curve of a mountainside and into the distance. When she closed the book, Dylan was still sleeping beside her, not having moved so much as a limb, and yet she could've sworn his eyelashes were longer, darker, like she'd inked them in. She thought, *I've got crush goggles on,* figuring her adoration had inflected her perception, an emotional mascara applied by always being a little turned on. She did not think, for even a moment—because why would she; why would anyone—that his lashes had simply grown.

—

"Don't go past Hiro's desk," Danzy warned the next morning when Bertie breezed in ten minutes late. She'd taken to sleeping at Dylan's place on weeknights, even though her apartment was closer to their relative offices, because he claimed that when they were at her house, they ended up overcompensating for how short their commute would be and failing to give themselves adequate time. "He's saaaaad."

"Is it another diet? Is he going macrobiotic or something? One of those Whole Body Perception jams where you eat sweet potatoes until you become a nicer person?"

"Right, and drink the blood of virgins till your lips are ruby red. No." Danzy leaned forwards conspiratorially. "I heard they're doing layoffs, actually."

"Oh damn." Bertie looked at her phone as if she might be able to convince it to rewind by ten minutes and get her to her desk on time. "He has such a thing about punctuality, I'm screwed."

"Come on, everyone knows you're in love right now. If he doesn't give you a break, he has no heart."

"I'm not."

"So in love."

"Who died and made you a romantic?"

"I'm just saying, even Hiro knows mercy. He's not going to fire you for a few minutes here or there."

At that moment, Hiro came around the corner, and both

women straightened up and smiled. He waved half-heartedly at them and kept going, eyes lingering on Bertie just long enough to make her blood freeze. When he was out of earshot, she exhaled.

"Where is this even coming from?" she asked. "Aren't we doing weirdly well?" The company remained profitable despite creeping manufacturing deficits, maybe due to a residual perception of their morality, maybe something else. Stock prices had gone up, actually, following a series of congressional subpoenas to discuss the corporate overuse of oil, electricity, and jet fuel for the executives. The hearings took place behind closed doors, and everyone said they were a joke. Bertie thought about the rocket, and how much the seats on board would be worth. Earth was dying, and space was huge. Maybe Congress had a reason for the gentle nature of its oversight.

Danzy looked thoughtful. "The commute times are . . . unholy. They can't blame you for that."

"They could tell me to stop staying at his place if it's making me late."

"Come on. No one's going to make you break up with your boyfriend."

Bertie sat down hard in her chair, letting it spin in a circle. She sighed. "Aren't you a little ray of sunshine."

"I am. And you're a, um, funny, er, a funny bunny." Danzy put two fingers behind her head in the bunny-ear position and wiggled them around.

Bertie squinted at her, suddenly cold.

"What?" she asked, her throat gone dry. Kate used to call her Bunny, but of course Danzy didn't know that.

“God, don’t make me say it again. I’m already embarrassed.”

“I just . . .” Bertie shook her head, to clear it. “Ignore me. I got a weird feeling.”

“Goose over your grave?”

“Hmm. Probably. Big old goose feet.” At that point, Hiro walked by them again on the way back to his office, and both women turned to their computers and began to work.

—

When Danzy drew the dinosaur, she always started on a piece of paper, making tiny thumbnails in which the dinosaur looked shocked. Small arms extended, mouth open wide, like a gingerbread cookie. She did hundreds of these sketches, some no more detailed than stick figures or bubble heads, before she committed to an idea. Bertie thought it was an insane workflow, but Danzy liked it; she said that drawing badly let her thinking “emanate,” whatever that meant. She was trained as an animator, not an illustrator, so iteration was in her blood. Bertie made two or three images and worked them half to death, but by the time Danzy moved to a tablet and stylus, she was inevitably able to whip off ten or twenty frames with surprising speed, all of them excellent. Each frame almost identical, but slightly different. Moving not towards perfection but towards movement itself.

To Bertie’s eye, Danzy’s version of the dinosaur was also less serious than her own. She doubted anyone else could tell the difference, since they both adhered to the same brand-style guidelines, but she knew. Danzy’s dinosaur was more carefree and not so pensive. He didn’t share the quality, important to Bertie’s dinosaur, of being both pleased and alarmed each time he found himself in a new situation, handling a quill, opening a treasure chest, parleying with an angry ghost. Bertie's dinosaur saw the absurdity in his own life, that his deadly claws should be used to stroke the strings of a harp; that a harp should exist. When asked for music, Danzy's dinosaur simply played. Bertie's contemplated.

But they worked together well. Bertie did more character design, Danzy did more scene and story. When they were assigned a project together, Bertie always caught Danzy's eye across the meeting, and Danzy raised her eyebrows in celebration. It was a form of cultish camaraderie that Bertie associated with her teen years—a need to attach, above and beyond what the situation merited—and she was happy to find even a small particle of it in her adult life. Sitting beside each other now, they passed a bag of unshelled pistachios back and forth without speaking, sucking and chewing on the nuts until they were left with one unsplit shell and a pile of wet, disgusting detritus. A long time ago, in high school, she and Kate had done something similar, Bertie remembered. With sunflower seeds, because they were both obsessed with a guy on TV who ate them religiously while he solved crime.

Danzy smashed the last pistachio open with the butt of her stapler, and when it broke into a dozen pieces around her desk, she screeched.

"Wow," Bertie said. "Wild applause."

"Clearly I don't know my own strength."

"Clearly." Bertie swept a bit of shell from her desk. "Okay. Have you finished the Small Business September options? I took another whack at a greengrocer—get it? Because the dinosaur is green? And I added a dogwalker."

"All hail the gig economy," Danzy sighed.

They exchanged images and went to work doing secondary angles of each small business owner, trying to stretch each other's perspectives and also extend the time it would take to finish the assignment and be given another. It was repetitive work, but Bertie felt a glow extending off of Danzy as they silently sketched, the brief but vital sense that Bertie was, for once, not so alone. *What does that mean?* she asked herself. *Compared to what?* But then she brushed the thought away.

"Who do you think is going to write copy for this?" she asked Danzy. "Susan, or Earl?"

"Well, Earl is the master class."

"It doesn't even matter. I could write the copy. 'A small business makes a mighty roar.' "

"Or 'Help us celebrate the places in our community where good service isn't extinct.' "

" 'Quality makes you stand out from the crowd.' And the dinosaur is looming over the crowd, selling donuts."

"I could eat the hell out of a donut right now."

"Hey." Bertie looked up. "Want to get a drink later at that new donut-whiskey bar? I've heard it's actually kind of all right. They do custom fillings, like chocolate and custard swirl, and jam and stuff." She and Danzy had never hung out outside of work and work events, and Bertie thought that was sort of strange. A missed opportunity. They liked to make fun of the same things, talk about movie plots and how they would've fixed them, show each other sidewalk sketches they'd made over the weekend, random caricatures of their coworkers passed back and forth during All Hands meetings. But Danzy seemed taken off guard by the idea.

"Really?" she asked, pulling a curl out and letting it snap back. "I always thought of you as Miss Work-Life Balance. Separation of the powers."

"Come on, you can get the late shuttle. I'll drive you back to campus."

Danzy snorted. "Drunky. You can't invite me out for a drink and then offer me a ride."

"One drink. Seventeen donuts. That's still under the legal limit."

"I just. I don't know. I have stuff to do tonight. Aren't you seeing that guy?"

Both of them leaned back and paused.

"Okay. Sure." Bertie turned back to her tablet and opened a new file layer. It was just a drink. Who cared? They'd never hung out before, and they still wouldn't. Danzy didn't want to, which Bertie told herself was fine. Even so, the warm aura of their work receded, loneliness sliding back in like a fog. There was something missing from her life, Bertie conceded. But what? She drew the pet store dinosaur as a pirate, with a parrot perched on his shoulder and another on his head. "Do you think of the dinosaur as a *he* or an *it*?" she asked, trying to change the subject.

Danzy seemed relieved. "A he. But honestly I kind of hate myself for it."

"I think the mighty T. rex can shoulder the burden of your gender norms."

"But what if he wants to dance ballet!"

"Like men can't? And I've done him with a tutu, actually. And a leotard. According to the brand book, he's genderless."

"How unusually progressive of us. Let me see the tutu."

They spent the next half hour flipping through each other's archives, marveling at the way their renderings had progressed in parallel. Outside the company, no one knew who drew what, and Bertie assumed that, to the "end user," all the illustrators seemed like one monolithic hand. But, of course, they were different people. *Not even friends, necessarily,* she told herself, in the manner of poking at a bruise. *Just regular colleagues, no big deal.* Did she still have any friends? During the bombings, a sort of buddy system had emerged, but somehow Bertie didn't get one. She was still too wounded then about losing her parents; she hadn't wanted to be caught in such close quarters with anyone. Now she had Dylan, but that wasn't quite the same.

"Anyway." Danzy closed her laptop, popped her tablet into a kitschy soft case in her purse. "I'm heading out. This day is dunzo."

"So no drink?" Bertie hoped it sounded casual, but Danzy's face tensed, ever so slightly. She never liked having to repeat herself.

"Not today. Maybe another time." She winked at Bertie. "Have fun doing it till dawn."

When Bertie left, twenty minutes later, she found Danzy still downstairs, chatting with Ruby by the juice fridge. She'd seemed like she was in such a hurry to be gone, but there she was, laughing and sipping a rosewater iced tea while Ruby counted off the bad local sports bars on her fingers: Sports Page, Sports Zone, Good Sport, and more. They both waved half-heartedly to Bertie as she went by, and she gave them a tight smile, pushing through the glass doors and shouldering her bag a little bit higher as a warm wind hit her face. She felt dizzy, or maybe just annoyed. The sky was too blue. Birds wheeled overhead, too far away to see what kind. In the parking lot, she flipped through radio stations in her car until she zoned out, coming to ten minutes later with a shudder, having spent the intervening time listening to monks chant on a local independent program and staring into space. She was gripping her steering wheel so tightly that her knuckles were bloodless.

"Okay," she said to herself, and checked her mirror before pulling out of the lot into traffic.

—

Bertie considered calling Dylan in consolation and having him meet her at the Caltrain station, but couldn't muster the social energy to explain her mood even to him. There would be so much commuter chatter on the way, so much conversation when she got to the city. She didn't want to be alone, exactly, but she didn't want to be with Dylan, either. Spending the night at his apartment would have entailed going to work the next morning without a change of shirt, since all her stuff at his place was dirty. She needed to do a laundry run, bring a gym bag. An annoyance she somehow couldn't abide.

It's okay to want to spend some time apart, she told herself, though, in fact, the idea sent a thread of panic through her. She didn't have that many people left to rely on. At home, she locked her apartment door and then fell onto her back on the couch, staring up at the ceiling. She turned on her smart speakers with a voice command, and the same monks came on, chanting. The station must've been doing a series.

Thoughts of Dylan ran through her head, though the images were not quite Dylan; it was like they were animated by an unknown artist. Their energy was circumspect, cryptic. When he smiled in her mind, his teeth looked sharp. She picked up her phone and flipped through to see if she had Kate's number. "Huh," she muttered to herself, when she couldn't find it. She got a text then, her heart buzzing along with her phone, but it was just political spam. *DO YOU NEED HELP?* the text screamed at her. *WE'VE GOT YOU COVERED.*

Bertie jumped up and went to the kitchen to make tea, but halfway through the process, she decided that she didn't want any more caffeine. It was too early for chamomile, and she was out of mint. She went to her bedroom and pulled on her swimsuit, a navy blue one-piece she'd had for five years, which was starting to stretch out at the hips, the belly. There was, she discovered, a run in the ass, but it wasn't that visible. Anyway, she was at home. Her complex didn't have a pool, but the one next door did, and was owned by the same company. When she moved in, the older woman who'd handled her paperwork—Bev, or Bethany—had winked and said she was welcome to use it any time. "No one will notice," she assured Bertie, which made Bertie wonder if it was, in fact, allowed.

Bev was correct, though: no one paid any attention as Bertie walked the half block between complexes, wearing flip-flops and her suit, towel wrapped around her waist. The courtyard that housed the pool was empty, which meant Bertie had her pick of chairs to throw her towel on while building up the nerve to dive in. It was a little chilly for swimming. The sun was going down—not down all the way yet, but low enough for the sky to be periwinkle, almost purple, clouds and dust. The pool was lined with rosebushes, which were covered in blooms just a bit past prime, bright pink and yellow flowers spitting their pretty guts into the air. It smelled ecstatic. Bertie jumped into the water, getting a head rush from all the chlorine. Technically, they weren't supposed to be maintaining the pool anymore; she'd seen a flyer tacked up on the community bulletin board. But someone had ignored the memo, compensating for the lack of fresh water with extra chemicals.

Two laps in, Bertie began to breathe hard. She'd never swum competitively, so her form was bad; instead of ducking underwater to make her turns, she just spun around with her head up and kicked off in the other direction. After another lap and a half, she floated on her back and let her strokes get lazy, watching the clouds go orange above her. The sunset exploded like overripe fruit. In high school, she and Kate had spent an entire summer trying to scam their way into people's pools. They drove to rec centers, made friends with a pretentious girl named Maureen whose family sold Jet Skis and all-terrain vehicles. One night they went to a party at Maureen's house with bathing suits on under their jeans, knowing that the only people there would be basketball players and winter sports types, talking in affected voices about the best snowmobile trails and the odds for their fantasy leagues. Plus the girls who loved them. There were a few such girls. Some, like Maureen, were themselves obsessed with the fresh powder up at Snoqualmie Pass and the goggle burn that declared a long day of downhill, but others preferred the après ski. Hot chocolate with schnapps. Making out in front of the fire. After each drinking a requisite Corona and lime, Kate and Bertie had snuck outside to finally, finally get in the pool, but when they opened the sliding glass door, the night had gone freezing.

“Pacific motherfucking Northwest,” said Kate, wrapping her arms around herself.

“It’s not so bad,” Bertie countered. She stuck a foot bravely into the water, then pulled it back. “I thought Mo said they heated everything!”

“Apparently yet another lie from the queen of the made-up boyfriends.” A month before, Maureen had confided in Kate that she was in love with an older man named Thomas, a Brit who worked as an i-banker and had a charming accent and a closet full of Brooks Brothers suits. Kate was still mad that she fell for it, which Bertie privately found unfair to Maureen. Maureen was a known liar. You couldn’t hold it against her.

“I refuse to accept this,” Bertie said. The week had been warm, tilting over to hot. At night she’d been sleeping in her attic bedroom with a fan blowing straight at her face, sweating up the bed. Now it felt like fall. She walked to the shallow end and stepped onto the second highest step, submerging herself up to the shins.

“You’re crazy,” Kate told her.

“Hey,” said a dude named, maybe, Philip? Andrew? Some prince name. He peeked his head out the door, then slipped through after them. “Are you guys swimming?”

“Not really, it’s kind of—”

“YEAH!” Philip/Andrew pulled off his shirt and jumped straight in, sending a wave over Bertie’s thighs and drenching Kate’s towel.

“Asshole!” said Kate, but Bertie laughed, and splashed her. They looked each other in the eye and then hurried to jump in after Andrew—Bertie decided that must be his name—leaping together, towards one another, practically into each other's arms. The water, it turned out, wasn't quite as cold as the air, and once they started racing each other up and down the pool, they got positively flushed. Andrew timed them, smoking at the sidelines with his elbows propped up on a ledge. He was haphazard, his mind fritzing out if they went past forty-five seconds, most often declaring an arbitrary winner. After being denied an obvious victory, Kate swam over and dunked his head underwater, to general applause, and later on that night Bertie heard she made out with him on Maureen's parents' bed.

The California sun disappeared behind a building, and Bertie began to shiver in the falling darkness. She flipped back over and swam breaststroke for a while, taking pleasure in the awkward, yogic angle of the frog kick, and the water, frictionless against her skin. The evening still smelled of roses, but now there was a top note of gasoline. In the deep end of the pool, she treaded water and took a gulp of air, then ducked her head down, exhaling and scrabbling with her toes for the bottom. In the muted space below the surface, Bertie imagined Kate's face. Pursing her lips into a mirror, assessing her bangs. Bertie knew it was a little weird, this sudden fixation, but Danzy was the one who'd brought her up. (*Your friend, wasn't she supposed to move here?*) And Danzy had only met her, what, once? When had that even been? Any image of Kate at more than eighteen years old was hazy, digressive.

Bertie broke the surface and gasped. She pushed herself out of the pool and rubbed the towel all over her body, wringing out her hair and then hurrying back to her apartment, scooting her flip-flops against the concrete. Making friends as an adult was too hard, but that was no reason to stalk your friends from high school, was it? At home, once again on the couch, she flipped through social media, trying to find a recent picture or address for Kate, some way to send her a private message, since her old email account had been deactivated. All she could find, after a half hour of searching, was a phone number listed under Kate's mom's name, though that was in the online Whitepages, which wasn't exactly a verified source. No pictures. No "friends in common." It was the best she could do.

It would be crazy to call her, Bertie told herself. Not even her friend but her friend's mother. She'd known Kate's mom, of course: a precise, buoyant woman with high expectations who, in Bertie's experience, was rarely home. What if she asked, *Why don't you get in touch with Kate directly?* What if Bertie was forgetting some reason that Kate was mad, and had blocked Bertie everywhere? That was actually the simplest explanation. These days people disappeared all the time, on purpose. It should've been harder, with so many digital markers everywhere, so many internet spiders feeling their way across your name, out there in the ether. But if you could just get rid of those markers, you were as good as gone. A few weeks before, killing time at her desk, Bertie had read an article about a woman whose banking records and credit history had been spontaneously deleted by some computer burp, who took the opportunity to move her whole life to Cancún, where she lived by the graying ocean and learned to surf. The perfect modern crime: accepting your own death. Though, of course, that woman came back. Otherwise, there would have been no article.

With shivering fingers, Bertie dialed the phone number. *Hi,* she imagined saying, *I'm looking for Kate? You know, your daughter?* She listened to the rings on the other end of the line, and closed her eyes, bracing herself. It rang and rang into the existential blackness of the satellite signal. Not two months before, a telecom satellite had fallen into the sea and sunk a ship; what were the odds?

"Hello," said a firm robotic voice. "The number you are trying to reach, two-zero-six-five . . ." The voice listed out the whole thing and then said, ". . . is not available. Please leave a message after the beep."

Why didn't parents ever set up their voicemail boxes? Eyes still pinched shut, Bertie left a brief message, including her number, and then hung up. She threw the phone down onto the couch and looked out the window, at the now-dark sky. It was probably late enough for chamomile tea. What was she doing?

She started to shake, and pulled an afghan over herself. She couldn't escape the feeling that everything was disappearing, and fast. Her phone rang and she dove for it, but it was just Dylan. It was, thank God, Dylan. His voice, when she answered, flowed through her like wine.

"Hi," she breathed.

"Hey, Bert, I was just thinking of you. I feel like I haven't seen you in forever."

Bertie laughed, wiping away a few stupid tears that spilled from her eyes. "It was just this morning, dummy."

"I know, but I missed you. What are you up to?"

"Um." She sat up. "I guess, I went swimming, and now," she cast around for something that wouldn't sound pathetic. "I'm going to draw."

"Oh!" Dylan seemed genuinely pleased. "That's awesome. Maybe we should do a couple of solo nights a week so you can get stuff done."

"Maybe. Yeah." It actually sounded like a good idea, and Bertie was filled with a sense of purpose. She would draw the woman who had disappeared, first from her computer, then from her life. "I'm going to do it all analog. I get enough tablet sketching at work."

"Well, I won't keep you. I can't wait to see what you come up with. Maybe we can also watch the same movie from our separate apartments, if that won't be too distracting, and then you can tell me what was wrong with it next time we're together."

"Slow-fi art critique, I like it." Had she just called her old friend's mom on the phone? What had she been thinking? "Okay, well I'm gonna go, then. Text me the movie."

"Will do. And, Bert, sweet dreams."

"You, too, you sloppy romance hound."

"Hmm. Strident but fair. Good night!"

Bertie clicked End and walked to her kitchen table, which doubled as a desk. She pulled some papers from a nearby drawer, plus a bag of pencils, a good gum eraser, her favorite pens. She was whistling by the time she brought in her computer and pulled up two tabs: one of the woman's face from various angles, and one of a movie streaming service. The night was black now, but she didn't close the curtains. She felt like she was floating again, but this time it was all warm. She was floating in nothing.

By the time she went to bed, it was well past midnight, and her eyes were burning with sweet relief.

– 13 –

The next Saturday, Bertie and Dylan decided to get breakfast tacos from a stand ten minutes from his house, which used the parking lot of a large Catholic church as their base of operations. "Except obviously not on Sunday," Dylan pointed out. He'd heard about the tacos from his boss, who made him take a company car all the way across town for an assortment of barbacoa and cabeza while working from the city that Tuesday. "It was fine," Dylan said. "I picked up his laundry on the way, so it was kind of a twofer." Dylan's subservience to his boss fascinated Bertie, but she couldn't quite bring herself to ask what it was that made him so loyal and invested, why he believed that a man who had to be drunk to do his job had such vision for the future. At least today it got them tacos. The stand grilled their own chilis and spring onions, and as the smoke drifted around them, Bertie's eyes began to water. Her phone rang from inside her jacket pocket, where her hands were stuffed for warmth, and she silenced it without looking.

At each corner of the lot, two policemen loitered together and watched the relative nothing that was taking place, so keen and calm that Bertie wondered if they were even assigned to these posts, or if they just showed up. Homeless encampments were arranged all along the parking lot's perimeter as well, but they were peaceful, men smoking cigarettes, mothers brushing their children's hair, buttressed by their shopping carts and plastic milk crates. The church set up a food bank after the taco stand closed every evening, replacing one hungry line with another.

Hooking her chin on Dylan's shoulder, Bertie said, "I'm going to eat five mental wellness tacos." She looked at the policemen, their faces eyeless behind sunglasses and motorcycle helmets; they did, in fact, make her feel a bit insane.

Nearby, a man was shaving with a broken razor, peering into an old driver's-side mirror he'd propped up in a camping mug. Good and bad neighborhoods had always smeared together in the city, but now, with the influx of refugees from the Midwest and the Central Coast fires, the blur was total. You could spend five hundred dollars on a dinner and walk outside into a tent city, call a car to take you to a start-up office that stood between a men's shelter and a bail bondsman. Not that Bertie could afford a five-hundred-dollar dinner, but sometimes her teammates all went out on the company dime. "Maybe six tacos," she murmured. The night before, there had been a bomb scare—not, it turned out, a sign of renewed hostilities, just an old piece of unexploded ordnance in the Marina. But it had taken the news about an hour to catch up with the investigation, and in the meantime Bertie and Dylan had huddled on the couch, unsuccessfully trying to pretend that they weren't scared. They'd heard the explosion from his house when the bomb crew set it off.

"What if someone's trying to blow up the Bay Bridge?" Bertie had asked. "What if there's, like, a biotoxin? I bet someone in town is working on something gross like that."

"They'd go for the Golden Gate," Dylan had replied, unhelpfully. "Just imagine the photos." And Bertie did, the big red struts cracking into the water as brittle as bones, wires snapping free in the gray sky. People threw themselves off that bridge all the time, and it did make a kind of sense to picture it tumbling to its own watery grave, especially since the news would be able to counterpoint their footage with vintage tourist shots and calendar pages. *Today, we mourn one of the city's true characters* . . . In the end, not much damage was done, though the bomb squad hadn't anticipated the collapse of the warehouse where the device was stored when they decided to detonate. A crew member was injured, and the neighborhood was shaken. If it hadn't been the weekend anyway, offices downtown would've closed.

"I feel," said Dylan, lifting Bertie's sharp chin away from his shoulder in the parking lot, "that mental wellness may not, in this case, go hand in hand with gastrointestinal wellness."

"Fine. Three tacos. But that's my final offer."

"I'm not criticizing, I'm just making an observation."

"Says the man who farts up the sheets every night, no matter what he eats."

"Why, what an ugly word."

"Fart?"

"Sheets."

"They're both ugly words," said Bertie, though she didn't believe this. Sheets made her think of endless, pristine paper; of sleet and snow and the scent of freshness. But she liked agreeing to disagree.

Dylan rolled his eyes. "I'm kidding." Then he perked up. "Oh, listen, it must be ten." The church bells were ringing loud above them, though you could hear the clangor muting as it hit the morning fog. People crouched on the curb with paper plates on their knees, taking messy bites of their tacos, sipping iced coffee mixed with horchata. They, too, paused to listen to the bells, and then cast nervous glances at whatever nylon tent was closest by, as if the chime had rattled them into an undue fear of being mugged for their breakfast. The actual residents of the tents looked like they could not have cared less.

As it happened, Bertie knew that the taco truck donated some of their leftovers to the food bank every night, and a minor scandal had erupted recently when groups of tech workers in ratty sweatshirts had been found waiting to take part in the free food. When asked why they would steal from the poor, they said they didn't think about it that way. They saw it as a life hack.

"God, this is going to take forever," she said. "Didn't we get here at nine?"

"You wish. Nine-forty."

"That's still a pretty long line."

"So entertain me." The bells stopped, then seconds later started again from the beginning. Bertie tried to take a selfie of the two of them, but as usual, Dylan turned away, muttering *Paparazzi!* He was sensitive about how poorly he photographed.

"Did you ever go to church?" Bertie asked. "We haven't talked about that."

"I just assumed we were both heathens." Dylan ran a hand through his hair and eased the line. It hadn't moved. "No, no specific churching. I guess I sort of have my own system."

"Hmm. Sure." The cashier's phone made a *cha-ching!* sound and the line advanced by one. It was all twenty- or thirty-somethings, plus the occasional silver-foxy couple at forty-through-sixty, childless, with their hands in each other's pockets. The kind of people who heard about good taco trucks through a whisper network. Bertie said, "You know, that reminds me, I had this idea once. I was trying to figure out how to make it into a comic, but it was more of a situation than a story."

Dylan looked interested. Bertie almost never talked about her works in progress, because deep down she worried that articulating an idea would kill its ability to surprise her, turning it into a synopsis, some shriveled thing. *You make art projects sound like vampires,* Kate had told her once, derisively. *Can't let 'em see the sun.* But when could that have been? She shook the thought off.

"So this thing. I feel sort of silly saying it out loud, but it was about . . . souls, I guess?"

"Oh." Dylan's face paled a little. "Cool." Hadn't he wanted to be entertained?

"I mean, since we're talking about it, right?"

"Right."

"It was this theory. I thought I could draw it in kind of a spiral, but I never figured out if it would be better to follow just one person, or if I'd have to show a bunch of them at once—"

"Um."

"Right. Yes. I guess I had this idea after my parents died." Still pale, Dylan squeezed her arm, and Bertie felt a small internal glow. He must be as hungry as she was, she thought. Hunger often made him look bloodless. "Some doofus at work was talking about the multiverse. A sci-fi nerd, like you."

"Hmm. Thanks."

"Sure, babe." She winked at him, hoping to look like the kind of person who could get away with saying *babe,* and smacked him on the butt. She didn't think she was pulling it off, but oh well. "Anyway, so I got to thinking, in science fiction, people who live through different timelines are always basically different people. Like if you change the timeline, you kind of kill the person and start again."

"I know you don't like sci-fi," Dylan said, moving her forwards again in line. "We don't have to like all the same things."

But Bertie was warming to her subject.

"What if, though, there is a multiverse? On a Hadron Collider–type level, I mean, where we're always splitting off into these different possibilities, with every choice we make." What, after all, separated the people in line for tacos from the people on the fringes? Not that much. All Bertie had to do was squint to see herself there, flipping through old magazines. Crumpling newspaper circulars up for kindling or even insulation, stuffing them into her jacket on cold nights.

"How is that different?"

"Well, instead of each of those people being totally separate, I thought, what if they all originally come from the same place? So one version of someone breaks their leg at age five, but another version ends up dancing professional ballet. One version dies in a car accident when they're thirteen, but another one skips that road trip and has a massive heart attack at forty. And so on. They're all different people. Like, a banker—"

"A baker? A candlestick maker?"

"No one makes candlesticks. But okay, they work in a candlestick factory. And they get tetanus because the conditions are unsafe. But at the start, every single version is connected, as a sort of big chubby baby soul that splits in all the different directions."

"I—"

"What?"

"Nothing." Dylan looked away, into the crowd. "I want to hear the rest."

"Well, think about how little kids believe everything is magic. They see fairies and talk to ghosts, and remember past lives and shit."

"Is that true?"

Bertie opened her mouth to reply, then shut it. They'd never discussed whether they wanted kids, and she realized this line of conversation was tripping a bit too close for comfort. Dylan's face was less doubtful than uncomfortable, perturbed.

"I mean," she continued more carefully, "I'm given to understand that children are weird. And all I'm saying is, maybe that's because they're still much closer together. Some part of them remembers being connected to their whole self, because they haven't had time to grow apart. And old people—maybe they start seeing things and forgetting stuff not just because their bodies are breaking, but because enough of their other versions have died and been reunited, and they know they're getting close."

Neither of them spoke for a moment. There were only a couple of people ahead of them now, and the scent of grilled pineapple made Bertie's mouth water.

"Maybe," she said, "heaven isn't harps and clouds. It's all the parts of you coming together and filling in the gaps. So you can see all the lives you ever could've lived, as perfectly and completely as possible. No regrets."

"Or all regrets," Dylan pointed out.

"Yeah, well, I'm sure at least a few versions of you would turn out to be total bummers," Bertie agreed. "That just comes with the territory."

"Wait, my versions specifically?"

"If the shoe fits," Bertie said, and just then Dylan, moving forwards in line, stepped hard on one of Bertie's toes.

"Ow! God!"

"I'm so sorry!"

She bent down and held her hands around the foot, as if doing so would radiate health back into it. "Well, now I know what me and all the other versions of me will talk about in the afterlife." But soon they were at the front of the line, where the array of taco and salsa options was so dazzling that she forgot to be mad, especially since Dylan offered to pay, which was really the least he could do.

As they settled onto the pavement, Bertie's phone buzzed in her pocket again, and Dylan nudged her shoulder.

"You've been blowing up all morning."

"It's probably just robocalls. I've been getting a ton of them lately." She fished her phone out and held it up. "See? A two-oh-six number. No one ever calls me from Seattle except telemarketers who don't know better. Don't they realize that our generation doesn't switch phone numbers when we leave home anymore?"

"Apparently not."

"Ugh." She moved to stow her phone away, but it started to ring again, from the same number. "That's it. I'm telling them to put me on their no-call list."

Handing Dylan her plate of tacos in a precarious juggle,

Bertie raised her eyebrows at him to make sure he wasn't going to drop them, then wandered over to the steps of the church before hitting Accept.

"Hello," she said crisply. "Who am I speaking with?"

"This is Laura? Barrie?" Bertie's heart lurched. It was Kate's mom's name, but the voice was much too young. Mid-twenties, tops.

"Oh, hi, sorry. I left you a message?"

"Yeah, but I don't think I'm the person you're looking for." On the other end of the line, the girl laughed. "I definitely don't have a daughter. Like, God forbid."

"Oh," Bertie said again, stupidly. "I mean, obviously, yes. You don't sound like her. I was looking for— It's a long story."

"Your friend's mom?"

"So not that long of a story."

"Sorry to be disappointing. I just thought you should know, so you wouldn't think she was blowing you off." The girl paused, then went on, "This will sound weird, but there's another person with my same last name who goes to my church. James Barrie?" Bertie felt the conversation drifting out of her grasp, and she sat down carefully on the steps. "Huh."

"Kind of a long shot, but I could ask him if he knows the person you're looking for. See if he has her actual phone number."

"No, it's okay. I don't want to waste more of your time. Thank you, though."

"I'll just let you know if I find something, okay?"

"That's really nice of you."

For a few seconds after hanging up, Bertie stayed put as her phone cooled off in her hand. *We are definitely all getting brain cancer from these things,* she thought. *And probably finger cancer.* She was surprised the girl had bothered to return a call from a random wrong number; the odds couldn't have been good that she'd find a millennial who did more than just text. Bertie wasn't even sure she'd have done it, had the situation been reversed. *This is Laura,* the girl had said, and for a second it was like talking to a ghost. Kate's mom, rewound and erased, or just peeled in half, leaving two translucent layers.

"Who was it?" Dylan asked when she sat down beside him.

"No one," she said. He handed back her tacos, and she reminded herself that she was hungry. Starving, actually. *They're mental wellness tacos.*

The fog wasn't burning off with the morning, which meant it would be cold and wet all day. Zipping sounds cascaded from all around them as the homeless men and women came to the same conclusion and tucked themselves in for an early nap. *This is Laura,* she had said, and for a moment Bertie had hoped. But no, it wasn't. It was someone else completely.

—

As the days went by, Laura didn't call back, and Bertie mostly forgot about her. There was, after all, enough to worry about at work, and once or twice a week when she was home, she had her own projects to pursue. Time took on the blurry, sleepy quality that she associated with the middle of the school year, back when she was eleven or twelve: every day she got up. Every day, she knew where she was supposed to be, down more or less to the minute. She received assignments, she worked on assignments, she finished assignments, she was assessed. Getting ready in the morning took the same amount of time even when she tried to shake things up by skipping a shower or putting her hair in a lazy braid instead of blowing it dry; inevitably, the other parts of her routine swelled to fill the space, as they had when her mom carried her downstairs in fifth grade so she wouldn't be late to meet the bus, but then let her watch cartoons until the moment they headed out the door. Sometimes she found herself sipping tea in the kitchen, staring out the window at the sidewalk that led out of her complex and humming the same song she'd heard from the monks on the radio. A tonal mumbling, coming from some part of her that her conscious mind could not access.

Driving to work, or anywhere, really, had begun to seem like a choreographed madness the whole city indulged in together. Gas was ten dollars a gallon, and according to the talking heads on TV, it really should've been twice that price. City clerks and public defenders had started riding the bus alongside schoolteachers and baristas, but the tech contingent, including Bertie, still clung to their cars. They could afford to, just barely. Not really, in fact. In other cities, cars frequently sat idle for so long that they stopped running: there were think pieces about the phenomenon. They peeled in the sun and got covered in rust, and all the news outlets warned that California would soon be the same, even though the infrastructure for public transportation was so bad. After reading one such story, Bertie had gone into her apartment's creepy storage unit to dust off her bike, but it was covered in spiderwebs, and when she wheeled it into the courtyard, the chain snapped off as soon as she spun the pedals. She kicked the bike and it fell down, skittering across the pavement. Everything she tried to change just reminded her how difficult change really was.

—

"Here's the thing," Hiro said. He was pacing in front of a whiteboard in the morning meeting, a marker stuck in his left hand as an afterthought. "I know things are not ideal. The company knows it, too."

He'd called this meeting before anyone got into the office, sending out an email at six a.m. with no clear agenda, just a time and a place. Now the whole team was fidgeting in the conference room's uncomfortable chairs, afraid the marker in Hiro's hand was there to diagram the departments headed for layoffs. The company's stock was still up—rising, actually, two and a half points in the past week and then holding steady while the market roller coaster-ed around it. (*Rocket*, Bertie thought.) But the layoff rumors persisted. How could things continue as they were, after all, with no checks or balances on their spending? Yes, the cafés no longer used Kobe beef in their sliders, but they still made breakfast, lunch, and dinner for anyone who was around, and offered real coffee and six kinds of tea. They'd only been relegated to Nescafé crystals for a few months during the coffee crisis, while most of the country went without; the cost, Bertie had heard, was on par with acquiring a mid-level startup.

"In times like these, people want to feel useful," Hiro went on. "You want to know that your job has some kind of meaning, and you're not just another butt in a chair."

"Don't people always want that?" Ruby whispered, leaning up to Bertie and Danzy from the row behind.

Danzy smiled without taking her eyes off Hiro. "Ah, an innocent," she said.

Bertie nodded. "Sweet honey of youth."

"Guys," Ruby pouted. "Be nice."

"The point is," Hiro said, pointing to them with the pen, now in his dominant hand, "there's more to life than just administering flu vaccines and rebuilding roads. The world wasn't built on roads."

"It wasn't?" Danzy whispered.

"No," Hiro continued. "The world was built on vision. And that"—he turned around and scrawled V I S I O N on the whiteboard—"is exactly what we have to offer to our fellow man."

Ruby raised her hand. "So this isn't about layoffs?"

"What? No." Hiro shook his head severely. "I'm not saying there won't be cutbacks or sacrifices. But every person in this room is a vital part of this operation. Don't you know what we're giving people?"

". . . Vision?" Bertie suggested.

Hiro looked flustered.

"Yes, of course, that, but also." He turned and wrote C O N S I S T E N C Y below V I S I O N, and next to that, L E V I T Y. Around each word, he drew a circle, and then he connected them with lines, creating a word cloud of unclear application. "The world is changing around us, and people are scared. Folks are losing their homes, their electricity is rationed, their water is rationed. There's oil insecurity. These people need something in their world to be exactly the same as before, something they can rely on. And that's where we come in. Bertie, can you get up here for a second?"

Bertie balked, looking around briefly in case there were someone else he might be talking to, but seeing that she had no choice, she hopped up beside Hiro and took the marker he offered. They exchanged tense smiles.

"Now, Bertie. Can you quickly draw . . ." He leaned over and whispered in her ear. She nodded. When she was done, Hiro turned to the group and asked, "Can anyone tell me what this is?"

"It's the dinosaur," said Danzy. "Nice one, girl." Bertie had added a top hat.

"That's right. That's right." Hiro nodded vigorously, as if the question had been hard. "Anywhere you go in America, and if you'll excuse me, I think in the world, people recognize this image. They know what it stands for."

Dino ethics? Bertie thought. *A megacorporation that grew so fast it doesn't know its own strength, and now lumbers across the planet smacking into stuff with its tail?* She frowned, as Hiro looked around the room with eyebrows raised. *Carnivorousness?*

"We are the consistency. When you look for us, on your phone, your computer, your smartwatch, your glasses, whatever, we're there. And this little guy"—he pointed at the dinosaur, which was big—"is levity." Hiro didn't usually use words like *levity*; he was straightforward and clear, all-American. They'd seen his high school pictures once, as part of a team-building exercise, and he had a letterman jacket. But now his face strained under the weight of its own sincerity. "This is the gift we have to offer a world in turmoil. It's our vision."

Having taken the marker back from Bertie, he tapped the word V I S I O N, leaving a smattering of little ink dots.

"It's important to senior leadership that everyone knows we're part of a team here, and what we're doing is important. Do you think you guys can all get on board with that?"

A sick sense crept up Bertie's spine. Even she had to admit, the dinosaur made her feel safe and warm. She trusted it, felt more intimate with it, than almost anyone else in the room. But Hiro seemed to think that feeling amounted to a form of heroism. She could practically see him clinging to his car, to his nicely cut shirt, with every word. *We deserve it*, he was saying. *Let's all agree that we deserve it.*

"What is this?" Danzy muttered under her breath as Bertie returned to take her seat, but around them, people were nodding enthusiastically, and even Ruby, behind them, shouted back, "Yes!"

"All right," said Hiro. "That's great to hear. I'm so glad to be part of this with all of you. I'm so proud of what we're going to accomplish together." He told them there would be cake in all the micro kitchens following the afternoon's All Hands meeting, and with that dismissed them back to their desks to continue inspiring, consistently, all the people of the world.

—

"So are we part of a cult now?" Danzy asked once they were safely out of earshot. She'd grabbed Bertie and Ruby, smiling as they shuffled out of the glass-walled conference room and into the buzz of the hall, but now they were one floor down in the women's restroom, and it seemed safe to speak freely. Danzy had even checked under the stalls.

"Excuse me, when were we not part of a cult?" Bertie addressed her hair in the mirror and deemed it flawed but acceptable. After that meeting, she felt like she had less to prove. "You drink the Kool-Aid in your onboarding training, and it's all downhill from there." The company's ethos had always been grandiose: from the beginning, they'd claimed they were going to change the world. Never outlining how, or whether it would be for the better. Why did they need to make everyone think they were ethical, instead of just being rich?

Bertie imagined the company, personified, leaning down towards her and whispering, *I could've made it so much worse.* Immediately, her arms went wild with gooseflesh.

"I don't know," said Ruby. "I thought it was moving."

"What?" Danzy turned and took Ruby's chin in her forefinger and thumb, an intimacy that Bertie noted in silence. "You cannot be serious, you sweet angel. That was the biggest load of crap I have ever been personally subjected to."

"So why do you guys do the job, then, if not that?" Ruby asked.

"The money," said Bertie and Danzy in unison.

"Obviously," Bertie went on, a little embarrassed, "I also think it's kind of fun. Comparatively. It's a good job. But I don't have some superhero complex where I believe the outfits I plan for an extinct cartoon animal are going to change the course of geopolitics."

"It was a really good hat, though," Danzy said.

Bertie smiled with false modesty. "Yeah, I thought so."

"You caught the light on the silk, which isn't easy."

"Well, thank you. It's rare for an artist to be appreciated in her own time."

Bertie and Danzy, busy amusing themselves, didn't notice at first that Ruby wasn't laughing along, or that she'd flushed deeply as she fixed her lipstick in the mirror. She was young and full of promise, with impeccable cat-eye makeup and jeans that were always tight from the wash. Her nails that day were polished blue, with a small bedazzling at the center of each one, and she'd come very highly recommended from the staffing firm that technically employed her. When Danzy finally turned to her and saw that something was wrong, she asked, "Okay, then why do you do it?"

"What?" Ruby pursed her lips, tetchy.

"The job, girl. Why do you do the job?"

"I don't want to say. You'll just make fun of me."

"We won't!" Danzy put her arms around Ruby from behind, resting her face beside Ruby's face "This is a place of trust. A safe space."

Ruby still looked skeptical but apparently decided that she didn't care.

"If you must know, I actually give a shit. I think my efforts have some meaning. In the wider context."

"The wider context of what, though?" Bertie raised her hands in a surrender stance when she saw Ruby's brow furrow. "Not being an asshole, I swear. I just don't understand what you mean."

"Right, like," Danzy indicated all around herself, "is this what you imagined for yourself? All this and more?"

"Pretty much. Why not?"

"It's just—so impersonal."

"In what way?" Ruby arched her perfectly shaped eyebrow and folded her arms across her chest, dislodging Danzy from behind her. "You think things are only fulfilling if they're about you? Like, oooh, I went home and I drew a picture and *no one will ever look at it*. Why is that more meaningful than making images that the whole world sees?"

"I . . . just . . ."

"Of course you don't have a response." Using a fingernail, Ruby removed some tiny imperfection from the corner of her eye, and then stepped back, satisfied. She looked like a different species than Bertie belonged to, all of a sudden. One that had uniforms, each identical figure nodding to the next and the next. She believed her loyalty would be rewarded. Though Ruby, as a contractor, did not at that moment have health insurance. "You guys are too jaded to care about anything but yourselves."

With that, she stalked out of the bathroom, leaving Bertie and Danzy to stare at each other, using the mirror as a prism for their shock. Finally, Bertie turned and said, "I guess you two won't be doing it till dawn anymore, will you?"

Danzy flushed. "Shit, was it that obvious?"

"I mean, yes. Supremely. Why else would she be that pissed?"

"She's young. Everything means something to her." Danzy leaned against the wall and looked at Bertie. "Do you know what she told me yesterday? She said, 'I thought I'd be on a magazine cover by now.' And I asked, 'Okay, for what?' And she didn't have an answer. She just thought someone would recognize her for something, and it was this big disappointment that no one had."

They both started laughing.

"She's what, twenty-three?"

Danzy nodded, unable to speak through her giggles.

"Oh my God, a magazine cover. For being what, such a team player? The little hypocrite."

"I know."

"The *cover*."

They laughed and clutched at each other with the fervor of

two bodies drowning, scrambling to be saved. *Rats on a sinking ship*, Bertie thought, with some satisfaction. Danzy got ahold of herself first, and took Bertie's arm as they left the bathroom. "Hey," she said. "I'm sorry I've been such a dick to you lately about hanging out. I was worried people would figure out about me and Ruby, and we were trying to keep it quiet."

"Oh. That." Bertie had actually forgotten. The badness she'd felt before was still there, but it was different. "Don't worry about it."

"No, we should hang out. We should eat whiskey donuts."

"You know, I went there with Dylan last week, and it was not good."

"Yeah, how's it going with that guy?"

"Kind of amazing, actually."

They passed the micro kitchen, where Ruby was performatively eating a pear and chatting with a group of employees around her age, all of whom were beautifully dressed. The tableau was almost Elizabethan, Bertie thought. Courtiers, lesser noblemen, who'd never known life outside of the castle. They all, like Hiro, thought they deserved everything they had. *And don't they?* she asked herself. It wasn't like anyone else deserved it more.

"The thing about Dylan," she said to Danzy, trying to distract the mournful look off her face as Ruby was lost from view. "Is that it's like he's known me forever. Like, he knows everything about me without me even having to tell him."

"That honestly sounds restful."

"Yeah, it is," Bertie agreed. "Most of the time it totally is."

– 14 –

In her dreams, Bertie experienced outlandish science fiction, bombs that went off and left her immobilized, bombs that crumpled her body with agony if she moved a single muscle. Ray guns that turned people into wave forms and transmitted them through telephone lines. Bodies becoming sensuous sine curves, minds disassembled and reassembled at the whims of physics. Sometimes she saw her parents, and had tea in their living room, and her mom drank rooibos, which Bertie was fairly sure was not a tea her mom had known about in her real life.

Why did you leave me? she asked them, calmly. And they said, *We had to, it wasn't our choice*, which was both a totally practical and a completely unsatisfying answer.

She saw Kate running through hallways and ran after her, saying, *Wait, I have your homework for fifth period, you forgot it in my car!* Her heart pounding wildly, because if Kate went through the classroom door, Bertie would never be able to reach her, and the consequences would be dire. She stood outside the door and hit her head gently against it, suddenly naked, as the men's swimming team filed past her in their meet-day sweats and stared with pity over their shoulders.

In one dream, her phone kept ringing and ringing, and she wanted badly to pick it up, but couldn't find it. A weight in her pocket turned out to be a pack of cards, a buzzing in a table drawer was a cooking timer, an actual ringing phone was someone else's phone, which they snatched away with a look of deep suspicion.

It became hard, in waking life, to know which things were too strange to be real, and which were just strange enough. One of the interns brought a new toy into the office that he could connect to his phone and use, like a laser pointer, to beam audio files directly into people's ears. A sort of weaponized Bluetooth, as he explained it. He kept doing it to Bertie, starting with the audio so low she assumed someone nearby was listening to headphones, and then slowly increasing the volume until she clapped her hands over her ears and shouted, "Damn it, Robbie!" Which made everyone look at her like she was crazy, while Robbie the intern laughed at his desk.

At the end of the day, she felt it happening again, a quiet chanting, or maybe it was humming, coming from all around her. Or within. She got up and went to the kitchen for seltzer, and the sound followed her, so she marched back to her desk and looked around for Robbie so she could say, *Ha ha, you got me, now cut it out.* But when she asked, it turned out that Robbie had already gone home, and it wasn't until she sat back down that she realized the music had disappeared as quietly and mysteriously as it had come.

She flicked herself in the temple. *Wake up,* she thought. *Come on, wake up.* But the fluorescent lights buzzed above her, and the seltzer was one of the bad-good flavors that tasted like sugar-free candy, all of which was too specific for a dream. Or was it? She flicked herself again, feeling a sudden hope that it might work, that this was not the right world, or not quite right, and that if she just touched the correct part of her face, reality would snap back into place. *Wake up,* she told herself. *Wake up, now.* But her eyes hurt from staring at the computer, and if she didn't leave soon, traffic would get even worse. Her heart wrenched within her; what if this was her chance? To—what? Fix it? Fix what? Her life?

Bertie's phone rang from inside her bag and she jumped, and answered it, but it was just Dylan. These days, it was always Dylan, and she was always so glad to hear his voice that her eyes filled up with tears. He was the steadiness that kept her blood pumping. He was the smooth road and the power steering in the car. He was bus schedules, and movie times, and traffic lights, and all the things that kept the world working, and the fact that all of that existed in him and no one else was just scary enough to Bertie—a perpetual bachelorette, not even a bridesmaid, most of the time, since bridesmaids at least got laid at the wedding—that his presence in her life was never boring. It was just as steady as a hum.

—15—

Bertie hadn't been so furiously creative since she was in art school, or maybe even before that, in high school, when the need to let something flow from pen to paper had been an itch as constant as puberty. She supposed it might be the effect of being in love—if that was, in fact, what she was in. Certainly the feeling she had was overwhelming, as love was supposed to be. And transformative, too, the hearts and stars she'd doodled early on in her notebooks turning into a circulatory system bleeding down the page and a supernova burning its ounce of atmosphere. At home, she often sat at the kitchen table until her drawing hand cramped, making tiny hatch marks to depict the soft jumble of a forest floor, or inking black the night sky in a distant ocean scene, moonlight spilling into the water. She kept a sketchbook at Dylan's house, in among her underwear and exercise clothes, and she pulled it out now whenever he fell asleep before her—which he nearly always did, right at the crack of ten p.m.—instead of popping in some headphones and catching up on TV shows. Or whatever, instead of gazing at him. It was hard to gaze at him, actually; sometimes, when she tried, he shifted. Or so it seemed. His bones uncoupling gently in the night—she supposed he probably ground his teeth.

She'd meant what she said, when she'd told Danzy that he

understood her unusually well. And it was sweet: it was. She could show up and throw herself into his arms, and he would know right away whether to say, "Bad day?" or "Someone's in a good mood!" or "You're right, your new conditioner does smell like Bubble Yum." But she hadn't quite been able to articulate the other feeling, which was equally real: that he didn't anticipate her needs so much as create them, threading a needle and slipping it under her skin, pulling her around with the gentlest of tugs. One morning he bought her an apple turnover so good that it overwhelmed her; she had to sit down as she ate it, taking deep breaths with every bite. Which—it was a pastry, just a pastry. When she asked what had inspired the choice, he said he thought she liked them. And didn't she?

Sometimes she woke up and saw him beside her and couldn't understand why he was there. "Am I mad at you?" she asked him, voice coated in sleep. And he would shrug and turn back over and disappear beneath the covers.

—

"What do you say to your boss," Dylan asked, "if he wants you to tell him where you've been all day?" Outside the weather was miserable, and they were splayed out head to toe on his bed, each with their own laptop, flicking idly through the internet. Bertie had just told him how she and Danzy had started sneaking off after lunch so they could chat at their leisure, now that they were friends again. The office park was so big that as long as you weren't in an overbooked conference room, no one would ever realize you weren't where you were supposed to be. There were love seats and massage chairs placed in random hallways, and in one building there were two kayaks full of pillows, side by side, so you could prop yourself up as if in a hammock, computer or tablet perched on your knees.

"That we're doing a sprint. Honestly, though, he doesn't ask questions. We're at least as productive now as before."

After finishing the small business illustrations, they'd tackled a project on teen bullying (the dinosaur was against it) and then sat calmly together while Bertie drew the dinosaur as the Sphinx—unlikely; anatomically impractical—and Danzy did the Colossus of Rhodes, which just looked like a really big dinosaur straddling a river while people gazed up in wonder from their boats. "It looks like he's going to stomp the townspeople," Danzy complained, but Hiro had loved it, and the picture ended up on the company homepage within the week. Bertie thought this had less to do with the dinosaur and more to do with the river, which was sparkling and calm in Danzy's rendering, neither spilling its banks nor diminishing to a trickle in the California drought. People did want to be inspired, apparently; they wanted to be soothed. She couldn't really blame them. After the warehouse explosion near Dylan's apartment, stores had begun selling out of essentials again, the aisles empty of bottled water and paraffin refills for camping stoves.

"Hey." Dylan rolled over onto his back and looked at her from upside down. He seemed hesitant, and grabbed her ankle with both of his hands until she screeched and kicked him, the tickle running up her leg.

"What? You just want to torture me?"

"No." He kept looking at her, still from that unusual angle, which made it tricky to guess his mood. His face had Picasso-ed out, becoming shapes and colors, colors and shapes. It was getting dark out. "I was thinking. Do you ever consider going on some kind of vacation?"

"God, yes, can you imagine the peace and quiet?" She scooted out of reach and tucked her feet underneath her, sitting cross-legged with her back to the headboard. "No one asking me dumb questions or accosting my bodily autonomy."

"Obviously I mean with me."

"Really?"

"Or else this would be a cruel taunt."

Bertie stuck her leg back out, so he could hold her foot: a peace gesture. She was pleased with the idea, but something about it made her nervous, and she chastised herself as a commitment-phobe. He'd been her boyfriend for seven months. "What did you have in mind? We've done the local color, all the beaches and things."

"I was thinking something bigger."

"Go big or go home."

"In this case, literally."

"So, what then? Not New York." A travel advisory remained over the city like a specter, in place since the early explosions. Journalists occasionally ran photos of an empty Times Square, quiet East Village streets, a subway car with open seats at rush hour. The scenes always framed for maximum shell shock. She couldn't ever go to New York. "What else is there? The desert? A lake somewhere?"

"What about Los Angeles?" Dylan suggested. Bertie froze. *He can't make me,* she thought, and then, *What is wrong with you?* Meaning herself. Why was she being so neurotic? This was a cute boyfriend thing. A very, very cute boyfriend thing. Still, a warning hummed in her sternum. As if, in addition to being cute, Dylan was threatening to push a big, red button. At the end of the bed, he appeared totally calm, running his thumb against the soft space where her toes connected to the bed of her foot.

"I've heard it's not safe there."

"Pshh. People say that about the Bay Area, too. They say that about everywhere."

"We did have a bomb scare recently."

"And it was fine." Was it, though? "My point exactly. Don't you want to see . . ." He paused, watching her. "Palm trees?"

"Come here," Bertie said, a little desperately. She tugged his arm, then crawled towards him, straddling his lap. She was constantly surprised by the comfort there was to be found in his body, the way his belly smashed against her own, the way his shoulder seemed as soft as a pillow. How her fingers fit everywhere, her tongue.

Dylan made a happy grumble and turned away.

"You can't distract me this easily."

"Oh no?" She kissed him, smoothing down his hair with both hands, feeling the veins that popped up at his temples whenever he started to get excited. There was nothing wrong with Los Angeles, except she didn't want to go.

"Don't you have a friend there?" Dylan asked, when she let his mouth free.

What she had were a few threads, connected to nothing. A job offer. Kate. A disappearing act and a person swallowed whole, left blinking like an underwater beacon. Bertie buried her face in his neck and shook her head. Outside, the wind blew against the side of the building. A storm had kicked up, more dusty than wet.

"Not anymore, I don't think."

"Who was it, though?" Dylan pulled her upright and fixed her with an inquisitive stare. "Do you remember what I'm talking about?" He was being strange, but he was strange so often. His energy had become expectant, of late, in a way that sometimes made her nervous he was about to propose.

"My friend Kate."

"Hmm. Who?"

"I've told you about Kate." He frowned, but there was a déjà-vu-yness to the conversation that convinced her she was right. With a gasp, Bertie felt her mouth start to water, her tongue turn bitter, and Dylan studied her.

"What's wrong, Bert?" He leaned in and kissed her. "You know that you can tell me anything."

What indeed might be wrong? All the most recent pages of Bertie's sketchbook were filled with drawings of Kate, every way Bertie could remember her. Kate wearing a bikini and voguing on her front lawn, or driving to a coffee shop with her brow furrowed, missing every stoplight. Kate in sunglasses, Kate with an enormous hat. Feeding a carrot to a donkey behind a fence on a school field trip they'd taken together, visiting a local farm to learn about independent agriculture.

She had one time, months ago now, called Laura back to see if she'd tracked down any information on Kate's mother, but she'd stammered her way through the question, embarrassed to be asking at all. It was ridiculous. Of course Laura had nothing to add, though she seemed to feel bad saying so. After hanging up, Bertie was so upset that she put her phone in her mouth and bit it, then ran to the bathroom to rinse off her tongue with mouthwash, having heard that cell phones were especially filthy objects, worse than a doorknob or a toilet seat.

"What if we went to Paris?" Bertie asked.

"Whoa. That's a step up."

"I know." She hadn't intended to ask it until the question was out of her mouth, but all of a sudden it made sense. The French graphic novel she was reading, Dylan's old expertise from visiting Montreal with his monster of a boss, who kept a mistress there for two whole years and set up business travel just to see her. Bertie brushed the tears from her eyes and felt the rise of new excitement. France had recently reopened its borders, and the tourist trade was bustling—at least relatively so. Most people weren't traveling much, but those who were considered Paris to be one of the most viable options. An enormous waste of jet fuel, but what if you were dead soon? What if everyone was? That was the general stance of the advertisements, suggesting the blackest truths with a wink. She'd learned this advertising technique was called "loss aversion," and couldn't help feeling the name was apt.

"Is that really what you want?" Dylan frowned, the skin around his mouth still pink from where she'd kissed him too hard. He rubbed at it absently. "If you're scared to go to L.A., then it seems like France would be way worse."

"No. Not true! L.A. has all that unexplained water pollution."

"Unexplained." Dylan rolled his eyes.

"Well, they don't know exactly what it is. And it causes all that fog!"

"I guess."

"Paris is inland."

"So no sea monsters."

"And we could go to the Louvre."

"Aha." Dylan sat up and dangled his legs off the bed, massaging his knees so hard that Bertie was afraid he'd pop off the caps.

"What's that supposed to mean?"

"Nothing. It's just an expensive trip to go to one museum."

"There's also the Orangerie. The Musée d'Orsay. The Rodin Museum. And really good food."

"You know how I feel about traveling overseas," Dylan said. "There's so much to—"

"What, so much to do in our own backyards? Come on. Don't force me to mock you." A warm liquid began filling Bertie from bottom to top, slipping in through the cracks and gathering in her buried places.

"I thought you'd want to see your friend," he said softly.

"I do. But." Bertie didn't know what to say. How to explain the sudden magnetic draw towards Europe, pulling her up by the skull, by the rib cage. She had no proof that Kate was even in Los Angeles, not really. But she couldn't face the idea of showing up and finding out she wasn't there: it would be too close to learning that Kate wasn't anywhere at all. "Well, whatever. You were the one who brought up a vacation."

"Maybe we should," Dylan said. "If you want it that badly." He seemed unconvinced, hunched over his knees and staring at the floor. "Maybe it's what you need."

"Think about it, at least." She grabbed her computer, flipping it open and tabbing through a few discount flight search websites. She could hear her pulse in her ears, saying, *Paris, Paris, Paris.*

"I don't know if I'm ready." He watched her. "Are you?" He whispered, "There's still so much we could do here."

But Bertie wasn't listening to him anymore. She was thinking, *Paris, Paris, Paris.* She was imagining sitting by the Seine in the dark, drinking wine straight from the bottle. Opening an umbrella under low gray skies, and running over cobblestones. She thought, *Who knows who you'll meet, in Paris.* Anything was possible there, in a city so old, so full of ghosts, that the ground could shift beneath your feet without appearing to change at all.

—

That night, with Dylan asleep beside her, she drew a careful pen-and-ink sketch of two figures in the rain, outside the Louvre. She pulled up a few photos for reference, but found that once she got started, she didn't really need them, not only because the details seemed natural but because she was more interested in the figures themselves. Two dark shapes, and a long line of other bodies that ran from the glass pyramid in the center of the courtyard, back to the street and around a corner, while pigeons flickered through the air.

One of the figures wore a neat skirt, while the other had a handkerchief tied around her neck, and Bertie took special pleasure in rendering the tucks and folds of the fabric, getting the pattern to bend and disappear convincingly into the knot. They were so familiar to her. She made the skirted figure smile, a sarcastic expression that the figure wore sideways, as if more amused by herself than anything. The other figure, though, looked wary, peering at something over her shoulder, just out of sight. Bertie had the urge to reach into the picture and touch that girl's face, just enough to distract her attention and bring her peace of mind. But of course that was impossible.

Dylan rolled over in bed and put his arms around her, trying to tug her into some sort of sleep sex.

"Quit it," she said, and pushed him away. She shaded in the windows on the top floor of the museum, light catching the glass so you could see a person inside, peering out.

"Mmm." Dylan shaded his eyes from the bedside lamp. "Turn it off. Come on, it's late."

"You're already asleep. You won't even remember this tomorrow."

"Mean," he said. But his head dropped back on the pillow. "Tell me ssstory."

"Not right now."

"Pls." In sleep, he breathed out through every word, so they either stretched or abbreviated, like a thirteen-year-old texting.

"Uh, once upon a time there was a guy who wouldn't shut up, and his girlfriend cooked him and ate him, the end." She looked closer at her picture, unhappy with the line of people. She added a man and his daughter nearby, throwing crumbs to the birds.

"No, a Bertie story."

"For real?" she asked.

"Mmhmm."

"You know all my stories."

"The one that hasn't happened yet."

Bertie sighed. "Fine. Once upon a time there was a girl

named Bertie, who went to Paris, France." She thought if she annoyed him enough, he'd get bored and let her get back to work. But he stayed quiet, listening, and so she continued. "What do you think she did in Paris?"

"Got away." He pouted in his sleep.

"Sure, I guess she had a real nice getaway there. Forgot her troubles."

"Remembered them."

"Dylan." Bertie shook his shoulder and he snapped awake. "That's enough. You're starting to creep me out."

"WhatidIdo?" He rubbed his eyes, and gave her a smile.

"Nothing," Bertie said. She closed her sketchbook and set it down on the bedside table, shaking out her wrist to release the pins and needles. Repetitive distress. "Never mind."

She turned out the light and spooned him, wrapping her arms around his chest and pressing her face to his warm back. He snuggled into her, and held her hands with his own. Normally this was her favorite moment of the day, breathing deep his sleepy humidity. But tonight he smelled off, like bread left too long in the bag.

"You're not really going to eat me, are you?" he asked.

"No," she said. "You taste inconstant."

"What?" He sounded alert now, but Bertie found herself drifting away.

"Go to sleep," she said. "I'm tired. We can talk about it in the morning."

– 16 –

The next day her stomach hurt, so they didn't discuss anything much. Bertie rolled out of bed with a grimace and caught her shuttle without any coffee, taking a single seltzer can from Dylan's fridge and only letting him kiss her on the forehead, which in retrospect felt a like a father's kiss, or a priest's. Not really boyfriend material.

The next day she missed a call from an unknown number, and when she called it back, the number had been disconnected, which either meant it belonged to a telemarketer or a very clever bot, using her cell signal to ping off some satellite and listen to nearby conversations for reasons Bertie could all too easily imagine. One thing she'd learned from living so long in the Bay Area was that all technology was a lock waiting to be picked, and the more you trusted it, the worse the unpicking would be. Dylan's boss, for example, had purchased a company that used location services on people's phones to deduce their grocery shopping habits and send them tailored advertisements in the newspapers he distributed online. Already he'd been contacted by two different law enforcement agencies who wanted access to the information, supposedly to assist ongoing investigations.

"And is he going to give it to them?" Bertie asked. "I would think they'd need a warrant."

"Not really. The terms and conditions of the app say that the information can be resold at the company's discretion."

"And people actually know that?"

Dylan shrugged. "He's trying to help. And the cops are just doing their jobs."

"So that excuses, like, invasion of privacy?"

"It's where they go to shop for potatoes," Dylan said, and when Bertie didn't seem convinced, he went on: "Look, if he doesn't do it, someone else will." Which was his answer to everything. It wasn't that Bertie had such high moral standards—her company was building a rocket to help rich people escape the smoking hull of the earth. Or, as they would say, experimenting with technology to expand the reach of human adventure. But Dylan's crypto-libertarian tendencies made her uneasy, his conviction that the ability to do something was always a good enough reason to do it. Apparently his boss was obsessed with the mechanics of eternal life, and Dylan kept talking about how close they were getting.

The next day she went home after work instead of staying over at his place, hoping to plan out at least a couple of pages of a new graphic novel. She'd gotten the idea for it on the shuttle bus, where she excitedly began doing character studies. It would be a buddy comedy, with two women around her age who bought a house together to live out their final days on a dying planet: the End of the World House, she would call it. Located in a small town in—maybe eastern Washington? Not the scrubby sagebrush desert, but an apple town near Grand Coulee Dam—the house would be in hilarious disrepair, and inside, the women would discover clues to an old mystery, racing to solve it against the clock of their own apocalypse. The townspeople wouldn't like them, of course. They would try to farm based on tips from a blog. They would plant beans and corn in the wrong season, pick okra out of people's yards just because they liked the flowers.

She was excited to get to work in earnest, sitting down with a pot of coffee and a grid-lined notebook so she could sketch the panels out more easily. On the bus, she'd planned out her characters, one dark haired, one light, to look archetypical. A sort of Betty and Veronica vibe, a fifties flavor. But with everything ready in front of her, she stalled. First her pencils needed sharpening, then she remembered her brush pens were new and she hadn't tested them out to get a feel for the different nibs. The idea throbbed in her fingertips, racing through her mind and warming itself in the darkest corners, but the moment she put pen to paper, it just—stopped. To encourage herself, she ordered a pizza, but then couldn't focus until it arrived. After which, of course, she couldn't draw with greasy hands. A beer sounded good, to go with the pizza. A little bit of internet browsing, to let her mind reassert itself after the beer.

Soon she was looking, for the fourth or fifth time, at the one photo she had finally dug up of Kate, a high school snapshot she'd scanned into her computer years ago and posted online for a #flashbackfriday. In it, she and Kate were sitting on a blue leatherette couch in the art room, flipping through a book. They both looked very over it all, their legs crossed above the knee and their boots too heavy for their feet. Bertie had, by that point, moved past her flower-dress hippie phase and on to her flower-dress intellectual phase, meaning she'd cut her hair and added steel-toed footwear to her arsenal. Kate had an eyebrow raised, and was pointing to something, and whatever she was pointing about, it was clear that Bertie emphatically agreed.

Adult Bertie tried to remember the topic of their conversation, but she couldn't. It was too long ago, and too inconsequential. She drew an illustrated version of the photo, and then tried aging herself and Kate up, as though they'd posed for the same picture ten years later, adding crow's feet and fixing their hair. She could only guess what Kate looked like now, but what she drew felt right. Enough so that she drew her again and again, in the mountains, behind the wheel of a car on the freeway, in an uncomfortable airplane seat with the tray table pressed against her knees. At the sticky bar in a basement club, smiling at a man whose face was obscured. Now her work was picking up steam, and though she didn't intend for it to happen, slowly the pictures of Kate moved closer to the panels she'd imagined for her book, until they were one and the same. Kate standing in a kitchen with her hands on her hips, wearing boyfriend jeans rolled up past her ankles. Kate wearing a baseball cap over her hair and looking uncertainly at an apple on an apple tree. In the book, she thought, Kate would be better at cooking and sweeping, but terrible on the farm, especially with animals. Choosing this for her, pinning her in place, gave Bertie a sugary rush of power.

She drew Kate at a table in the dining room of the End of the World House, sipping coffee from a ceramic mug. Across from her sat the novel's other character, and it was almost without thinking that Bertie drew herself there, in that body, stirring cream into a cup of tea. The tea bag hung over the side, and Bertie was twirling the string around her spoon to hold it in place. Reaching out to pick a bit of lint off of Kate's sleeve. It was too much. She tore the page out and crumpled it up. Tossing the paper in the sink, she went and got the matches she kept in the bathroom—*Toilet matches*, she'd hissed at Dylan once when he had, aromatically, failed to use them—and lit the paper on fire, letting it burn to a fragile ball of ash, which she doused with a spray from the faucet.

Maybe she had intended it. Maybe she'd intended it all along. It felt like a form of theft, to take Kate's face and use it for her own purposes, especially given the fact that she couldn't exactly ask permission. But now that she'd begun, Bertie found she couldn't stop. There were a thousand images in her head to replace the one she'd burned. She would begin at the beginning. A dark road at night, and a pair of headlights burning through the gloom. A structure illuminated by the twin beams, along with a cat, asleep on the porch of what we now see is a house. At the end of the road, the end of the world, as far as the viewer is concerned.

The cat stretches, arches its back, and slips away into the night. The headlights turn off, and once again the land is in shadow. Two shapes, human and therefore irregular, move up the steps, and one of them digs through her pocket for the keys. A panel shows the other figure in silhouette: despite the lack of clear features, we sense that she's rolling her eyes. This has happened before. "Just a second," comes the first speech bubble. "I know I put them right here." "It's okay," says the second figure, no longer annoyed. "They left a spare under the turtle." The sun is coming up now, so what was black is misting into gray. An elegant hand lifts the shell off a stone tortoise and finds the house key nestled inside. She fits the key into the lock, and moves to flick on the lights. "Here goes nothing," she says.

They walk into the great room, and we finally see their faces. Bertie and Kate. Kate and Bertie. Together, they smile. The keyless one, Bertie, turns to Kate, and her expression says: *This is home*. "Okay," she says. "Let's go pick bedrooms." And without another word they sprint up the stairs, playing a game they've played a hundred times before. Racing each other to be first to nowhere, pushing shoulders into the wall and pulling on each other's arms to gain the advantage.

—

The next day Bertie was supposed to go to the city after work and see a movie with Dylan, since the art house theatre in the Castro was doing a Bergman retrospective and they were both embarrassed they'd never seen his films. *Films*, Dylan called them. Never movies. All morning Bertie chatted with Danzy, sketching Kate at different angles with a bandana tied over her hair and a paint roller in her hand. "Those are good," Danzy said. "What are they for?" And Bertie said, "Oh, nothing, just a personal thing." Finally, she made up her mind and hid in the bathroom with her phone, texting Dylan the sad thermometer-in-mouth emoji along with the message *Boo I'm sick. Better not infect you*. Then she held her breath.

Oh, he replied, and the typing bubbles murmured for what seemed like an extra-long time. *U can wear a plague mask?*

Lol, she texted, frowning on the toilet.

Thought u wanted to see the movie?

I do, but don't want you to get sick

Ok. Dylan usually texted without punctuation, so Bertie

knew that this was a disappointed *Ok*; she knew that she was meant to know. *Well there's another one on Saturday*

Date!! she said, hoping her relief played as excitement.

Have a surprise for u then

Ooh tell me

Better in person, he said with a winky emoji and then the one wearing a monocle. She sent back a heart and then stood and tucked her phone into her back pocket. It buzzed again, but she didn't look, so it wasn't until later that she saw he'd written *Feel better* along with a bunny emoji, the one that looked like a little white rabbit that's always late for important meetings, and always desperate for tea.

She spent the rest of the day buoyant, and when she went home, she blocked out three full pages, pausing only to search again for Kate online. And though as always her searches returned nothing, for once she wasn't so upset. Instead of dwelling, she put a pair of sunglasses on Kate's face, and sent her out to walk among their skinny apple trees. She left herself on the porch with a glass of iced tea, picking dirt out from underneath her nails. That Bertie watched as Kate strolled into the late-afternoon sun, crushing dry grass under her heels. With just a shout, she could get her attention; with just a joke, she could make her smile.

This is kidnapping, she chastised herself, but it had been a long time since Bertie was filled with such a sense of purpose. So what if this wasn't the real Kate? It was a real Kate. A person with her name and her face and her dislike of cars that tried to take over the driving process by shouting out directions and beeping until you buckled your seatbelt. Even if the real-real Kate wouldn't have painted her finger- and toenails before going out to sow seeds in the garden, this Kate did, and that was enough. This Kate had the real Kate's dark sense of humor, and her physical grace. Under Bertie's hand, she floated across the apple orchard, feet barely touching the ground.

Bertie imagined her knocking on the frame of the cartoon strip, asking to please be let out. *I'd love to,* Bertie replied. *But I don't know how.* Instead she drew Kate startling as a rabbit scooted past her leg, brushing her gently with its haunch as it launched itself into the field. As Kate caught her breath, another ran by, and then another, till she was knee-deep in rabbits, testing her weight against the apple tree branches, trying to avoid crushing any soft limbs. A frightened rabbit bit her leg and she screamed—in the next panel, the rabbit screamed, too, and the jagged speech bubble was shared between them, their fear intermingling, blood to blood. Bertie threw down her pencil.

There was a headiness to this. The power, after so much searching, to keep Kate in a single place. To define, even, what that place was, who was there with her, what would happen next. But that headiness was frightening, too. She felt a pulsing sense that Kate, wherever she was, was in danger. Maybe she herself was that danger, even. She was the one who was holding the pen.

Don't be silly, she thought. *It's just a picture.* In the next panel, as if to prove the point, she drew herself jumping up and looking out to Kate, asking, *What's wrong? Are you okay?* Kate stood, panting, in grass that had been beaten down by dozens upon dozens of small feet, a bead of blood trickling down her calf. They looked at each other. For some time, they said nothing. "Bunny—" Kate began.

Bertie's refrigerator clicked on and the kitchen was filled with its soft whirring, pleasantly tactile and distracting, enough to break her concentration. She looked at her phone and saw that Dylan had been trying to tempt her with texts about the surprise she was not yet allowed to know. A present, unopened; a detective; a dark and empty hole. She was a little impressed with herself that she'd worked straight through, hadn't even heard the buzz.

Her fingers hovered over the phone as she tried to decide what to say back.

– 17 –

"I thought this project was dead," Bertie moaned, as she and Danzy walked into a conference room that had been booked on their behalf sometime late the night before. The local business illustrations, yet again. "Or finished, anyway."

Danzy sat down heavily and sighed. "It was both. But someone on high"—here, she pointed upward, like an angel indicating heaven in Renaissance portraiture—"decided to resurrect it."

"Why does this always happen with the worst assignments? They come back and back and back."

"Nothing outlasts . . . small business marketing."

"I mean, if they wanted us to draw more options, they could've just said so. I don't see why we have to talk about it for half an hour."

Just then the videoconference clicked into focus, and Susan appeared, her bathrobe a maroon chenille, and her expression every bit as irritated as Bertie and Danzy's.

"I know," she said. "Don't tell me: this meeting could've been an email."

"Wait, so you didn't call it, either?" Bertie asked.

"It just showed up on my calendar this morning. It was actually the exact same event as our kickoff meeting, if you looked close. I thought maybe it was a glitch."

"But you came anyway?"

Susan rearranged her bathrobe dismissively. "I'm paid by the hour."

"Can I ask you something?" Bertie said.

"I guess."

"Is that, like, a fashion statement?"

"What?"

"The bathrobes."

"The what?"

"You know, you're always wearing these bathrobes. Why do you have so many?"

"I don't." Susan flushed. "I have this one. I only wear it when it's cold. Jeez, I didn't know you were paying such close attention."

Danzy touched Bertie's arm. "Bertie."

"No, I'm sorry, I just—" She brushed off Danzy's hand. "You have that one? But what about, like, all the other ones?"

"I don't have other ones. Why would I spend my money on that?"

"You—" Bertie looked at Danzy, her forehead creased, but Danzy seemed confused. "Really? I wasn't trying to be a jerk, I was just curious."

"Whatever." Susan raised her eyebrows, and the sound of her typing came through the speakers. Bertie imagined an email being sent to someone. A chat message full of OMG OMG. "Let's just get through this."

"I'm really not—" Bertie said, but Danzy shook her head.

"So," Danzy said. "Here's the list I've been working on. A baker—maybe cupcakes, or is that too played out? Either way.

Um, a garden store employee. A mechanic. A barista. And what do you think about an organic farmer? Sheep's cheese or something?"

"Sounds good to me," said Susan briskly. "Do you want me to get started on copy for those now, or wait till you've done some illustrations that I can riff from?"

Bertie sat and watched them tossing ideas back and forth, discussing the endless marketing job as if she weren't even there. Susan's dog, Herb, came and sat down next to her, panting into the camera. He seemed perfectly healthy. No more limp, no uncanny wisdom in his eyes. He stared straight at Bertie, his face pulled into a doggie smile. Bertie felt dizzy. Her mouth tasted like metal.

"Okay?" Danzy nudged her in the ribs. "You'll take the garden store and the coffee shop? Three of each."

"Sure," she said. Her voice echoed strangely in her ears.

How many times had Bertie drawn the dinosaur as a barista? Dozens. Hundreds. She would give him an apron with a chain store–adjacent logo, and show him rendering a stegosaurus in latte foam. She could have him pulling out a chair for a customer with his tiny arms, or sweating over the milk steamer, tongue stuck out between his sharp teeth. *Nothing I do*, she thought, *matters in the slightest*. Even if the versions she drew today were masterful, moving, the marketing equivalent of a Beethoven symphony, she would have to draw another one later, and then another and another. The world would keep spinning its exact same direction.

She got a text from Dylan.

SECRET TIME

I couldn't wait anymore

I got us tickets to Paris

Bertie stared at her phone as Danzy and Susan hashed out the due dates.

Wow, what?? she sent back.

Yeah!! And a day at the Louvre, just like u wanted

She asked, *Do you want me to pay you back*

And he said, *Of course, lol*

He went on, *Didn't want u to think I was too scared to do it*

She: *I didn't really think that*

He: *Good bc I'm not scared in the slightest, u should remember*

Bertie threw down her phone. "What is happening today?" she muttered.

Danzy glanced at her, then smiled and waved goodbye to Susan, who disappeared with a flash into the blackness of the screen.

"You, dude," Danzy said. "You're happening."

—

At lunch, Bertie eluded Danzy and sat by herself with a fresh notebook, drawing picture after picture of Kate. She was in a fever now, picking at a salad and soup and sketching the tired bags under Kate's eyes as she was awakened each morning in the End of the World House by a murder of crows. The crows perched in the trees outside her bedroom window, cawing, and when she tried to sleep on the dusty couch in the living room, they flew around and found her there. Bertie took a spoonful of soup, and Kate moved from room to room, rattling the doors in their frames, struggling either to get out or to keep someone from getting in.

Bertie tried to be pleased about Dylan and the tickets to Paris. But it was such a strange thing for him to do. Usually he didn't even make dinner reservations without double-confirming that she was free, and now he had booked an international flight, a museum, presumably a hotel. Bertie's mom once told her that her dad had proposed to her on their first date, and she'd been so creeped out that she wouldn't see him again for a year. *So what changed?* Bertie had asked, but her mom was always vague. *He apologized*, she said, and when Bertie replied that it didn't seem sufficient, she'd said, *Well, he seemed sincere.*

Kate, in her drawings, tucked herself into the corner of the sofa with a blanket wrapped around her shoulders, staring out the window at three crows hopping around on the hood of her car. Where was cartoon Bertie? real Bertie wondered. She ought to have been there with a shotgun, bracing Kate up with a mug of whiskey. But she couldn't put herself in the room. By now, even that other Bertie had begun to feel like an interloper: someone standing between her and Kate. They were together, being hounded. They were both confused about how they'd ended up in the places they were in.

She thought: *What are the good things about Dylan?* He always bought her tacos. He made decent breakfast, when they had the time. He thought Dunkin' Donuts coffee was worth drinking, which she didn't agree with but was nonetheless charmed by. Her phone buzzed, but it was just a news alert: there was a new crack in the Antarctic ice shelf, and someone at CNN had set up a countdown clock to help the general public appreciate how soon it was projected to break off the continent and raise sea levels by ten inches, at least. Maybe there would be a tidal wave: it was apparently possible. Bertie imagined a wall of water coming at downtown San Francisco, all the tourists huddled up in the SF logo sweatshirts they'd hastily purchased at nearby gift shops because they thought that coming to California meant that they could just pack shorts. She saw it all the time. Their eyes so miserable in the mist and gloom that the advancing of a giant wave would seem less frightening than inevitable, a hundred simultaneous memento mori social media posts going out about how the coldest winter they ever spent was this summer, right here, right now. Dylan would find that funny. He hated the way the tourists clogged up the roads around Fisherman's Wharf.

Over margaritas, once, she and Kate had agreed that in the case of an apocalypse-level event, if there was enough advance warning, they'd both dress up really goth, with thick black eyeliner, and stand together, faces powdered pale and turned towards the storm. But wait. When could that have been? They never drank margaritas in high school: margarita mix, maybe, but not actual good ones, since Bertie's household lacked a decent blender and Kate's mom wasn't quite cool enough with underage drinking to allow more than half a glass of white dinner wine.

Was it that time she visited, whenever that was? The day that Danzy met her? Bertie couldn't remember, but the vision she had of herself, licking salt off the rim of the glass, seemed too serene to belong to a person reconnecting with someone after the passage of many years. Wasn't there always a warming up period? Friendship was not like riding a bike. You could forget how to do it. You could spend too much time apart. That was why she didn't want Kate to move to L.A.

What? Bertie thought. Kate was already in L.A. Definitely. Probably. She rubbed her face until it went red, then put her lunch tray on the conveyor belt that brought all the dishes back to the kitchen, to a staff of washers and dryers she'd never seen, and who might, for all she knew, be robots. The ultimate contract employees. She went and told Danzy she didn't feel well and was going home early to take a nap. "Frankly, I think that's a good idea," Danzy said. "You're being extremely weird today, and Hiro's kind of on the warpath. If you've got some exotic flu, he won't be happy if you share."

"Jeez, I swear, I've seen Susan in like a million different bathrobes!"

"You really haven't. But anyway, who cares?"

Bertie grabbed her coat and laptop, not even bothering to shut it down in her hurry to go. Each door she passed through, beeping her name badge against the electronic locks, was like another step outside her body. The great *ka-thunk* of each door closing behind her like the *ka-thunk* of that body falling to the floor.

Outside, things were better but no less strange. Instead of going home, she stopped to look up when the next shuttle to the city left, and from where; by speed-walking, she was able to catch it, and settle into a window seat a few rows back. "Headed up to Frisco, huh?" asked the shuttle driver. He was an older man, the kind who liked to flirt with young women because he knew they wouldn't take him seriously, and also wouldn't have the confidence to tell him to stop. She was probably just at the edge of his age range. Bertie smiled and shrugged. "Yeah," he said, agreeing with himself. "We used to call it Frisco. Still can't get used to anything else. It just sounds right." The bus hissed as the suspension system kicked in, and pulled out onto the South Bay streets, and then the highway. Already, at two p.m., the traffic was at a standstill. "Used to work down by the Wharf," the driver continued, looking at Bertie in the rearview mirror. She glanced around at the other people on the shuttle, but they were all wearing headphones. Even the policeman, stationed at the front of the bus—this was a new thing, wasn't it? Why did it feel like the police were always getting closer?—was bobbing his head in time with some private rhythm. He had on sunglasses, too: no eyes.

"You got a fellow up there in the city?" the driver asked.

"I'm just going to get some work done while we drive," said Bertie. She opened her laptop, but since her own headphones were still on her desk in the office, left in the rush, it was the most she could do to dissuade further conversation.

"You know, it's funny," the driver chuckled to himself. "I keep getting older, but you all stay the same age." He flicked his eyes, Bertie was relieved to note, back to the road in front of him, the endless sea of taillights disappearing into the fog. "All you kids running around, ruling the world. You don't ever seem to learn."

"Learn what?" Bertie silently cursed herself for engaging, but she couldn't help it. "Please enlighten me."

"Oh, it's all just work, work, work with you kids. Not the way we did it in my time. We took some hours out of the day to live a little."

"People tell you a lot about their personal lives, do they?"

"Some do, some do." The man winked in the mirror. "But let me tell you, I can see a lot just by paying attention. And I know, if I could live my life again, I wouldn't do it the way you all do. Over and over, always the same. Not for all the money in the world."

"No one would live their life over again if they had the choice," Bertie said. Normally she would've just ignored him, but today his words drilled into her brain, with unearned significance. Maybe she was getting a migraine. "That sounds horrible."

"I don't know. Some would. You could make different decisions, if you wanted to."

"Well, I don't." Was that true? She couldn't really be sure, but she wasn't about to voice doubts to this man.

Through the windshield of a nearby car, Bertie saw a woman carrying on a conversation with no one, twisting and twisting her radio dial, while in front of her, another woman in a black sedan was painting her nails on the steering wheel. A man one lane over was singing, passionately. Each car its own universe, a microcosmic example of how to live through this moment, on this stretch of road. As much infinity as anyone really needed.

The shuttle driver said something then, so softly Bertie didn't catch it. Just the last few words, which sounded like: ". . . when she comes."

"Wait, who?" she asked.

"She's coming back around for sure, mm-hmm."

"Sir?" said Bertie.

"What's that?"

"You're just—uh. Never mind."

To her relief, he began whistling "She'll Be Coming 'Round the Mountain," occasionally muttering more of the lines, and at last turning his attention to the road. Bertie, shaken, leaned her cheek against the cold Plexiglas of the window. The weather was unusually bad, not just cloudy but full of thunderheads, white on top of gray, so it looked like bits had been erased from the sky. Bertie knew that, to paint it right, the white clouds wouldn't just be white, but white with blue and purple and yellow. But they looked blank. As if pieces were falling out of the universe in some predictable pattern.

When the bus stopped a few blocks from Dylan's apartment, Bertie hustled down with a terse "Thank you," making sure not to look either the driver or the cop in the face. She checked her phone: it was only four, which meant Dylan wouldn't reasonably be home for a few more hours, but she walked straight to his door anyhow, and buzzed. *Why don't I have a key yet?* She wondered. *I have a drawer, but no key. I'm going to have to pay to sit in some coffee shop.*

Instead, to her surprise, he buzzed her up and opened the door, saying, "Bert!" as if he had expected her. "You finally got here."

"Uh," she replied. What did he mean by that? "The traffic was bad."

"Ha. Yes. It's always bad, isn't it?"

"Pretty much."

He inspected her closely, seeming nervous. "Well," he said. "Good things come to those who wait, I guess." He held up her sketchbook, taken out of her drawer. "We can discuss this, now that you're here. That'll be fun."

As he dangled it in front of her, Bertie grabbed for the book, but Dylan evaded her, and flipped it open to the most recent pages. If he'd just asked, she would have gladly shown it to him, but now she did not want him looking inside. A shard of something cracked off within her, leaving an emptiness, like the space behind the clouds; a piece falling free.

"Is there something you want to tell me about this?" he asked her. "Like why you're drawing the same person a million times? No, actually, don't bother." He leaned in. "I knew you would feel it, eventually."

"I—" She fumbled with her words. "I'm doing a graphic novel. That's one of the characters."

"Oh, hmm, sure."

"No, really. She's based on my friend . . ." Within her, fingers grasped for a cliff's edge. She was falling over. It was already too late. *Too late,* she thought, again. But for what?

Dylan sighed. "I know who she is."

"You do?" Bertie saw a picnic table, a pile of meat. Images, here and gone. She worried she might be about to pass out.

"She's Kate. The Kate you don't want to see in Los Angeles. The Kate you haven't spoken to in years."

Haven't I? "Why were you digging around in my drawer?"

"That's a pretty good dodge, but it won't work."

"I'm not cheating on you, if that's what you think."

"But you sort of are? You weren't sick last night."

"That's not what cheating is."

"You're lying, though. You're lying to me. Your mind is full of secrets." He tapped her on the forehead, and she flinched. Then he massaged the tense line of his jaw.

Bertie grabbed the notebook from him and sat down on the couch, clutching the book to her chest. All day things had been going wrong, she'd been going wrong, and now Dylan's skin was covered in a film of sweat. He looked seasick, taking on a green tint. He tried to smile, but it came out strained. A serial killer face, she thought, like Ted Bundy might wear when he wanted to imitate human emotion. But of course that wasn't fair. She was the one who had lied.

Why did she come here? She couldn't remember.

"Are we going to Paris?" she asked.

"Of course we are," Dylan confirmed. "The great getaway. We're going to lock ourselves to bridges out of romance."

"That's—not what people do."

"That's not what a love lock is? Two people, tethered together forever, the old ball and chain?"

"What's happening?" Bertie whispered. She opened the sketchbook and flipped through a few pages so quickly, it looked like Kate was shaking her head in warning. To the left, to the right, eyes wide. Like someone running away from a monster in a story. *He's right behind you*. But he was, in fact, in front of her.

"I'm sorry," Dylan said. "It's really too soon, but things are starting to fall apart. You do feel it, don't you?" He looked concerned. "It's always like this before it resets, if you pay attention. Different versions crashing together. It's dangerous for us to stay any longer."

He went on, "And for what, really? The whole point of our time here was to be together. Not for you to go gallivanting off with Kate, or inventing a new Kate, or whatever you're doing." Then he paused, and took a deep breath, visibly pulling himself together.

"What are *you* doing?" Bertie asked. She snapped her fingers in his face, and it felt familiar. Everything felt like it had happened before, in a slightly different way. "What is this?" *Snap, snap, snap.*

"You came to my apartment," Dylan said matter-of-fact. "You're my girlfriend. We've been dating for almost a year. But not," and now he looked at her with great meaning, "quite a year."

He began to pace back and forth in front of the couch. "The deal was a year. If you could last for a year, I'd give you what you wanted."

Bertie breathed. "Javier."

She wasn't sure what it meant. None of her coworkers were named Javier, she didn't think. Though there were a lot of them. Maybe he was one of the new hires, the ones who cycled from team to team for three months apiece, leaving chaos in their wake. Maybe he was a friend of Dylan's, someone she met once and then forgot. But that wasn't what it felt like. Javier, whoever he was, belonged to her. His yellow teeth. His skeleton smile.

"That's right," said Dylan. "Here it comes."

"We didn't have a dating contract," Bertie hissed. She didn't want to think about this Javier person, wherever he might be. She wanted to stay here, in this room, with the earth steady beneath her feet. "I don't remember signing on a dotted line."

"You know, I can see now that I've let this go on for too long. That party was how many months ago? Seven? Eight?"

"This is my life. You can't just come in and mess with my life." How would he, though? Bertie licked her lips. They were so dry.

"Why, Bertie," Dylan said. "Whatever do you mean?"

"I mean—all of a sudden, you're crazy? That's not fair."

"Oh, please. You've been making excuses for me for weeks now."

Bertie sat back. It was true. Excuses for him, or for herself. She had bunkered up, and it had felt good. Her body vibrating like a string.

"You've been trying to reach her," he went on. "Some part of you remembered that you were looking for her, and it kept right on looking, the best way it knew how. And the more you found, the further you got from me. You've been sleeping in my bed, but your mind is a thousand miles away. Five thousand, actually." He looked miffed. "Dylan," he mimicked. "Let's go to France. Not for any particular reason."

Bertie cringed, though she wasn't sure why. "Don't be mean." His tone was harsh, but something about what he was saying rang true.

"I'm not being mean. If anyone is, you are. I gave you everything you could want: your life, a chance to make your art. A world where both of those things were possible. I loved you."

"You love me?" It hurt. She wanted it. But it hurt.

"Have I not said that this time?" He rolled his eyes. "Yes. Sure. And you love me, too, I think. We work together." Kneeling beside her, he took her hand, but the gesture curdled. "Maybe that part will stay with you, when we go back. That's what I hope, anyway."

"What are you talking about?" she asked. And he smiled. Angry. Hurt. Threatened. Sad. An animal about to bite.

He snapped his fingers.

"This," he said.

– 18 –

The doorway was right in front of her in the museum hallway. Dylan was by her side, one hand on the knob.

"Are you ready?" he asked. She was dizzy. It was strange. But she nodded. "All right," he said.

The door swung open.

—19—

Without a second thought, Bertie ran past him into the room, which was, to her surprise, quite small. An office, practically a closet. Javier had stuffed himself into the corner beside a filing cabinet and turned his face away from her. His eyes were clamped shut, as if he believed that it made him invisible.

"You're still here!" Bertie shrieked at him. She grabbed his shoulders and shook him, screaming so loudly she spat in his face. "You did this. This is your fault! Give her back!"

Javier cowered further, retreating every inch he could, or every centimeter, Bertie supposed; this was France, after all.

"You brought us to Paris?" she said. "You took us hostage? For what? Why are you doing this? Where is she?"

Mushing his mouth together, Javier sputtered something in soft, impenetrable French.

"Speak English," Bertie reprimanded. "I know you can."

"'Our Father, who art in heaven, h-hallowed be Thy name—'"

"No! Stop!" She couldn't believe his nerve. Shaking him again, Bertie pulled Javier closer to her face. "That's not for you. Nice people only, for Jesus. That's got to be the rule."

"Well," said Dylan, approaching from behind. "Hardly."

She ignored him, focusing on Javier, who had finally opened

his eyes and was looking back and forth between them in a panic. "Why are you doing this?" Bertie asked again.

"I thought she was pretty," Javier said, his voice soft.

"That's not a reason."

"I wanted to show her the museum, give her a present. A private Louvre. The jewel of culture. The jewel." He paused. "I was the head of security. Bringing in women was the biggest advantage."

"So you trapped us here?"

"We're all trapped here." Javier turned and grabbed Bertie's shoulders in return, so they were holding each other, on the edge of an embrace. "There's no way out. Even when I manage to leave, they bring me back again."

"Who is *they*?"

"I don't know. Je ne sais rien." He looked at her meaningfully. "*Rien.*"

"Wait." Bertie released his shoulders, and stepped back, towards the door that led to the hallway. He knew nothing? Surely he knew that she had been in his way, standing between him and pretty Kate. That was a motive. Right? The office was small, the ceiling low. It felt like something that had been added into the walls centuries after the palace was built. For unimportant people, a place to keep them out of view. "If you didn't do it, who did?"

Her stomach dropped as her adrenaline plummeted, and things started coming back. She had just been in Dylan's living room. She took the shuttle home from work, and was supposed to draw the dinosaur tending seedlings in a garden, or maybe walking through a greenhouse full of tropical leaves, as though he were back where he belonged, in his own era. Dylan had been waiting. A *loop*, she told herself. *It was a loop.* She took another step away.

"Don't leave," whined Javier. "I don't want to be alone here. With just *myself*."

"Then why did you hide?"

"I was scared." He cringed. "Nothing here is like how I thought it would be. How it's supposed to be." Which seemed like an understatement. *You were wrong*, Bertie told herself. *Sleight of hand. Misdirection. Eyes on the wrong prize.* But her body rejected this assessment. She'd hated Javier for so long—lifetimes, it seemed—she couldn't just stop.

"How long have you been watching us? Kate and me?" she asked him. "Did you somehow follow us from home? Have you been in California?"

"Why would I go there?"

"I don't know, you tell me."

"Bertie." Dylan put a hand on the small of her back, and she shrugged away. He sighed. "Bert, you have to see he doesn't know anything. This is a dead end. He must've gotten stuck when you did. Collateral damage."

She spun on her heel to face Dylan. "Then what was it all for?"

"What all?"

"The year. That whole year of my life that I traded away."

"You asked," he said. "You wanted me to get you through the door. I made a deal I felt was fair."

"But you knew. That he was just some guy."

Dylan shook his head. "I don't really understand why things

happen in this place the way that they do. It seemed possible to me that he knew something. And like a win-win. Figure it out. Get a year with you."

Bertie leaned against the wall, catching her balance as her head went all swimmy. "Oh my God. We were in love. You made me be in love with you. None of it happened." His apartment and its smell of moldering plants. Her hand on his arm at the party, so warm. Plus everything else. Danzy putting on lipstick, and kissing at her reflection in the mirror. A hundred yogurts in the micro kitchen. Sunset outside her apartment, with a cat yowling under a bush. Her graphic novel, the one good thing she'd made in years.

"It was all real."

"That's even worse." She pushed the heels of her hands into her eyes, hoping that when she opened them again, it would all become clearer, but it did not. She was still standing on the edge of a hallway in the hollowed-out Louvre, and Kate was nowhere.

"Take me to her," Bertie said. "Do that. Whatever the deal needs to be, bring me to Kate."

"I can't." Dylan frowned. "How many times do I have to tell you? I honestly don't know where she went. It's . . ." He ran a hand through his hair. "When I stepped into your loop, she was *gone*. I don't know where she went. It was like she got swallowed. Fell into a hole. I didn't want that to happen to you."

"You said you were trying to pull us apart. That somebody wanted you to." Bertie had assumed that someone was Javier. It made sense: Dylan's declaration that the loops were not exactly for her benefit, followed by Javier's sudden appearance. She clasped her hands together, holding them so tightly that it hurt. "Whoever it was, they asked for that. So I'm un-asking."

"If I could take it back, I would," he said. "But it's too late. Something got messed up in this place, and I have no idea what it is. Anyway, I can't pull someone into a loop who isn't even here. Who might be . . ."

Dead? Bertie thought. *Like my parents?* The one thing he might have changed in her life that she would actually be grateful for.

"She's alive," Bertie insisted. "She has to be. I can still feel her. She—" Bertie closed her mouth.

Javier started crying, still tucked into the corner of his office. At the bar, so long ago, he'd been the picture of confidence, striding across the room with his imperfect face, his wallet full of cash. He had the look of a man with good black-market access, used to getting things his own way. Now he was this. A child. A nothing. How dare he be scared.

"This is all your fault," she told him. "I don't care if you didn't mean it, we wouldn't be here if not for you."

"Poor Katherine," Javier said. "Poor beautiful Katherine. I can't find her."

"You," Bertie spat. "*You.*" She ran over and started pounding him with her fists, on the shoulders, the chest. The fact that he was just some idiot somehow made her madder than ever. "You all just do what you want." He rolled up into a ball and took it, lying on the floor. "I want to live forever! I want to get laid!" She kicked him in the ribs, and in his spine till Dylan came and picked her up from behind, pulling her away as she kicked the air. She shivered in his arms, wanting to hit him instead, but knowing it would do no good.

"All right," Dylan said. "Come on, Bert. Hush now."

He set her down, and out of habit, she spun around to press her face into his chest, then changed her mind and pushed him away, pacing down the hall and back. Outside Javier's office, the ceilings were high and arching, the space an empty echo chamber, amplifying Bertie's footsteps. She had too many people inside her. The Bertie who'd arrived in Paris, the one who'd been alone when Kate disappeared, the one who'd bought Mexican Coke from the corner store with Dylan. All of them stomping up and down the hallway.

"Do you take pleasure in this?" she asked Dylan. "Watching us suffer?"

"Hey now," he said. Stress was starting to show in the corners of his mouth, pinching and puckering. "I'm trying to help." Which he clearly thought was true. Bertie clutched her head and moaned.

Her stomach clenched in the way it always did when she got up too early, four or five a.m. for a flight, too early for breakfast, or even tea. Every few seconds something came back to her: she and Kate in a golden hall. She and Dylan, on a cold beach, while the sun went down. All the police who were roaming the city, and riding the Caltrain down to the suburbs, walking down Castro Street in Mountain View as if their riot gear might go unremarked.

"I have to get out of here," she said. "I need air."

"All right." Dylan straightened up. "Where do you want to go?"

"I don't know. I don't know."

If she ran, he'd chase her. So she wouldn't run. Keeping her steps as steady as a bride, she walked down the hall to a corner, and turned it. Around her, portraits of knights, pictures of fruit, ships fighting through the waves and crashing on distant shores. Dylan followed behind her, and she let him. Not sure that he was even what she wanted to get away from.

"Bert," he said. His body was hesitant as he stopped beside her, his posture an apology, the edges of him soft, like a text with no punctuation.

"What?"

"This is too much, isn't it?" She snorted, but he ignored it. "It's a lot for me, too," he said. "Jumping back into the middle of things, like this. It makes me feel sick to my stomach, actually. Like I can't tell if I'm hungry or ill."

He was always hungry, wherever they went. He snuck candy bars into the movies, and also bought popcorn. He put emergency snacks in her purse. She wanted to tell him this, to laugh at him, but her heart was clamped shut so painfully. A wince inside. Where was Kate? Nowhere. Everywhere. Bertie was so tired.

"I had a thought," he told her. "You can say no."

"I should hope so," she muttered, hugging herself close. All her life she'd tried not to be bitter, brittle. But circumstances had conspired.

"What if." Dylan paused. "What if we started over one more time, together, before we decided what to do next? To give ourselves a calmer frame of mind."

Was he kidding? He didn't seem to be.

"And then what?" Bertie asked. Though it was not completely unappealing. A bed. Soft Parisian sheets. Waking up for coffee and croissants.

Dylan shrugged.

"We'll figure it out, I guess."

Bertie rested her fingertips on her temples, and closed her eyes. It was a posture she'd seen witches make in cartoons, and exhausted housewives on sitcoms. Women with headaches.

"And if I wanted to leave after?" she asked. "Go home? Just by myself?"

He looked uneasy. "You can't get back to where you started from, I don't think. Too much has shifted."

"But to go back to my life? No more starting over?"

"I don't know." Dylan bit his thumb. "I wish you wouldn't, though. I don't want you to get lost, too."

And of course. Dylan didn't know if she could leave him, because he didn't want her to. He was perfectly happy to be trapped together in the loops. "We could get things just right," he went on. "Don't you see? Live in the perfect moment, forever. Our *favorite* moment." Which was, at least, a sentiment she understood. How many times had she tried to re-create a perfect day? Countless times. Getting the same coffee, wearing the same sweater, hoarding totems and tokens against disaster.

They would wake up, and the walls would be purple, the light muted through the curtains. Out in the hall, the smell of fries left over and congealing on plates, the quiet shuffle of housekeeping moving from room to room, touching the *Do Not Disturb* signs, *Prière de ne Pas Déranger.* They'd be in the same bed. Dylan might roll over and kiss her shoulder, as he did sometimes, when he had permission to wake her up. She often slept later than he did, especially on weekends, and that would carry over to vacation. Out of bed, she might take a shower, she might pad around in her bathrobe, look out the window at the street. Maybe it would be raining. Maybe a bomb would go off. Maybe they'd order room service, and get mediocre eggs.

They would drink coffee. Schoolchildren would parade down the sidewalk and laugh at their own secret jokes. She and Dylan would decide to walk to the museum, because what better thing was there to do in Paris, in this lifetime, on this particular day? It would be like getting drunk: letting yourself, just briefly, forget.

Okay, she was about to say, *Okay, why not,* just this one more time. She did want to forget, after all. If she was honest with herself, she'd wanted it for a long time. To let the knowledge of the world leak out of her ears in a mercury puddle, and drip down a drain into nothingness. Release herself from knowing. Release herself from being who she'd been. But when she looked up at the wall behind Dylan, she found that the person she'd been was not done with her.

"Oh—" she said. "Oh."

Because there were her comics. They were framed and hanging, real and here. Every page she'd drawn of Kate: the dark, the car, the house, the cat, the rabbits in the apple orchard, the couch, the crows, each stroke of the pen. As if they'd been pulled here by the magnet of her desire.

"What's this?" she asked. Reaching up, she took the first page off the wall.

"Hey," he said. "Can you do that? To the art?"

"It's not the art," she said. "It's mine."

As she ran her fingertips over the ridges of the frame, which was heavy and golden, not quite the right style, Bertie felt as if a glass of water had spilled over her head, over her mouth, down the back of her shirt, getting stuck in her bra. Cool water pooling up in every crevasse of her body, slowing her down to this moment, this place.

Dylan, sensing a change, stepped closer to her. "Come on," he said. "Let's get out of here. You were going to say yes."

But Bertie just stared at the page in her hand, so nicely mounted, lovingly preserved. It was like having a part of your dream walk out into the waking world—a nice part, for once. With some reluctance, she put it down, leaning the frame against the wall, and stepped back so she could see all the pages at once: everywhere, Kate pointed, Kate turned, Kate indicated from within the story that she was ready to be free.

"I really don't think you should touch it," Dylan said, nervously.

She turned to look at him.

"Why not?"

"Well." He frowned. Always such a stickler for the rules. Do what your boss says. Don't touch the pictures. "In a museum. Do you usually touch the art?"

And of course she did not. But what of this was usual?

One picture in particular caught her attention, in which Kate finally snapped and threw a clock through the window at the offending crows. The glass shattered all around her, up and out and into her hair, and Bertie thought, *Ah*. In the story, this moment was supposed to be a hinge, the event that helped her characters decide they would need the townspeople after all, and that they were perhaps not completely sufficient unto themselves. Here, it meant something different. She wasn't supposed to touch the art. It was separate from her. It came from a different place. A different time.

Bertie walked over to a window across the hall, where there was a Grecian sculpture of Artemis, goddess of the hunt. Posed with a cavorting doe: hunter and hunted together, at peace. As if that were possible. Bertie and Kate had been nervous when the security guard—so efficient, she was practically motorized—disappeared after locking them into the museum, and they'd come up with a contingency plan to smash their way back out if they had to. She hadn't thought it would work with Dylan here, but maybe she'd been giving him too much credit.

Looking back at the pages, her pages, on the wall, Bertie's heart filled up with pride. She might never see them again, she thought. She took it in, and took a breath. Then she shoved the statue as hard as she could. "No!" Dylan cried. It went through the window with a loud crack, and shattered on the cobblestones below. A group of women looked up from the street and saw her, and to Bertie's surprise, they smiled.

"What have you done, Bertie?" Dylan's voice was agonized. "Why would you do that? You wrecked it."

"I'm sorry," she said. And for a moment, she really was.

Behind her, Bertie heard a soft *ding* and turned to find an elevator that hadn't been there a second before. At least, she didn't think so. Cold light spilled through the crack between the doors. The floor hummed, as if in thrall to some great machinery, and Bertie's hands shook. She could feel it: the way the world was always about to turn, one way or the other.

Then the doors opened. And there was Kate.

– 20 –

"Bertie?" Kate asked, her eyes widening. Then her face broke into a grin and she threw open her arms. "You're here! You came!"

She was dressed as if she were on the way to work for a morning full of high-level meetings. A pair of copper red high-waisted pants and a ribbed black sweater, black boots—all poached, it seemed, from the couture stores inside the museum, just near the exit. Bertie wobbled slightly at the sight of her, standing there in an empty elevator with the spiritual air of someone about to take their first sip of morning coffee. But then Kate gestured towards herself. "Come on," she said.

And what else could she do? Bertie jumped onto the elevator and let the doors close them in. Dylan saying, "Wait, Bert—" behind her, his voice disappearing as they slid away.

Kate looked thoughtfully after him as he vanished.

"Do I know that guy?" she asked. But then she shook her head in a *who cares* way and pulled Bertie into an embrace. "I missed you, I missed you," she said into Bertie's neck, and Bertie was struck dumb with it. The emotion, the avalanche of words that would've rushed out of her if she'd so much as opened her mouth. So she didn't. Instead she hugged Kate back, as the elevator hummed around them. She breathed the scent of her friend, which was the scent of fresh bread baked in winter, and of mints pulled out of a very clean handbag, and cold lake water wrung from a swimsuit. Filaments of every possible pleasure. Kate took a step back then, holding on to Bertie's hand. "I thought you were still mad at me," she said.

Which finally broke the spell. "What?" Bertie asked. "Why would I be?"

"You don't . . . ? Um." Kate squeezed the hand she was holding. "Bunny, I'm so happy to see you."

Which wasn't an answer. Bertie was about to press her on this—her mind was indeed in the process of formulating that more insistent *Why*—even, perhaps, a *Why the fuck*—when the elevator shuddered to a stop on a new floor, and the doors opened to reveal a woman, waiting, with her hands folded behind her back. She was wearing her hair down, and a bit of it had gotten in her mouth, and she was, with a grimace, wiping this strand away when Bertie saw that the woman was also, unaccountably, Kate.

"Wait," Bertie said.

"Oh," said the Kate in the elevator. "Wrong floor." She hastened to press the Close Doors button, and it responded swiftly, but not before Bertie saw the face in front of them opening in surprise. A few seconds later they reached another, empty, floor, and elevator-Kate pulled Bertie out onto it. "There's a nice place to sit over here," she said, walking towards a nearby door and beckoning that Bertie should follow.

But Bertie found she couldn't move her legs. Was this shock? *Kate.* Her joints went soft. *It's Kate.* Then: *They are?* She swayed in place. Kate cocked her head in concern, as Bertie, dizzy, leaned against the wall. "I'm just," she said, and drew a deep breath. The light seemed to be dimming around her by degrees (*There is another Kate?* she wondered. *What? How?*), and she slid down into a sitting position, putting her head between her knees the way she'd learned in soccer practice, a remedy for the girls who started to pass out if they exerted themselves too soon after eating. Which they all had done, none of them good yet at regulating their behavior.

Now, Bertie felt herself about to throw up, and put a hand over her mouth. Thankfully it didn't quite come. The sickness simply burned in her throat, and she hunched her shoulders tight, all the way up to her chin. The present Kate slid down to sit beside her. She placed a hand on the back of Bertie's neck.

"Bunny. It's okay. You're okay. Shh." She held the back of her other hand to Bertie's forehead, as if it were a cool washcloth.

"What's happening?" Bertie asked. "Who was that?" She knew she should be overjoyed to see her friend in any form after such a long time, but instead she felt like she was getting a fever. The hot and cold blood. The clammy palms. Her skin prickling under Kate's casual touch. She, Bertie, had been more of a surprise to Kate than Kate's exact double, on another floor of the museum. And even she had not been much of one.

"She was . . ." Kate paused. "Me. A different me." Then she added, "I think that one worked in finance. Our mom must have been so proud." She pulled back and clasped her hands between her knees, looking at Bertie over her shoulder. "You really don't know any of this? I assumed . . . I just figured . . ." Her face began to flush.

"I've been looking for you," Bertie told her. "You were here?

The whole time?" Ignoring for a moment the notion of a plural *you*.

"Of course," Kate said.

"So what *happened*?"

"Christ. A lot. Can you be more specific?"

But Bertie shook her head and tilted her chin up to the ceiling, trying to keep her roiling nausea at bay. When she first laid eyes on Kate, in high school, she'd thought, *Nope.* Not because she didn't seem cool, but because she seemed too cool: the violet hair, the wristlet of leather and metal, came together with the wry twist of her lips to tell Bertie, *This is not a safe place for you.* Maybe she'd sensed, beneath everything else, a history that couldn't be squared with her own cozy family life. The divorce, the moves, the dislocation, all as essential to Kate as her smile. And now, years later, here she was, still so much greater than the sum of Bertie's parts.

With a sigh, Kate spoke. "I was trying to find you, dummy. That's what happened to me. I only stopped because . . ." She paused again, and when she continued, her voice was quieter. "I didn't think you wanted to be found."

Bertie raised her eyebrows, and Kate went on:

"After I got off that elevator and you weren't there, I thought for sure you were just taking selfies by the statue. Because it's got good light, or whatever. Lots of angles from the stairs. But it doesn't take that long to take a picture, and when you still hadn't shown up ten minutes later, I went looking for you, and that's when I remembered: your camera wasn't working."

Kate looked at her. "Of course, you weren't at the statue, either. I thought you were being such a huge dick."

Bertie laughed bitterly. "Actually, I thought you were."

"Hilarious," Kate said. And then she took a moment to compose herself, winding a stray piece of hair around and around, into a small coil. "You had been so mad about L.A.," she whispered, almost to herself. "I know you were trying, but you also kept disappearing, and I just figured, when I couldn't find you, when I realized what I'd done . . . I figured you were angry, and you'd left me, and it was my fault." Which Bertie didn't know how to reply to, though Kate didn't seem to require a response.

She'd wandered around looking for a way out, but kept getting lost, deeper inside the museum. "I kept thinking: someone will come for me. Eventually, if nothing else, the museum will open, and then the police will come, and then the FBI or whatever the French version of the FBI is, and they'll find you, and we'll both leave. If the museum just opens. But it didn't. I thought you'd finally come back, but *you* didn't. The bathrooms still worked, so I had toilets and water. And there was enough food in various cafés and things that I didn't starve. But it got really old."

Kate exhaled. "I hated it, then. God, I hated it. I refused to look at almost any of the art, because doing that would mean I was trying to appreciate where I was, and I just couldn't see my way to that."

"So what happened?" Bertie ventured. Meaning, at least in part, *Don't you still hate it now?*

"I guess, I gave in? One day I got tired, and sat down on a bench, just to zone out for a little while. And without really meaning to, I looked at the picture in front of me, which was a woman making, I think, lace, bent over all this pretty fabric with needles and pins."

"Vermeer," Bertie said.

Kate nodded.

"She was so focused. She seemed—I don't know, at peace. Like what she was doing was just what she was meant to do, and here she could do it forever and ever, and I thought that was a beautiful thing. It wasn't my usual kind of art thought; I mean, you know me. I mostly make a joke and move on. This was magnetic. I couldn't look away. I have no idea how long I spent staring at that picture, but when I looked up, there was—" She coughed. "Well, me."

"But how?" Bertie said. "Just—how?"

"Believe me, that was also my question, after a period of significant freak-out," Kate replied. She paused, gazing into the middle distance, as she had while blasting the Ramones from her mother's borrowed car. Tugging the frayed sleeves of a black sweatshirt over her fingers. "This is what I think. You know how soap bubbles all stick together? How they have those swirls of color?" Kate checked for assent and then continued. "They're separate bubbles, but where they touch, they can share things. Pass stuff back and forth. And the place where they connect: this place is like that."

"This is the Louvre," Bertie said. "This is a *museum*."

"Yeah, but come on." Kate gave her a look. "It's different. You can feel that, I'm sure." When Bertie didn't answer, Kate frowned. "Well, whatever. It is. And after we finally both calmed down, she and I—the other me and I, I mean—talked about it. From her point of view, she'd come to the museum with Javier, and not you at all. He left her to go get a bottle of wine, and she was standing there looking at the picture, and there I was."

"Oh, shit," said Bertie. It hadn't occurred to her that there might be loops happening that had nothing to do with her. But of course, there must be. She and Dylan had collided like atoms; they had gone off like a bomb. Creating not a crater in the ground, but a little black hole in time that swallowed Kate up again and again. Different Kates, even. Loops in, what—other worlds?

"Yeah," said Kate, agreeing with *Oh, shit*. "Pretty much. All of us have a story like that."

All. That was interesting.

"So it's not just the two of you?"

"We thought so, at first," Kate said. "But we've found so many more of us. This place draws us in, from all the different lives we've lived. All the different versions of us who found a reason to be in this museum. Some came with you, like I did. Some by themselves, or with other people. We're arriving all the time."

She looked down at her hands. "Sometimes I can remember things that I never did, in my life. Which some other version of me did do. They're blurrier than my own memories at first, but after a while, I can't tell the difference. Some of us have even brought things with us, actual objects from our lives, and they feel—so important to me now. Like a nerve in my body that was always invisible, but has suddenly been exposed. Everything that's important to one of us, all the others start to feel it." She flicked one nail against another. "That's how I found you, just now. You picked up that drawing, and I felt it. I would have felt it anywhere."

Bertie imagined Kate, refracted like light. Fractal, emerging endlessly from a single point. Time had bloomed around Bertie's body. Kate, instead, seemed to have bloomed around time. Bertie shook her head. "I can't even believe you're here. I can barely believe you're real."

"Sometimes," Kate said, looking into her eyes, "I wonder if any of this is real."

For a moment Bertie wasn't sure how to answer. One morning in Paris, she and Kate had gone to a bookstore that was also a coffee shop, and picked up six different pastries to split. A pistachio raspberry tart. A chocolate croissant. A regular croissant. Tarte aux pommes, which Kate had eaten most of, going so far as to slap Bertie's hand away from the last bite, and two religieuses, giant choux pastry towers meant to look like nuns, filled respectively with coffee and chocolate cream. Sitting across the road from the remains of Notre Dame in a little park garden, they'd attracted wasps, despite the bad weather, and by the time they finished their meal, both of them were buzzing with sugary energy.

Did you know, Bertie had said, that my company is making a machine that can create virtual realities based on synthesized pictures and sounds from the internet? It's the first step towards an actual simulated place to live in after death.

So, heaven? Kate had asked.

Or hell.

Kate snorted. But why? Aren't we all supposed to be afraid of the singularity, and being absorbed by robots or whatever?

Apparently not, Bertie had said, though she'd certainly heard post-techno-bros at parties expound on this very theme at length. She went on: they think the world as we know it will end no matter what, and this is how the human race will survive. In this endless, looping space. It's still super-secret and mostly theoretical. I only know about it because they're giving all us nobodies tickets in a lottery to be included in the test. If it goes well, that means we'd be the first members of some new society.

Or . . . it could go badly and you'd be trapped in a digital hellscape for all eternity?

Yeah, or that.

Kate had snuggled against Bertie on the bench and bitten her shoulder. Don't do it. You're not no one, Bunny.

"Kate," Bertie said, now, gathering her strength. "Listen, I think I can get us out of here. I've been through the museum exit, and I'm pretty sure I can find it again. And Dylan seemed"—oh, God, she hadn't explained Dylan yet—"distracted, so . . ."

"Bertie." Kate sighed. She stayed seated, and made her words delicate. "No. I should explain."

"Later, we can talk—"

"Bunny, no. I . . ." She put her hands over her face, then pushed them back over her forehead, tugging gently against her scalp. "Wow. I was so sure you were mad, for so long, and now you're not, and it's actually worse."

"What am I supposed to be *mad* about?"

"This." Kate looked at her evenly. "No one is keeping me here anymore. I'm not trapped. This is where I want to be." She bit her thumbnail, and made a face like it tasted terrible, but she was going to see it through. "Don't you see? The others. They're me. They're *me*. I can know every possibility, every moment of time that's mine. I don't have to have just one future, now. I can see them all and keep them close to me."

Bertie felt her head shaking again, back and forth, though she couldn't remember deciding to move it. A disconnect between her body and mind. None of this was right.

She said, "But I found you. I kept looking. You're coming home with me."

"No," Kate said. "Bunny, I'm not."

"What do you mean?" Tears stung Bertie's eyes, and she wiped them away angrily.

"It's not . . . oh my God. It's not about you. Can't you see that?" Kate puckered her mouth, trying to make her cheekbones more prominent, her lips plumper. Bertie had seen it so many times, in the bathroom at her house, or Kate's house, or a restaurant. Everywhere. On the internet, on her own phone, saved to her favorites, her very favorites of all time.

"I can't believe this." Bertie stood up. She was shaking all over. "I can't believe you. All this time I was looking for you." She took a step back. "You've always been so scared of getting stuck."

"I was stuck, Bun. I'm not anymore." She swept a hand out, indicating—what? The paintings in their golden frames, the hidden doors leading to secret places. Different worlds. And Kate would slip between them forever, because she had clipped herself free from the leash of her life. *Including me,* Bertie thought. The tightest, most insistent leash of all.

Well.

Bertie closed her eyes. She counted to ten, letting the tears drop down her cheeks and off her chin, trying to keep her breath even. Once more she imagined herself on the back of a rocket, departing from Earth, whipping through a space so cold it burned and peeled her fingers away from the metal. She was so used to holding on that it hurt just to think about. But what if she didn't? What if she just let go?

Before either of them could speak again, they heard footsteps coming down the hall. Rapid, pattering like rain.

"Bertie!" Dylan turned a corner and ran towards them, his face panicked, his cheeks red. "Oh my God," he said. "I found you. Thank God." He stopped and rested his hands on his knees, crouching and panting. Then he saw Kate, and he startled. "Oh, shit, she's here." As if he'd known her all his life.

"I remember you, now," Kate said, getting pale. "I knew I'd seen your face before. You were in the courtyard, weren't you?"

Bertie paused. Something was shimmering between Kate and Dylan, and she didn't like it. Smoke in the distance. Barbecue. Dylan grabbed Bertie's hand, and in her surprise, she let him. Feeling the warmth shared back and forth between them from the moment they touched, until she pulled her hand away. Dylan flexed his empty fingers and winced.

Then, suddenly, she knew.

Bertie turned to Kate. "You were the one. Who wanted us apart." She spun back to Dylan. "It was her. You were doing your *good deed* for her. Not Javier at all." *Why can't you just let me be?* Kate had asked, as they stood at the threshold of the museum. Not so different from what she'd said in defense of her move to Los Angeles. *It's not about you, okay? Sometimes I just want to make my own decisions.*

From the start, Dylan had refused to look for her. Dylan, who could skip the tracks of time, had said he couldn't, or wouldn't, find Kate.

"I was just annoyed with you," Kate said softly, now. "That morning, outside the museum, I just wanted to get you off my back. It's just something people say." She licked her dry lips, and Bertie could hear the echo of it. *Let me be.* "I didn't think anything would actually come of it."

"Why were you happy to see me then?" Bertie asked. "Here, I mean. What did you think was going to happen?"

Kate sighed. "I thought—" She stopped, and tugged on her lip, and Bertie understood. She had already chosen to stay, long before Bertie showed up. Before Bertie gave up her life for her. "I thought you came to say goodbye."

Bertie's head swam. She looked at Dylan. "And did you know?" she asked. "That she was here the whole time?"

He looked ashen. "Not exactly, no. I thought I was just giving her a break from you, while we hung out. Remember," he tilted his head towards Bertie, "I didn't know you'd ever figure out what was happening. I had no reason to want her gone forever. But then, when you did figure it out, I just . . . didn't press the issue. I didn't understand why she was gone. Letting her stay gone seemed like the easiest way to keep us together."

"So if we'd just looked for her when I wanted to, I could've maybe . . . convinced her . . . I don't know. I would have had more time."

"Bunny," Kate said. "No."

"If you'd *listened to me*," Bertie went on, to Dylan.

He closed his eyes.

"You would have been so mad if I'd told you," he said. "I wanted to, I really did. But I never seemed to find the moment."

"Why not at least try, though?" Bertie asked.

And he just shook his head again.

"I wanted to make you happy."

Which was the stupidest, truest thing.

The earth had begun to vibrate, Bertie thought, but then she realized it was just her body, angry and sweaty, on the verge of passing out. She strained to hear any sound from outside the museum—a car, a bird, the wind—but there was only the hum of the radiator and the slam of her pulse in her eardrums. Why had she ever even wanted to come here? To see art. To see someone else's inspiration, but in its worst, its least natural form. The point being not that it was beautiful, but that it was chosen.

She said, "I just—" and reached out a hand. The nearest painting was a giant illuminated image of rebel angels falling to earth, which seemed appropriate. "You're both just—" She shook her head, then pressed her palm into the center of the painting. "You're both terrible."

Again there came the same soft *ding*, and this time when the doors of the elevator opened, Bertie threw herself into the arms of two women who stood there waiting. Both of them with a familiar face, but neither of them the woman she knew. They caught her, and the doors slid shut. Behind them, Kate and Dylan could only watch her go.

— 21 —

When she woke up, it was raining. Sheets of water fell against the window, uninterrupted by the gargoyled stone overhang, and blown irregularly by heavy gusts of wind. Bertie lay on her back. She didn't often sleep that way—she was a side sleeper, and being on her back made her feel like a corpse. Now, though, she sank into the expensive mattress, weighed down by the comforter and radiant with the heat of her own body.

Out in the hall, she heard a door open and close, a muffled conversation taking place. She thought, *I don't have to get up. I don't have to do anything.* On the bedside table by her head, her phone buzzed, and she picked it up to see a push alert from the airline: her plane was due for an on-time departure at ten p.m., and she was invited to check in. It was only nine in the morning, and the whole day stretched out in front of her, so long as the hotel would store her baggage after she checked out.

Bertie picked up the landline beside her and called down to room service, ordering a pot of coffee, brewed fresh, and an omelet with green onion and chèvre, plus a side of fries. There was no fruit on the menu, since fresh fruit was still hard to come by: all of it either shriveled by drought, or poisoned by the lingering radiation from a dirty bomb. But her hunger was greasier than that, anyway. Eggs and bread, potatoes and oil. Bertie rolled onto her side and dozed until she heard a knock on the door, and when she hopped up to unlock it, an efficient young woman rolled the tray into her room and stayed just long enough to receive her signature on the bill. The rain got heavier as Bertie plucked the silver dome off the top of her breakfast, and she went to the window to watch a river of water flow down the street, everything pixelated by the storm.

What will you do today? she wondered. *Will you tour the Catacombs, so you can stay dry? Rain and bones. Rivers and stones.* She dipped a fry in ketchup. *Or will you take a taxi to Montmartre and spend your last day in Paris drinking wine in a café, pretending to be artistic? Maybe you could even smoke.* There was something alluring about that, contrasting the heavy rain with a mouth of fire. Bertie yawned. She was still sleepy.

The coffee was good. It wasn't easy to find plain black coffee in Paris, she'd discovered: there was espresso, and sometimes a French press, but rarely just a regular pot of the sort she was accustomed to. The one she set each night so it would be ready when she woke up in the morning, now that beans were available again. There were benefits to going home. Here, the coffeepot had been covered in cling wrap before being set on the room service tray, and it cost seven euros, but it was worth it as a treat, so much better than the pod machine that was provided in the room, gratis.

When she thought of home, the bottom fell out of her stomach, all the way down to the end of time, but she turned away from it, back to the ceramic cup in her hand, the low morning light.

There was really only one thing she could do today. But she didn't want to think about that yet, either. Instead, after eating, she took a long, luxurious shower, shaving her legs and deep conditioning her hair before blowing it dry in front of the mirror, so it was stick straight and staticky warm. She folded all her clothes into her suitcase except one pair of black jeans and a cozy sweater—not too heavy, but not scratchy, either. A black-and-white chevron knit, made fisherman style, which smelled ever so faintly of campfire. Bertie twisted her hair into one long strand and let it fall over her shoulder. Her packing done, she curled up on the bed in her socks, and looked out the window until she could no longer deny that her time in the room was over.

—

"Bon matin," the concierge wished her, after he accepted her suitcase. She'd settled the bill. Her taxi would depart from outside the lobby at seven p.m., allowing her a generous amount of time to reach the airport and then her gate. She took the umbrella he offered on loan, and opened it above her in the street. Immediately the rain hit the nylon like a shower of coins. The air was cold, and Bertie could feel it condensing on her nose and cheeks as she started to walk. She knew the way. There was only one way.

She stopped at a familiar café for a hot chocolate with whipped cream. Across the street a group of three women streamed into another restaurant, shaking rain out of their hair beneath the awning before they were lost behind the fogged-up windows. Cars whisked by in the street, sending up sheets of water, but the pedestrians all seemed unbothered. It was the middle of the work week. They were all heading for the office, or dropping children off at school, tapping something into their phones, as they walked a path so familiar it was burned into their brains, and they could follow it without thought or worry.

The streets looked different in the day than they had the night before, when she left the museum, hurried along by a pair of silent women in her best friend's body (which: *Get your own face,* Bertie had thought. How could they be what Kate chose? Wasn't it just a form of escape? Of running away, with just yourself for company? Wasn't all time just no time? They reminded her of the people she saw in San Francisco, rolling the tinted windows up in their cars as they drove past the tent cities that kept blooming up, bigger and bolder, everywhere), and then fell to her knees on the pavement, as the topiary maze behind the Louvre shifted its shadows towards her in the moonlight.

Bertie wiped the last bit of chocolate and cream from the bottom of her cup with a pointer finger, and put the finger in her mouth. The strange Kates had not given her any message, or even spoken, they had simply taken her—away from the Kate she assumed was her own, away from the art—shoes clicking briskly down the hallways once they left the elevator. As her Kate and Dylan got farther away, Bertie felt alone in a way she hadn't for a long time. The museum door closed after her with a soft click, and when she picked herself up and looked, she could see nothing behind it but empty space. An occasional light from some alarm or system blinked from a box on the wall. She smelled the air. There was nothing special. Mown grass, mud, and a city sweating oil, but that was all.

Walking through the park, she'd passed a pair of dark figures pressed together in the trees, laughing sweetly, and had hurried away from them before they realized she was there.

Beside her in the café, a man jostled for space with his elbow, as if willing her out of existence. Bertie set aside her cup and threw down some change for the waitress, which she knew was not required in Paris but couldn't convince herself was actually unnecessary. She'd spent too many years in coffee shops, waiting for the barista to turn around and make eye contact before putting a dollar bill in the tip jar. Anyway, she was going home tonight. The Americanness she'd been so keen to shed at the beginning of her trip could slide back over her and take its natural place, glowing over her skin. She should get warmed up for being crude again, taking up space. Soon she would be driving to work in the morning, nosing her car into a crowded lane as assholes behind her leaned on their horns and frantically flashed their brights to spook her.

She left the café and walked to the river, where she stopped to lean over the wall and look at the water. So many bridges. Along the road, a few of the braver tradesmen were opening up shop, unlocking their green wooden carts full of paperback books and Toulouse-Lautrec prints and stashing the plastic rain cloths out of sight, then setting out Eiffel Tower key chains along the edges, wherever they'd stand. Below the Pont des Arts, the Seine was also green, a tugboat chugging along and leaving a veil of wake. Today Bertie would be approaching the Louvre from the opposite side, walking through the back instead of going around to the Rue de Rivoli. It felt a little like sneaking, but she held her umbrella up protectively and continued anyway.

The Cour Napoléon was full of people, separated into several lines—one extending back to the street, and another switchbacking several times in front of the glass pyramid. After inspecting the various instructional signs, Bertie chose the longest line and stood in it. There were no familiar faces in the crowd. Every few minutes, someone would arrive and brandish a printed piece of paper at a tall male guard, entreating him to let them in the third and shortest line, but invariably he diverted them to the longer line, with Bertie. The grumbling was general. It was still raining, not quite so hard. People were swathed in cheap translucent ponchos, and a pair of children were wandering around selling umbrellas that said: *Paris, je t'aime.*

At ten o'clock, Bertie's line moved forwards past the ticket counters, where she purchased a one-day pass and walked down the spiral staircase into the belly of the museum, the arterial center that let you choose your path, your destiny. She turned towards the Denon Wing. (No bank of elevators this time. That was interesting.) Did she like the *Mona Lisa* because it had been ingrained in her mind since birth, or because it was well made? She decided not to care. The room was already packed with tourists raising their phones above their heads to get an unimpeded shot, and in the crush, the tiny portrait looked less imposing in its beauty, more like a trinket or icon being worshipped into pieces. It looked vulnerable, which of course it was. She knew from art school that the painting had been stored for many years in a bathing salon at the Château de Fontainebleau, and it seemed entirely possible to Bertie that in that time the steam had peeled something away. She saw some resemblance to a soft-boiled egg. Everything bleeding together across circumstance and across time; a concept that was always the same, no matter how often it was reproduced.

She wandered for four hours. She looked at Raphael's Saint George slaying a dragon (*The monster is right behind you*), and at three fat angels surrounded by flowers, labeled *The Triumph of Love*. (*Bertie, do you hear me? I said, I love you.*) She looked at a marble death mask, a king painted in the guise of a saint, a woman being drowned in a deluge while a man tried to pull himself out by her hair. What she saw most of all were the other people moving through the museum like a river, endlessly replenished. There were so many of them, and tomorrow there would be more. The art, the same. The people, different. Two men walked by her holding hands, one wearing a sweater the color of wine and the other a blue suit jacket over a gray T-shirt.

All the babies that day seemed to be wrapped in the same white cotton, which was printed all over with stars or hearts or whales or birds, and strapped tightly to their mothers' chests.

When she was done, she left. It was so easy. Outside, the rain had stopped. She hung her umbrella from her elbow, and went to a café fifteen minutes or so away, where a waiter came outside and wiped a chair dry before seating her there and bringing a menu, never once asking her preference, inside or out. The air was fresh and wet. Bertie ordered a white wine and a pâté with salad, something she knew she could not reproduce back home without a lot of effort. She also ordered hot tea to brace her up after the hours of walking and admiring. Occasionally passersby looked at her out of the corners of their eyes, and she ignored their appraising glances. How had she ended up here, in Paris, all by herself? She knew the answer but couldn't explain it. The path was still a mystery.

The wine went quickly to her head. Paris, she thought, was

the place you went for romance. The place to be with the person you loved most in the world. Sitting in her still-moist chair, Bertie laughed quietly to herself, and appreciated that the other customers—all of them tourists, sitting outside at the rain-dappled tables—pretended not to notice. She had lost everything, but she found she didn't mind. She minded her parents being gone. But the rest—not so much. She would always mind the loss of those two people who had seen her feet when they were baby feet, her fingers when they were small enough to bite off with ease. Her parents were the only ones who knew her well enough to imagine what her own baby might look like, and with them gone, Bertie had stopped trying to imagine it herself, but now she thought about it again, and the thought was: maybe. A little Bertie, iterating always. There were so many ways to live forever, and also none.

She walked by the Seine, and through the streets, up and down hills. She ate a pastry and wandered through a much-trampled garden; the paths flattened by feet, the beds by rain. There were enormous signs up, advertising the skeleton of a dinosaur. She walked for so long that it took her by surprise when her phone buzzed in her pocket, alerting her that it was time to go back to the hotel. She hadn't noticed the sun getting low. She had to hurry, her lungs burning as she speed-walked through the Latin Quarter, and arrived with frazzled hair back in the lobby, with only minutes to spare.

"Merci," the concierge said when she handed him the borrowed umbrella. He was a different concierge than had been on shift in the morning, and he took the umbrella delicately, with his fingertips, as if it might infect him. "Also, mademoiselle, a package arrived for you."

"For me?"

"Oui." He nodded his head in acknowledgment and swept behind a door, emerging with a thick manila envelope, which he handed to her before turning away.

To Bertie, the envelope said, and she shoved it carefully into her purse. The taxi was already there.

"Il vous attends," the concierge suggested. He wheeled out her suitcase. *He is waiting for you*. Bertie shivered as she stepped into the cab, but the driver was anonymous, and promptly agreed to take her to the airport. As they drove, her fingers caressed the edge of the envelope. Finally, she opened it.

My dearest Bunny, read the letter at the top.

I hope you don't just tear this up. At least look inside the envelope. I think you'll be happy. I know you well enough for that.

Dutifully, she tipped the contents of the envelope out, and gasped, making brief eye contact with the taxi driver in the rear-view mirror before they both looked away.

On her lap lay every page she'd drawn of her new graphic novel, which she had last seen on the wall of the Louvre in golden frames. That morning, as a face in the crowd, she'd looked for the wing of the museum where they'd been hanging, but she couldn't find it, or it wasn't there, which was really no surprise. She didn't think they'd be at home in her apartment, either, spread out on the kitchen table awaiting her return. In fact, she'd assumed they'd been reabsorbed; that whatever power had folded space and time back up within the museum had folded them in, too, with her best friend, all possible versions of her, and with her boyfriend, or whoever he was.

But here they were.

I found these after you disappeared from the museum. I know you don't remember it that way, but that's how it was for me: you were there and then you were gone, and I had nothing. Yes, I wanted to be on my own, but that was a wish, like pennies tossed into a fountain. I didn't intend for anyone but you to hear it, let alone answer it.

You remember how I told you that some of us, the other versions of me, have been able to bring things with them into the museum, from their lives? These pages are a part of that. I didn't understand it at first, because I spent such a long time thinking I was alone here. But now I know.

The first page appeared maybe a few days in, and I kept going back to the wall to look at it, and slowly new pages would show up. It reminded me of our dumb plan to buy a house, do you remember? I mean, you must. Obviously. But back then, I couldn't tell if you were making the drawings, or if they just existed for me, like a figment of my imagination or a manifestation of my hopes. And actually, for a while, they made me angry, because I assumed you were nearby but refused to see me: that you were sneaking in and putting up the pages and then sneaking away. I finally decided that if you were, I probably deserved it. After that, I was just happy to see them, because they let me know you were okay.

Anyway. In those days, these pages were the only thing that let me feel close to you. The only art I could or would see. They were really the only thing that reminded me I'd been a person, once—since, after so many days without talking to another human being, I started to feel a bit . . . I guess, feral. I would prowl through the halls and growl at my shadow. My tights had ripped the very first night, and I ended up finding some pants in an old storage locker in a subbasement. At least they were clean, for a little while.

I started sleeping on the floor in front of your pages, to see if I could catch you when you came to add new ones, and apologize. I didn't expect you to stay with me, or anything, I just wanted you to hear me out. You have to understand, my hope was never that we'd be apart forever. Even when I was moving to L.A., I didn't feel the way you did, that it was the end of everything. I saw it as a beginning. That joke is on me, I guess, given how things have turned out.

You never came. I'd stay all night, and sometimes in the morning a new page would be there—or, like, three new ones—and I wouldn't have heard a thing. I thought, maybe if I could've kept myself from sleeping? But I already felt crazy enough, like some hunter/gatherer from the Stone Age who got moved to the wrong place in time. The museum stopped being a museum, for me. It was more of a habitat. I made little nests, and I foraged for chips and stale bread, and I drank a lot of root beer. I'm pretty sure I got like four cavities in the first month.

But the one thing that still seemed precious to me was these pages.

Bertie rested her forehead against the window of the cab while she read, trying to keep from crying. If she cried, her tears might smear the ink in the letter, or dot the illustrations, and she wasn't willing to give up either one.

Bertie, I know you're mad at me, but I need you to understand that my love for these drawings is the reason I know I have to stay. When that other me showed up, at that painting of the lacemaker—I think you said it was a Vermeer?—I took one look at her and ran away. I didn't know what was happening, but I knew I had to protect these drawings from whatever it was, and so when she caught up with me, I threw my arms out, as if that would stop her. But she looked at the pictures, and burst into tears. In her life, you aren't even friends anymore. Can you imagine that? But she still couldn't look away, and I know she'd protect the pages with her life.

We aren't the same. But we are one person. I don't know if that makes sense.

Anyway.

Not long after that, another of us came along. She walked right up to us while we were foraging for snacks, and said hello, as if it were no big deal. I threw a handful of salted peanuts at her head and screamed. But then—we all just laughed. I mean, what else can you do? When you see your own face?

This new Kate had been given the pages by her Bertie—the you she knew in her own life—and happened to have them in her bag when she walked into the museum. That's how they'd been appearing: she'd been putting them up on the wall any time she found a frame that fit. We'd found the pictures before we found her.

I was always surprised she wasn't more possessive of them, but from the beginning it was obvious that the pages were something we all had in common, the first thing that taught us we could come together as one. I thought—we thought—if this place could bring us something as important as them, it must be good.

It must be a good place, after all. Deciding that was a powerful experience. We agreed then that we would never go back.

Oh, Bertie. I know you won't like hearing that.

There's so much I still don't understand about what happened to you. None of it was how I thought it would be. Dylan didn't stick around after you left, so I couldn't ask him any questions; I watched you go, and then when I turned to say something to him, he was gone, too. I wouldn't trust him, Bertie. Then again, if I were you, I also probably wouldn't trust me.

But the pictures. These pictures. I'm not sure what it will mean that I'm giving them to you, but it seems like the ultimate act of protection, to send them to their proper home. Or anyway, it seems like the right thing to do. I hope you love them the way I do, and that you finish making them. Maybe someday I'll even get to read the end. Do Kate and Bertie survive? Do they learn how to grow crops, and make friends with the people in town, or do the animals come and take over the house and leave behind their skin and bones? How would you draw the end of the world, what would that look like to you? I'm not sure anymore that it's real. Maybe when one world ends, another one begins, but I have to admit, I love this Bertie and I love this Kate, and if they died, I think a piece of my heart would die with them. Maybe you always mourn the lost thing, despite the new.

I love you, Bunny, my dearest Bun. I'll miss you. I'm glad you're alive.

Your friend, always,

Kate

– 22 –

When she was a child, Bertie would wander through the woods near her house, and everything smelled green. She watched birds jump from branch to branch, watched them sail silently on wind that was untouchably high above her, and felt that the world's order was revealing itself to her, secrets untangling beneath her fingers like knots being pulled free in her own hair.

It was not a feeling she would find again. As she got older, she mostly got more tired. Her face didn't age so much as deteriorate, despite her attempts to hold it together with various unguents bought on the internet. She would think: after the weekend, it will be better, after vacation, in the new year. For a while she had Kate, but that couldn't last, and indeed it had not. Now she stood in the Charles du Gaulle Airport, yellow beneath the fluorescent lights, and searched with increasing desperation for the line that would take her through security to her gate. She didn't need the world to be green again; just a little bit greener. But how could it be? She genuinely didn't know.

"Hey, Bert."

He was there, standing behind her by an ATM with a line ten deep. Dylan had no suitcase, because of course what would he carry? Just himself, and his jeans, and his shirt, and those all came along naturally. He looked abashed. In one pocket he had his phone, and in the other his passport, since men's pants had pockets deep enough to hold such things. Bertie turned away and walked towards a concourse, which she quickly deduced was the wrong concourse, and when she turned to backtrack, there he was again.

"We're on the same plane, you know."

"I know," she said. Though, in fact, she hadn't been sure she'd ever see him again. "I'm not an idiot."

"We don't really have to do it this way. We could go back to the beginning. Or even back where we were right at the end. No jet lag—wouldn't that be nice? All you have to do is agree. To want it." He looked hopeful, and it looked stupid on him.

"I read somewhere that jet lag isn't just the body lacking sleep, but more the confusion of the person's cells," Bertie said. "The confusion that the cells could travel so far with so little effort expended. Like, there is no circadian rhythm for that. For waking up after ten hours and having gone three thousand miles."

"Well, it's really more to do with how you digest and how that relates to—"

She ignored him, which was becoming easy. "So my point is, can you imagine how confused my body would be if I moved instantaneously? Didn't even choose to get on a plane, but just let you snap your fingers and bring me home. There is no rhythm at all for that."

"For finger snapping?"

"Oh, go crawl back into whatever hell you came out of."

"Bertie, come on, you're not being fair."

"I'm not being fair?" She spun around, and put a finger to

his chest. "You took advantage of me. That's not something I can forget. You can't erase it. And I know you've tried."

Bertie looked at the ticket on her phone and then up to a board listing gates and flight times. Suddenly, the correct security line was right in front of her. She'd been staring at it so intently, she hadn't known that it was there. Dragging her roller bag, she got into the line, and Dylan followed.

"But you love me."

"I don't know that."

"You do. And I love you."

"You only ever say that to me when you want something. It's kind of hard to take you seriously."

He grabbed her shoulder, but realized quickly it was the wrong move when she turned on him, angrily, and the others in line saw what he was doing, and started to frown. The world closing in on him, too aware he was there.

"Bertie," he said. He removed his hand.

"Here's what's going to happen," she told him. "We're going to get on this plane. I'm going to order a wine, and watch, like, four movies, and fall asleep during the last one. You're going to sit there. And then, when we get home, we're going to go our separate ways."

"But I don't know what will happen to you, if you're not with me. If we can't control the loops."

"You don't have to know."

"I could just—" He held out his hand. "I could change your mind. If you gave me a chance. One more time, from the beginning, and neither of us would know. We'd just meet, like two normal people, and we'd see where it goes."

"Dylan." She sighed out through her nose. The sound that obnoxious men made in yoga to emphasize that they were engaged. She imagined him following her off the plane, trying to get in her cab at the airport, or taking his own and following her back to her apartment, and barging through the door. He would stay until she called the police on him, and could she really do that? She wasn't sure. He was right about one thing: there was a part of her, an untrustworthy part, that wanted him to stay.

The thing was, she could still see, inside him, the little boy who once stood on the edge of a forest and smiled at the camera as its lens flared in the light. *That's not a good enough reason*, she told herself. The innocence of the child was not, of course, mutually exclusive with the crimes of the adult. But perhaps it meant something, how deeply they were intertwined. She was scared, too, of the world she knew not existing. Though of course, it stopped existing all the time.

"Okay," she said, slowly. She had an idea.

"Okay?"

"Okay, but we do it my way. We do it now."

"Like, this very minute?"

"Here we are in line, two Americans on their way back home from Paris. What better meet-cute could there be?"

He frowned. "And could we keep the same seats? Next to each other?"

"Sure. That's part of it," Bertie said. He brightened up. "But this is part, too: afterwards, you have to let the rest just happen. However it does."

"The rest, how?"

"I mean, this would be it. No more loops. I think—" She

remembered him, breathless, telling her, *We could live forever.* The excitement that had colored his face. "I'm pretty sure that if you can start a loop all over, you can leave them all behind. I think the only reason you've never stopped doing this is because you didn't want to."

Dylan took a step back, and in that moment she knew she was right. The other people in line were fastidiously ignoring them at this point. One couple had begun talking in rapid German, inching farther and farther away.

"And you know what?" she said. "I think I get it. Way more now than I did before." *Eternal life,* Bertie thought. *A brand-new world.* She sighed. "But it just—it won't work for me. You and I would have to start fresh." She looked at him. "You would live this life, same as me, and then you'd die, no matter what else happened. You'd just have to agree."

"Oh."

She watched him reel. It was a lot to ask. But he'd asked a lot of her, too.

"It's the only way I could trust you," she said. "Otherwise, some part of me would know, and you know I'm right. You saw what happened with Kate. How I looked for her. I could always feel that something was missing."

"I see." He started to look green. "So we'd start from now."

"Rip off the Band-Aid. You wouldn't even have time to be scared."

He looked at her. "Is that true?"

"I didn't." She looked back. "I was never scared, at the start. You might be scared later. Probably. But for different reasons."

It occurred to Bertie that this might be the last flight she ever took. Oil prices kept going up, and ticket prices with them. The airport still seemed to be operating normally, but if you looked closely, you could spot marks of decay. An out-of-the-way window mended with duct tape. A flight attendant's uniform fraying at the edge. It was a bad world to bet on, but all her chips were already in.

"Or I could just go," he said. "I could just leave right now and do other things, however I wanted."

"You could," she said. "You could certainly do that."

"I need to think. Just for a minute."

"Well hurry." Bertie turned and surveyed the line. She felt completely calm, now. "There are only a few more people ahead of us. You don't have much more time."

—

When she was a child, Bertie would wander through the woods near her house, daylight shining in through the pine needles. She remembered that now, sitting in the lounge at the airport and waiting for her flight to board. She wasn't sure quite why. It was the whiff of something in the air, or maybe a sound. It was oddly familiar. She looked up at the ceiling, and there they were: two birds, caught up in the rafters. Not songbirds, though, like the ones that had danced through the trees of her childhood. Two pigeons. Cooing and ruffling, one of them grooming itself beneath a wing. No one else was paying attention yet, but as Bertie watched, a dropping fell from the pigeons' roost in the ceiling down to the floor near a man's suitcase. Someone would have to flush them out with a tall, tall broom.

She opened her purse and checked for the pages: a graphic

novel she'd been working on, and had risked bringing on vacation so she could continue to make progress in her rare abundance of time. Bertie fingered the pages in the envelope. They were still there, and safe, thank God. Why had she thought they might not be?

At the podium, two airline workers were sorting through something on a computer. Bertie shook her head. She was tired, and felt strange, as if she were at the end of her flight and not the beginning, but maybe she was just too aware of her own bad breath, a mouth that tasted like tinsel and wire. The flight crew called out the first-class boarding group, first in French and then in English, then Spanish. A German couple mumbled something to each other. Bertie was in the fifth boarding group, but everyone got into line as soon as the first passes were scanned, and she scrambled to the end of it, anxiously eyeing people's phones to see if passengers in groups six and seven had somehow made it into line ahead of her. She hated how anxious she got, waiting to board a flight, but the feeling was amplified now into a queer certainty that she would never get on the plane, never get home. Sweat began to pool at the small of her back, and her breathing sped up as people moved slowly forwards, step by step.

Above her, the pigeons were still sitting and talking to each other. No one else seemed to have noticed them yet.

"What are you looking at?"

A man behind her, American, too, by the accent, followed her gaze up to the birds and whistled softly. "Well, they're out of place, aren't they?"

"I hope they don't die," Bertie said, and then she blushed. "Sorry, that was morbid."

"Nah, let's live in hope together."

"Mm-hmm."

They continued to move silently up the line. Bertie was relieved to see that people who got to the front too early were shunted off to the side to wait. The man behind her began to hum. Not very loud, but still a bit too audible for Bertie's taste. She glanced behind her with a tight-lipped smile, and he smiled back, which was unfortunate. The humming continued. When she looked again, he seemed to get the hint, and stopped. No luggage, Bertie noticed. Not even a carry-on bag.

"Sorry," he said. "I hum when I'm nervous. Bad flier."

Bertie couldn't help herself. "You checked your bag, huh?"

"Oh. Yeah. I don't fly often, so I'm still in the habit. I'm kind of a holdover from a different time."

"No one really flies that much anymore."

"I guess," the man said, pleasantly. Bertie gave him a more careful once-over: round face, light brown hair, thinning. A little husky, but it looked good on him, or good enough. He had on a gray slim-fitting sweatshirt, which embraced his belly but also his broad shoulders.

"You got the comfy clothes memo, at least," she observed. "Not flying in a suit jacket or whatever."

"No. I was here for fun. I wanted to see it while I could."

"Me, too," Bertie said. A few beautiful things, on the other side of the world. Soon enough, that might sound like a fairy tale.

"Now who's morbid?"

"Pretty much everyone on Earth." Which wasn't exactly true. A lot of people pretended nothing was wrong. A lot of people were optimistic. At least in this quiet moment, when hostilities were at a standstill, and most people had enough food. Though who knew how long that would last?

The man hugged himself, and therefore his sweatshirt. "I got this special for the trip, actually. It's not my usual thing. But so soft!"

Bertie laughed. She couldn't help but find it inviting, the look of his arms holding him close.

"Is this . . . your first sweatshirt?" she asked.

"Maybe," he said, mysteriously. "Hey, where are you sitting?" And there it was, the reason Bertie usually didn't talk to strange men. They always found a way to cross the line.

"Uh. Let's not make this weird," she said. The guy looked harmless, kind of sweet. But how could she know for sure?

"Okay, sorry." He paused. "It will be weird now, though, if by some freak chance we are sitting near each other."

She raised her eyebrows. "Well, whose fault is that?"

"I'm in"—he looked down at his phone—"50C."

"Oh," Bertie said. "I'm 50A." Her anxiety began to creep back in, prickling up the back of her neck and knotting in her low intestine. Or whatever was there to knot, in the area of her uterus. Maybe she was getting her period. That would be just her luck, on a thirteen-hour flight. "Look, I just, um, I need to answer some emails."

"All right," the man said. "Sure." He looked at his own phone, and Bertie turned back around to face the front of the line, sliding through social media app after social media app, maneuvering her face into a contemplative expression, instead of merely hypnotized.

Despite her fears, Bertie got on the plane and even secured

a good overhead space for her bag, sliding it in on its side and rolling her eyes at all the bags pushed in on their bellies, taking up twice their allotted space. She was too conflict-averse to fix them, but luckily a pair of flight attendants were moving through the cabin, pointing to offending bags and saying, "I'm just going to flip this, to make space for our other guests!" before hauling them into realignment.

It turned out 50A and 50C were actually side by side, a window and an aisle in a two-seat row, set off from the middle row that went six deep across the center of the plane. Bertie sat down by the window, and the man from the line settled himself beside her a few minutes later, sneaking by a guy in a ball cap who was trying to shove an oversize duffel in beside a skateboard and a roller bag; he stepped back every time the skateboard moved, as if it were about to wing out and whack him in the forehead, but it never did, which meant he was the main obstruction.

"Oh, boy," said the man from the line, wiggling his eyebrows at the duffel-bag man in the aisle. "This has been a bracing day."

Bertie yawned performatively. "Yeah, red-eyes are not the best."

"I'm Dylan."

She sighed. "Bertie. Roberta. But no one calls me that."

"Nice to meet you, Bertie."

"Sure." She smiled and put in her headphones, flipping through the movies on the screen on the seatback in front of her, while Dylan fussed with the pillow and blanket supplied by the airline for overnight flights. He tried putting them behind his back. He tried in the seat pocket. He tried on his lap. Bertie wondered for a moment what would happen if she took them out of his hands and stowed them under the seat for him, to the side so he'd have plenty of space for his feet. She'd spread her own blanket across her lap already, but he seemed to have developed no preferences of his own, as if he were new not only to flying but also to having a body: *Do I like heat? Cold? Pressure?* A *breeze?* These seemed not to be questions that he could answer.

When she was in high school, Bertie had intended to come to Europe with her best friend, Kate, but it hadn't worked out. They didn't have the money, and it was probably for the best, since now she didn't even talk to Kate. No bad blood, they'd just gone different ways, and at this point she wouldn't have known how to find her if she'd wanted to. Which she mostly didn't.

It would've been nice to have someone like Kate with her here, though. Or better than Kate, her friend Danzy from work, or her old roommate Angel, from her earliest days in San Francisco, who she'd become close to only after moving out of their shared apartment. Bad bedfellows, it turned out, but just fine when they met on neutral ground. Angel had quit her job at a major law firm a few years earlier to become an assistant district attorney, and she and Bertie had frequent, spirited debates about the definition of prosecutorial overreach. When they did so, Angel was generally kind enough not to point out Bertie's total lack of legal expertise, which made Bertie think she was probably also kind enough to be good at her job.

If Angel or Danzy were here, they'd make a little nest out of their blankets and decide together how to best combine the snack options with the free alcohol to dull their brains for the flight. But Dylan was so nervous that his nerves were trembling all the way over to Bertie, and she didn't know him well enough either to tell him to cut it out, or to give him, like, a hug. He looked so sad. Bertie's own anxiety sweats had cooled once she was in her seat, but she could see perspiration beading on Dylan's brow, and the consternation on his face as he tried to jam one half of his seatbelt into the other.

She popped out one headphone.

"Hey," she said. "You know, it's going to be okay."

"Is it?" He clicked his seatbelt closed at last and briefly shut his eyes in gratitude. "I mean, I know. But really. Neither of us know."

"Well, okay. We could die. But we could die any time, and we mostly don't."

"So far."

"Right up till the moment we do."

"Comforting," Dylan said, and though his voice was sarcastic, Bertie could see a bit of the strain dripping out of his face, the vein in his temple receding until it was more of a color and less of a shape. He closed his eyes again. "Okay. Thank you."

"Any time." Bertie put back in her headphone, but watched Dylan out of the corner of her eye. He was rubbing the sleeve of his sweatshirt between his thumb and forefinger, touching it like a prayer bead.

—

They took off. Bertie watched a movie, got a wine and a side of seltzer, ate a chocolate bar from her bag. She took out her phone, switched to airplane mode, and took a picture of the clouds out the window, their undulating whites and grays, so she could draw it later, at her leisure, and experiment with crosshatching in the shadows. It was while she was watching movie number two that Dylan fell asleep beside her, and his head flopped over onto her shoulder. He nuzzled her shirt with his cheek, still sleeping, the way you might crush your face into a pillow to get the best angle, or press the softness against your skin. An almost familiar feeling.

"Mmhey," he whispered. Surely not to her, but to some person in his dream. A person he knew well, who would happily accept the weight of his sleeping self in a cramped space full of recirculated air, the kind of air that came out from the vents so cold that it went to your bones. "Tell me ssstory."

For a second, Bertie actually considered what she might tell. Maybe the story of how her pregnant mom had been certain she was having a boy, and told Bertie's dad with such conviction that he assumed she'd had a blood test. They painted Bertie's bedroom blue in anticipation of her arrival, and got her a blue terry-cloth elephant and a mobile featuring stars and planets and a single light-up alien ship. Her tiny female body had been a surprise, as it would be for her so many times thereafter. Never one to be wasteful, her mom had kept all the decorations—"I don't really believe in boy and girl colors anyway," she told Bertie once, as they were looking through a scrapbook of Bertie's first year. In many of the pictures, baby Bertie was wearing T-shirts or onesies that said *Future Ladykiller* or *Mommy's Heartthrob.* Her mom had frowned. "They were gifts," she said. "From people we're not friends with anymore."

But that wasn't really a story, it was just a point when Bertie's life could've turned one of many different ways. She had looked just as natural in the Ladykiller T-shirt as a baby boy might have, and when she was fifteen, she'd painted her bedroom forest green and hung up her own sketches alongside pictures of folk artists and a single Disney animation cel, framed: a birthday present from her dad. And anyway, what would any of that mean to Dylan? He was a stranger, and he was asleep.

Gently, she moved his head off her shoulder and watched him resettle the other way. He pulled the blanket, which he'd finally opened and draped across his body, up to his chin, and sighed.

Bertie turned and looked out the window at the darkness, which could really have been covering anything. A mountain range. The ocean's blue, pelagic deep, in which great whales troubled the waters with their great, untroubled frames. Forests of kelp a mile wide, dragged through the currents like tulle on a gown. A secret valley full of songbirds, hidden from sight until the end of human days. She couldn't know exactly what she was looking at, any more than she knew what it meant. But okay. Why not. For now, in the dark, everything was possible. No story ended, they all just went on.

Acknowledgments

The longer I'm alive, the more difficult it becomes to express sufficient gratitude for anything, but it still feels worth it to try.

Thank you to the Jentel Arts Foundation and The Lighthouse Works for providing the time, space, and support that allowed me to finish very early and very late versions of this novel. Thanks also to my fellow residents for listening to me enumerate my work-related anxieties, and for occasionally taking me to the Legion bar for pool to calm the hell down.

Thank you to Emma Patterson, an outstanding agent and friend, without whom I would be lost. More specifically, thank you for reading a shocking number of drafts of this book with me, and for always having thoughtful feedback and genuine excitement to share. Your faith and support mean more to me than you can know.

Enormous thanks to Carina Guiterman for her enthusiasm, intelligence, and editorial vision, which were evident from our very first conversation and which made this a much better book. I feel incredibly lucky to have benefited from your insight as we navigated the complicated terrain of revision, and more simply, I am happy to know you.

Thanks also to Lashanda Anakwah, Kassandra Rhoads, Elizabeth Breeden, Samantha Hoback, Beth Thomas, and everyone at Simon & Schuster for your incredible support. Sincere gratitude to Dave Litman and Jackie Seow for a cover that absolutely slayed me.

To Branden Boyer-White: first reader, life's companion, and (along with Shannon Watters) a vital port in a storm. Thanks could never be enough.

To Katie Coyle, Lea Beresford, and Rufi Thorpe for reading early versions of this manuscript and offering generous advice (and funny texts). I am so lucky to know all of you.

To Lyndsey Reese, Rachel Andoga, and Sam Martone for letting me moan about it every time I got stuck in the museum, and for being invaluable treasures. To Reneé Bibby, Sara Sams, Kate Spiliopoulos, Lynn Steger Strong, Edan Lepucki, Allegra Hyde, Mairead Case, Erika Swyler, Caroline Casey, Rachel Fershleiser, Reese Kwon, Danielle Lazarin, Esmé Weijun Wang, and Kimberly Madison for life-saving conversations of all kinds. To all my friends, simply for existing.

To my family, for lots of reasons.

To all the trees that died to make the paper that made this book, and all its many printed drafts.

To Dave, whom I love more than anyone.

About the Author

Adrienne Celt lives in Tucson, Arizona. She's a cartoonist and the author of two previous novels: *Invitation to a Bonfire* and *The Daughters*, which won the 2015 PEN Southwest Book Award for Fiction. Her work has appeared in *The O. Henry Prize Stories*, *Esquire*, *McSweeney's Quarterly Concern*, *Strange Horizons*, and elsewhere.